CAST INTO DOUBT

CAST INTO DOUBT

Patricia MacDonald

This first world edition published 2010
in Great Britain and in 2011 in the USA by
SEVERN HOUSE PUBLISHERS LTD of
9–15 High Street, Sutton, Surrey, England, SM1 1DF.
Trade paperback edition first published
in Great Britain and the USA 2011 by
SEVERN HOUSE PUBLISHERS LTD.

British Library Cataloguing in Publication Data

MacDonald, Patricia J.
  Cast into doubt.
  1. Mothers of murder victims – Fiction. 2. Mothers and
  Daughters – Fiction. 3. Family secrets – Fiction.
  4. Suspense fiction.
  I. Title
  813.5'4-dc22

ISBN-13: 978-0-7278-6958-6   (cased)
ISBN-13: 978-1-84751-306-9   (trade paper)

All Severn House titles are printed on acid-free paper.

Severn House Publishers support The Forest Stewardship Council [FSC],
the leading international forest certification organisation. All our titles that
are printed on Greenpeace-approved FSC-certified paper carry the FSC logo.

MIX
Paper from
responsible sources
FSC FSC® C018575
www.fsc.org

Typeset by Palimpsest Book Production Ltd.,
Falkirk, Stirlingshire, Scotland.
Printed and bound in Great Britain by the
MPG Books Group, Bodmin, Cornwall.

To our 'Mimi', Mary L. Hackler

ACKNOWLEDGEMENTS

Special thanks to two Tonys: Tony Canesso for his help with this book, and Tony Cartano, for all his help these many years.

PROLOGUE

Prajit Singh didn't want any drama on his shift. He needed time to concentrate. So far, it had been a quiet night, and that was the way he preferred it. Drivers came and went, coming in to use the restrooms, and pay for their gas. Kids hung around drinking slurpees from the machine at the back of the store, and harried moms came in to pick up a quart of milk for breakfast, or some small bags of chips to toss into the kids' lunches. Old people bought newspapers and poor people bought lottery tickets. Prajit used the in-between time to work on his studies. He was in medical school, and the work was grueling. He always had a textbook open under the counter. The venous systems, or the lobes of the brain, or grimace-inducing photos of virulent skin conditions were always peeking out from the shelf under the cash register. Prajit was a juggler of time and responsibilities and other people's needs. He was so used to being exhausted and over-burdened that it almost seemed normal to him now.

The door to the convenience store opened, and a young guy came in. Short hair, blue work shirt, angry expression. One of those white guys, born to the privilege of being an American male of Anglo-Saxon descent, who looked unhappy with the way the world was going these days. Prajit knew that he, with his brown skin and accented English, was probably seen by this guy as part of the problem. Prajit also knew, with a secret sense of satisfaction, that someday he would be a cardiologist or a urologist or a thoracic surgeon, and this guy would be sitting politely in his examining room, waiting for his help. Every time Prajit got discouraged, or fed up with the whole routine, he reminded himself of that. The customer approached the cash register and paid for his gas. Prajit thanked him politely. The guy grunted in reply, and then headed down the first aisle toward the back, where they kept the beer. Prajit went back to his reading. Tonight it was diseases of the gastrointestinal system. There was a lot to absorb, he thought.

Pun intended.

All of sudden it began. The raised voices. As soon as he heard them, Prajit remembered the two kids he had seen slipping in earlier, hunched under their hoodies and watch caps, and speaking in whispers that occasionally became harsh, muffled laughter. They had headed down the beer aisle too. Prajit had forgotten they were there. He glanced up at the tilted mirror above the cold case and saw that the two kids and the straight arrow guy were getting into it.

Prajit's heart sank. He didn't need this tonight. It was late. All he wanted to do was to finish his shift and go home. Not that it would be peaceful there. His young wife, Ojaswini, and their baby seemed to have taken over the entire apartment with diapers and bottles and toys everywhere that the baby was even too young to play with. Prajit tried to stay sanguine. These were the difficult days. They wouldn't last forever. One of these days the boy would be old enough for school, and Prajit would be a resident, working twenty-four seven in the hospital rather than in this twenty-four hour a day market. His nights as a clerk would be just a grim memory.

Prajit heard a shout, and looked up at the mirror. The straight arrow had shoved one of the kids out of his path, and he wasn't going to get away with that. Not without a fight. Prajit came out from behind the counter. 'Please, please,' he called out. 'If you wish to buy something, please bring your purchases up to the counter.'

His plea for civility was being drowned out by shouts and loud curses. Reluctantly, he started for the first aisle, hoping that he didn't get into the middle of a melee. Why was it that people with nothing better to do than fight always ended up here, in this convenience store? He answered his own question. Mostly, he realized, because it was the only place open around here at night. The store belonged to a friend of his parents, a businessman who had come to the US with nothing, and ended up rich, just as all the stories of immigrants predicted was possible. Normally Prajit was grateful to have a job, especially since his boss was flexible with his schedule. He knew Prajit was going to medical school. He approved. But at the same time, he expected all his employees to work hard, guard the money, and keep the peace. Sometimes that was easier said than done.

Prajit turned the corner of the first aisle, his hands raised in a pleading gesture. 'Gentlemen, please,' he said. 'Take your argument outside. If you wish to make a purchase . . .'

'If you weesh to make a purchase,' one of the punks mocked him in a singsong voice.

Prajit raised his hands in an attitude of surrender. 'Please sir. Just bring your items to the counter. I don't wish to have any problems.'

The thug was not as young as Prajit had first thought. He had a heavy shadow of a beard, and bright, angry eyes.

The white guy in the blue shirt turned on the punk. 'You think you're funny?' he demanded. 'This man here is just trying to make a living. He doesn't get paid enough to deal with the likes of you. Why don't you do us all a favor and beat it?'

Prajit was shocked and oddly warmed. He had misjudged the customer in the blue shirt. Here this man was defending him. Just when you thought you knew about people, it turned out you could be all wrong.

The guy in the blue shirt tried to push past the smaller of the hoodied thugs. The other one yelled a curse at him. The customer did not reply, but flipped his middle finger at them.

The bigger guy pulled a gun out from under his sweatshirt.

Prajit's eyes widened. He instantly remembered the words of his employer. 'If they have a gun, bow to the gun.'

'Please fellows,' Prajit pleaded. 'Let's calm down. I don't want to have to call the police.' The shorter, quieter one turned and looked him in the eyes. Too late, Prajit realized that he had made a mistake. Too late. His words stuck in his throat. 'No, no,' he tried to say. 'I mean no offense . . .!' And then, he heard the shot.

ONE

The sound of a noontime television anchor chirping about her upcoming guests drifted into the bathroom as Shelby Sloan leaned across the wide, marble-topped sink toward the mirror, applying her mascara. She had slept late, run some errands, and taken a spinning class at the gym. Now, she was showered and just about ready to depart. Shelby stared at her expertly made-up face critically. At forty-two, Shelby's skin was radiant and unlined. Her thick, shiny blonde hair curved smoothly to her shoulders and remained one of her best features. In her twenties, when she was a single, working mother, barely able to buy groceries and pay the rent, she had always assumed that she would look like an old hag by the age of forty, but, despite years of work, night school, child-rearing and too little sleep, the passage of time had been kind to her appearance.

A knock at the front door of her condo startled her. She wasn't expecting anyone.

Probably Jen, she thought, with a last minute question or two. Her best friend, an interior decorator named Jennifer Brandon, worked at home and lived on the same floor of the building as Shelby. She was going to water Shelby's plants and take in the mail while Shelby was at Chloe's. Both single, they spent a lot of time in one another's company, by design or default, for an evening of wine and dinner. Shelby smoothed down her cashmere sweater over her pants. 'Coming,' she called out. She glanced at her watch. Chloe was a stickler for punctuality. She needed to get going.

Shelby opened the door to find Talia Winter, her older sister, standing there. Talia never bothered with pleasantries. 'I'm on my lunch hour. I called Markson's,' she announced, naming the Philadelphia department store where Shelby was the chief women's wear buyer. 'They said you were on vacation.'

'Yes, I am,' said Shelby. 'Today is the first day.'

'You didn't answer your phone.'

Shelby sighed and stepped aside. It was true that she often

did not answer when she saw her sister's name on the caller ID. Talia only called about one subject – their mother, Estelle. Talia still lived in the run-down family house in Northeast Philadelphia with their alcoholic mother, who had, six months ago, been diagnosed with end stage liver disease. She was not eligible for a transplant because she still refused to give up drinking. With no family or home of her own, Talia had spent her adult life catering to the needs of Estelle Winter – a woman who had been either disruptive or absent in their lives for as long as Shelby could remember.

Talia stalked past Shelby, went down the hall and stopped in the living room of Shelby's spacious high rise apartment. She looked around critically and her gaze fell on an overnight bag that was packed and sitting on a gray suede chair.

'Where are you going for your vacation?' Talia demanded. She was fifty years old and looked sixty. Her short, sensible haircut was salt-and-pepper. She was dressed in her work clothes, a shapeless polyester pantsuit and plain blue shirt, probably purchased at Wal-Mart. Her unsophisticated appearance was deceiving. Talia ran the computer lab at Franklin University in Center City. She had a PhD and was considered to be an expert on artificial intelligence. Talia had always had a brilliant mind and an abysmal lack of social skills.

Shelby tried to keep her tone reasonable. 'I told you. Chloe and Rob are going on a cruise. I am taking care of Jeremy while they're gone.'

'You need to come and see Mother,' Talia said. 'She's getting worse by the day. She spends most of the time in bed now. Yesterday she didn't recognize me.'

'I'm sorry, Talia, but I can't,' said Shelby. 'I told you about this months ago. I gave my daughter and her husband this cruise as a Christmas gift. They've been planning it for months. And I've been looking forward to spending this time with my grandson.'

'I wouldn't mind a vacation myself,' said Talia pointedly.

'So take one,' said Shelby. 'It would do you good.'

'With mother this sick?'

Shelby sighed, and did not reply.

'Besides, I could never just go off and leave her with strangers,' said Talia.

'They're not strangers. She knows those caregivers as well

as she knows anyone else. They come every day.' Even as Shelby pointed this out, she knew that it was futile to try to reason with Talia.

Talia looked at Shelby as if she had not heard a word. 'You can bring the boy with you if that's what you want. It's her grandchild, after all.'

Shelby wanted to shout out, *never*. I would never subject my grandson to her. But Shelby knew better than to get into this with her sister. She would never completely escape the web of guilt and duty that kept Talia prisoner in that gloomy house with their incoherent mother. But Shelby did her best to resist it. Since Estelle's diagnosis she helped pay for care-givers, and she made the occasional perfunctory visit, but that was all. Talia was apparently intent on sacrificing her life for their mother. Shelby refused to feel obliged by her sister's choice. If that's what she wanted to do, that was her business.

'I'm certainly not going to bring a four-year-old around someone who is that ill,' said Shelby. Not to mention drunk, she thought.

'Never mind what would be good for mother,' said Talia.

Shelby raised her hands. 'I'm not discussing this. I have to get to Chloe's. Why don't you get in touch with Glen? Maybe he'll come see her.'

'Oh, Glen. Right.' Talia snorted, put her hands on her hips and glanced around the apartment. 'It crossed my mind that he might be here with you.'

Shelby looked at Talia in disbelief. 'Why would he be here? You think he's hiding from you? You know that Glen does what he pleases. I haven't seen him in months,' said Shelby. Their younger brother, Glen, though highly intelligent, was jobless, aimless, and had no permanent address. In his late thirties, he still had many friends who let him crash on their couches or housesit their homes. He showed up periodically and always persuaded Talia that he was worried about their mother, and undyingly grateful for Talia's stewardship. Shelby perceived little sincerity in his show of concern. He did it to keep the peace. 'Look Talia, I have to be going.'

Talia peered at Shelby. 'Why doesn't the kid come here?'

'The kid?'

'Your grandson.'

As she often did, Talia had stumbled upon, and prodded, a

sensitive subject. Shelby would have preferred to have her
grandson at her own, comfortable apartment. But her daughter,
Chloe, had gravely insisted that she didn't want any upheaval
in Jeremy's life, so Shelby had agreed to stay at their row
house in Philadelphia's Manayunk neighborhood. Shelby was
not about to argue the point. She was simply glad to have a
whole week with her grandson. 'He goes to school near their
house,' Shelby said, hating the defensiveness she heard in her
own voice. 'It's just easier this way.'

'Sounds to me like she doesn't trust you with her kid,' said
Talia.

'Well, you're wrong,' said Shelby. 'Now, if you don't mind.'

'I have to get back to work anyway. I don't know why I
wasted my lunch hour coming here,' said Talia. 'I should have
known better.'

I don't know why you came here either, Shelby thought.
She picked up her bag from the grey suede chair. 'I'll walk
you out,' she said.

Chloe was standing outside her tidy, gray stucco-front row
house when Shelby arrived. She made a point of looking at
her watch. Chloe had asked Shelby to be there promptly, so
that she could accompany Chloe to pick up Jeremy at his
preschool. That way, Shelby would know how to get there
in the week that Chloe and Rob were away on their cruise.
Shelby glanced at the dashboard clock. The unexpected visit
from Talia had thrown her off a little bit. And the city traffic
had been heavy from her apartment in Society Hill to the
gentrifying blue-collar neighborhood across the river where
Chloe and Rob lived. She had cut it close, but she was not
late.

Shelby felt the usual pangs of love and anxiety as she gazed
at her daughter's serious expression. Chloe had long hair that
waved around her oval, freckled face. She was lean from years
of religiously eating healthy foods and daily jogging. She was
dressed in her nurse's scrubs, which she wore for her part-
time job in an ob-gyn's office. At twenty-four, Chloe was the
image of her father, Steve, a customer Shelby met at a South
Street coffee house when she worked as a barista her last year
of high school. Shelby and Steve were married on Valentine's
Day at City Hall, along with about thirty other couples who

wanted a Valentine's wedding. Steve left soon thereafter, despite the fact that Shelby was pregnant.

When she learned of Shelby's pregnancy, Shelby's mother, Estelle, counseled abortion. When Shelby refused, Estelle washed her hands of her middle child, and her grandchild. Shelby threw herself into night school and hard work to provide for her daughter. Eventually, she gained degrees, promotions, and a handsome salary. Once, Shelby overheard Chloe's best friend, Franny, whose parents rented them the rooms over their South Philly pizzeria and often minded Chloe after school, ask why they could never play at Chloe's apartment. Chloe explained to Franny that her mother was never home because she would rather go to work. Even now, the memory of those words was painful. 'That's not true! That's not fair!' Shelby had wanted to cry out. But what was the use of protesting? The only thing that mattered was that her child saw her life that way. As the years passed, and Shelby managed to save enough money to move them out of that rough neighborhood, Chloe began to understand why her mother worked so hard. But the pain of that childish assessment lingered in Shelby's heart.

Shelby found a parking space down the block, got out and stretched. She walked back to her daughter and held out her arms. Chloe gave her a quick, fierce hug. Then she pulled away. 'We have to go,' Chloe said.

'I hope I'm not late,' said Shelby. 'Talia stopped by.'

Chloe rolled her eyes. Talia had gone about her life as if her niece did not exist. Her indifference bordered on cruelty. 'What did she want?' Chloe asked.

'She wanted to guilt-trip me about my mother,' said Shelby. 'What else?'

'Did she have any luck?' Chloe asked.

'What do you think?' Shelby asked. 'Hey, honey, I need to run inside and powder my nose.'

'What about Jeremy?'

'It will only take one minute,' said Shelby.

'He'll think I forgot about him,' said Chloe.

Shelby recognized the anxiety in Chloe's eyes. Chloe tried to be a perfect mother. She had cooked and pureed Jeremy's baby food from organic vegetables, rushed him to the doctor if he so much as turned pale, and was a housekeeper whose neatness bordered on obsession. She only worked part time at the medical practice so that Jeremy wouldn't have to spend his time in day care. 'No honey, we'll be there in plenty of time. He'll be OK. Can you let me in?' she said.

Chloe gave a small sigh and led the way back to the front door. It was a narrow, low-ceilinged house which, along with its neighbors, had been built on the hillside that rose above the Main Street of Manayunk. This part of the city, along the banks of the Schuylkill River, had once been a neighborhood of factory workers. In recent years it had become a popular neighborhood for young people with more energy than money. Rob, a social worker, had bought this house with Lianna, his first wife. When their daughter, Molly, was eight years old, Lianna, who suffered from headaches, sought treatment from a highly recommended neurologist named Harris Janssen. At the time, Chloe was a receptionist in Dr Janssen's practice. She watched the affair unfold, and ended up giving advice and comfort to Lianna's miserable husband. Lianna divorced Rob and married the neurologist who was treating her. Now, Lianna, Molly, and Harris lived in a sprawling stone colonial in the upscale suburb of Gladwyne.

Not long after, Chloe and Rob were married in a quiet cere-mony and Chloe moved into the Manayunk house. She removed every trace of Rob's former life except for Molly's room which Rob had insisted be kept exactly the same for his daughter's visits. It was in Molly's room that Shelby would be staying while she cared for Jeremy. To Chloe's annoyance, Rob had insisted on asking his daughter's permission, but Shelby was not offended. On the contrary, she thought it showed a healthy respect for Molly and her space.

Chloe's house was, as always, immaculate, the walls hung with the quilts she had made herself, and a ceramic pitcher of perfectly fresh flowers on the dining room table. You'd never know a child lived here, Shelby thought. Their apart-ments had always been chaotic and strewn with toys throughout Chloe's childhood. She could never understand how Chloe managed to keep her own house perfectly tidy. Shelby made a quick trip to the tiny downstairs powder room beneath the staircase while Chloe waited, and then they went back outside. Chloe got into the front seat of her own car, which was parked in front of the house, on the passenger side. Shelby walked around and opened the driver's side door.

'Do you want to take my car, honey?' she asked.

Chloe looked at her in disbelief. 'Your car does not have a car seat, mom. A child cannot ride in a car without a car seat,' she explained, as if Shelby had suggested decapitation as a method of curing a headache.

'Oh right, of course,' said Shelby. 'OK.'

Shelby pushed some food wrappers aside and got into the driver's seat of Chloe's car. She was struck, as she had often been in the past, by the fact that the inside of the car was a mess. It seemed to be the one place where Chloe's compulsive neatness was not in control. The front and back seats both were littered with empty water bottles, juice boxes, food wrappers, catalogs, and papers. There was change scattered over the floor mats as if someone had opened the door and hurled in a handful. Shelby glanced over at her daughter. 'Don't you want to drive?' she asked. 'You know the way.'

'I'll give you directions,' said Chloe. 'You'll need to drive my car this week, because you cannot take Jeremy in your car. Not without a car seat.'

'I won't. I promise,' said Shelby.

'So, you need to get used to this car,' said Chloe.

'I think I'll get the hang of it pretty easily,' said Shelby.

Chloe frowned. 'Every car is different.'

'Sweetie, it's not like I'm trying to fly a plane here. It's a car.'

'I'd feel better,' Chloe insisted, 'knowing you had already tried it.'

'OK, sure,' said Shelby, turning on the engine.

'Take the first right and then you're going to go three-quarters of a mile,' said Chloe, 'until you see our church. You've been there before.'

Shelby nodded and began to drive. She knew that Jeremy's preschool was located in the church basement. It always sounded strange to her ears to hear Chloe talk about her church. Shelby had not raised Chloe in any religion, but when Chloe married Rob, she adopted his faith. His parents were missionaries in Southeast Asia, and Rob's background had been extremely religious. Shelby made it a point to be respectful of their choice, even though it seemed foreign to her. She glanced over at her daughter, and was shocked to see tears standing in her eyes. 'Chloe, what's the matter?'

'I just hate leaving Jeremy. It's going to be so hard on him to be without us for a week.'

Shelby felt vaguely insulted at the image of Jeremy, miserable in her care, but she knew it was just Chloe, dreading the separation. Mother and son had spent very little time apart. 'I'll keep him busy. Don't worry,' said Shelby. 'He'll be fine.'

'I hope so,' said Chloe.

'Aren't you excited about the cruise?' Shelby asked.

'It will be good to get away for a while,' Chloe admitted.

'No going to work or making beds or meals for a week,' said Shelby.

'I could use a break,' Chloe admitted with a sigh. 'Not from Jeremy but . . . We never have time alone. Rob and I. I think we need that.'

'You should call me more often. You know I'm happy to watch Jeremy.'

'I know how demanding your job is,' Chloe said, sounding vaguely rueful.

'Didn't you tell me that Molly was old enough to babysit these days?'

Chloe shrugged. 'She's only thirteen. I have to go pick her up, and take her home to their big mansion and make small talk with Lianna. Not exactly pleasant.'

'I suppose not,' said Shelby.

'And now Lianna is pregnant. And, of course, she has to go to Dr Cliburn,' Chloe said, referring to the ob-gyn for whom she worked. 'So I have to see her there too. I just hope she doesn't decide to run off with him now`.'

'Come on now,' Shelby chided her with a smile.

'Well, I wouldn't put it past her,' said Chloe. 'Men never see through her. They all think she's so . . . perfect. Even after what she did to Rob – leaving him for Dr Janssen – he won't allow any criticism of her.'

'Well, she is Molly's mother. And Rob respects that. He's a very concerned father,' Shelby reproved her gently. 'To both of his children. You're lucky. A lot of men wouldn't care.'

Chloe's voice sounded small and bitter. 'Like my father.'

Shelby always felt guilty for the effect that loss had had on Chloe's life. 'I'm just saying that you married a good man. You made a wise choice.'

'Over there,' said Chloe, pointing at a buff-colored brick

building with a large, unadorned cross at the peak of the roof.
'There it is.'

Shelby obediently pulled over to the curb, where all the
other parents were waiting. Chloe gazed through the windshield with a blank look in her eyes. Her long, thin fingers
twisted in her lap. She was wearing an oversize, beat-up leather
jacket, one of her flea market finds, over her scrubs, which
made her look small and fragile.

Shelby frowned at her. 'Are you OK, honey?'

Chloe did not reply.

Just then, the doors of the parish hall opened and kids began
to pour out. Shelby studied each little face, her heart
hammering like a teenager trying to catch a glimpse of a boy
she had a crush on. Suddenly, she recognized him, and at the
same minute he spotted his grandmother.

'Shep,' he cried joyously. Misunderstanding her name,
Jeremy had dubbed her 'Shep' when he first could speak, and
it had stuck. Jeremy began to barrel toward Shelby, blond hair
falling across his forehead, a sheet of manila paper sporting
a colorful drawing clutched in his hand.

'There he is,' Shelby cried.

'I know, Mom,' said Chloe quietly. 'I know my own child.'

TWO

That night, when Rob came home, Chloe pulled a home-
made casserole from the oven. 'There'll be plenty left
over for tomorrow,' she said pointedly to Shelby as
she placed the serving dishes on the table in the tiny dining
room.

'Don't worry,' said Shelby wryly. 'I'll make sure he gets fed.'

Chloe lit the candles on the table and avoided her mother's
gaze. 'I don't like him to eat processed food, Mom,' she said.
'I know it was the easiest thing when I was little and you
were working, but Jeremy's used to fresh food.'

Shelby took a deep breath and tried not to take offense. It
was true, she reminded herself, that she had cut a lot of corners
in the kitchen. Chloe wasn't saying it to be mean.

Rob, sandy-haired with strong features and mild, blue eyes, had been washing his hands in the kitchen. He came into the dining room, loosening his tie and unbuttoning the top button of his chambray shirt. He always wore a tie to work at the senior center, even with his work shirt and jeans. 'Hey, your mother knows how to take care of a kid. I mean, you turned out pretty well.' Rob held out a chair for his mother-in-law at the table, and Shelby sat.

'Pretty well,' Shelby protested with a laugh, but Chloe did not smile and her face reddened.

'Let's sit down,' she said. 'Jeremy, come to the table.'

'I'm sitting next to Shep,' the child crowed, and everybody smiled as he clambered up on to the chair beside his grandmother. Shelby thought about her own mother, whose life revolved around gin and petty grievances. She had never apologized for urging Shelby to abort her child, and never showed any interest in being with her granddaughter. There was a time when Estelle's indifference could still hurt her. Over the years, Shelby had hardened her heart against her mother. Her loss, Shelby thought. She had chosen the bottle over seeing her only grandchild grow up.

After dinner, Rob offered to take Jeremy to an ice cream store on Main Street while Chloe got packed. Shelby followed her daughter into her tiny bedroom and lay across the bed, resting on one elbow while Chloe dragged suitcases from the floor of the closet.

Watching her daughter carefully setting out piles of clothes, Shelby thought about how much needless worry she had expended on Chloe's future. Instead of going away to college, Chloe took a course in medical recordkeeping, went to work, met an older man who was on the rebound, and ended up pregnant. Shelby feared that her daughter would end up alone with a baby, uneducated and destitute, just as she herself had been before she pulled herself out of it and made a success of her career.

Chloe insisted that her mother was wrong, and that her life would be completely different. Over the last five years Shelby had been forced to admit that she may indeed have been wrong. Chloe seemed to thrive at work and motherhood, and Shelby had come to think that Rob was a genuinely decent guy.

Chloe held a summery dress up to herself and looked into

the full-length mirror, cocking her head and frowning. 'I
don't know about yellow,' she said. 'I'm so pale. And these
freckles . . .'

'You look good in every color,' said Shelby.

'Oh Mom,' Chloe sighed, folding the dress up and putting
it to one side.

'Did you buy any new clothes for the cruise?' Shelby asked.

'I don't need new clothes,' said Chloe.

'I know. But I gave you that extra money so you could buy
yourself a few pretty things.'

'All I wear to work are scrubs,' said Chloe. 'Besides, I used
it to fix our hot water heater.'

'Oh honey,' said Shelby. 'You should have told me. I'd have
given you more.'

'You've given us enough, Mom,' said Chloe. 'I'm fine as
I am.'

Shelby got up from the bed and put her arms around her
daughter. They both looked into the full-length mirror. Shelby
knew that she could still turn heads, but nothing could compare
to the healthy perfection of youth, which Chloe had. Chloe
needed no makeup or sleek clothes to enhance her beauty. 'Of
course you are. You are perfect as you are.'

Chloe met her mother's eyes gravely in the mirror. 'No,
I'm not. I'm anything but perfect.'

'You stop that,' said Shelby. 'You're always so hard on
yourself.' She peered at her daughter's somber expression. 'Is
there anything wrong, honey? You seem . . . a million miles
away.'

'I'm fine,' said Chloe. 'I'm . . . not used to traveling. I don't
want anything to spoil this, is all.'

'What would spoil it?' Shelby asked.

'Nothing. I've just been looking forward to this. Being alone
with Rob. Kind of like the honeymoon we never had.'

'Well, I want you to enjoy this cruise, and not worry about
anything. Nothing at all. Just enjoy the weather and the free
time and forget everything else for a week. And Jeremy and
I are going to have a great time. The week will fly by.'

Chloe's eyes filled with tears. 'I know,' she said. 'I know
I can count on you.'

Shelby had to struggle to fight back her own tears at this
unexpected endorsement.

'That's right,' she said, squeezing Chloe tighter for a moment before letting her go.

Early the next morning, amid a flurry of instructions, last-minute rechecking for passports, reminders, and lingering hugs and kisses for Jeremy, Chloe and Rob took off in Rob's pick-up truck for Philadelphia Airport. They would fly to Miami where they were to board the cruise ship. Chloe waved at her mother and her son from the passenger window until they were out of sight. Jeremy cried awhile when they left, but he allowed himself to be soothed by his grandmother, especially when he saw the *Pirates of the Caribbean* action figures she had brought for him in her luggage.

The next few days passed quickly. Shelby definitely noticed the difference in her energy level when it came to taking care of a toddler. It had been one thing when she was nineteen. It was a little bit more taxing at forty-two. After he was done with preschool, they would go to the library or the park or the playground, all of which were in walking distance of the house. She found a joy and peacefulness in this routine that she had never felt when Chloe was four years old.

When she looked back on those times now, it seemed that she was always in a hurry in those days. Shelby wondered if that rushing might have been the source of Chloe's lifelong anxieties. In those days, Chloe always wanted one more push on the swing, and Shelby always had her eye on her watch, and a long list of things she needed to do on her mind. At the time, Chloe had seemed unbearably stubborn to Shelby, dragging her feet when she was ordered to hurry up and come along. Maybe, Shelby realized, she was just frustrated at the never-ending interruptions of her happiness.

Now, with only three days left until Chloe and Rob returned, she found herself savoring every moment with her grandson. As Shelby sat rocking back and forth on the swing set in the thin, April sunlight, Jeremy climbed up and slid down the slide repeatedly. Nothing else seemed to matter, to either one of them.

Shelby's phone rang, and she glanced at the caller ID. She saw, with a sinking heart, that it was Talia calling. Not again, she thought. In some ways, she really felt sorry for her sister. Long ago, Shelby had decided to pour all her love and concern into her own daughter. But for Talia, her mother had remained the center of her universe, the organizing principle of her life. Now, Estelle Winter was slipping away, and Talia's devotion seemed both futile and sad. But not sad enough that Shelby wanted to participate. Like their mother, Talia had shown zero interest in Chloe as she was growing up, and had never even commented on the birth of Jeremy. She has her concerns, I have mine, Shelby thought. She hesitated, and then let it ring. This time with Jeremy is precious and nothing's going to spoil it. Talia can wait.

'Shep, look at me. Look at me, Shep!' Jeremy called out.

'I saw you,' Shelby called out. 'That slide is fast.'

'Really fast,' he corrected her.

She smiled at him, tickled by his pride. 'I know.'

'Can I go again?' he asked.

'Go again,' she said.

'Watch me.'

'I'm watching,' she said.

When the sun was going down, and it grew too chilly to stay any longer, they walked home. Shelby made her grandson hot dogs and beans for supper, and watched cartoons with him until it was time for his bath. She read him his favorite stories and tucked him in with bunches of kisses. She tiptoed away from the door, and went downstairs to clean up the kitchen. Then, she remembered Talia's call earlier. She knew she should at least call her sister back. She punched in Talia's number at the lab.

'Dr Winter's office.'

'Talia?'

'No, this is Faith, her assistant.'

Shelby had spoken to Faith before. Faith was a grad student, well into her thirties, who kept the lab organized.

'Oh, hi, Faith, is Talia there? This is her sister, Shelby.'

'No, she has a tutorial tonight.'

'Oh, sorry,' Shelby said. 'I don't have her schedule.'

'She'll be back in about an hour. I can have her call you then.'

'That's all right. I'll catch up with her another time,' said Shelby. 'Just tell her I called her back, OK?'

'I will,' Faith promised.

Shelby felt lighthearted when she hung up. She had not neglected to call her sister, but, at the same time, she didn't have to talk to her. There was a part of Shelby that almost admired Talia's fidelity to their mother. But she could never understand where it came from. And she definitely didn't want to participate in it. Well, she had made the call, and now she needed to make no excuses for why she wanted to simply stay put, eating hot dogs and watching cartoons.

That night, Shelby decided to stay up late and watch an old Michael Caine spy movie. Since she had arrived at Chloe's, she had made a point to go to bed early, partly because she needed enough rest to keep up with Jeremy, and partly because Chloe's house seemed chilly and lonely once her grandchild was asleep for the night.

Shelby could have sat in the living room and watched the larger TV, but she decided to watch upstairs in Molly's bedroom where she was staying. Chloe had often complained that Molly's mother spoiled her, giving her anything she wanted since she'd married a wealthy doctor. Molly had her own television and a laptop computer in her room here in Chloe's house. When Chloe was a teenager, Shelby had always insisted that Chloe work to earn such luxuries, and she understood her daughter's dismay. But she had to admit to herself that it was kind of nice to be able to lie in bed and watch Molly's television.

Shelby locked all the doors downstairs before taking her shower and checking on Jeremy, who had fallen asleep instantly. She showered, toweled her hair dry and combed it. Then, she donned her pajamas and robe and shuffled into the bedroom. Chloe had cleaned the room, put fresh new sheets on the bed, and made sure that everything was in its place. Chloe had apologized profusely for the teenage décor, but Shelby found it kind of amusing to be sleeping under posters of Miley Cyrus and the Jonas Brothers. She climbed on to the bedspread and pulled one of Chloe's log-cabin style quilts over her. She set her cell phone on the night table, as she usually did, just to feel safe in the unfamiliar house. Then, she turned on Molly's TV set and let herself be absorbed by the movie. At some point, the rigors of the day overcame her, and, without quite knowing it, Shelby nodded off to sleep.

The ring of her cell phone at her elbow awakened her with a start. She was chilly. The quilt had slipped off into a heap on to the floor beside the bed. The early morning local news was on the television. How long have I been asleep, Shelby wondered, feeling disoriented? Through the tree branches outside the bedroom window, Shelby could see that the sky was pewter gray, with streaks of shell pink.

She looked at her watch. Six ten a.m. She picked up her phone and squinted at it. The number was unfamiliar. 'Hello?' she asked warily.

There was a moment's silence. Then a voice said, 'Shelby, it's Rob.'

'Rob!' She was instantly alarmed at the sound of his voice. It was Chloe who usually called.

'Something . . . has happened. I don't know . . .' A loud droning sound drowned out his voice.

Shelby's heart started to pound. 'Rob, I can't hear you. What's the matter?' she demanded.

Rob sighed. 'I thought you should know . . . Listen, something terrible has happened.'

Shelby could barely squeak out the next word. 'What? What is it?'

'We've turned around . . . we're headed back to St Thomas.'

'Who's headed to St Thomas? Who's we? Where is Chloe? Put Chloe on. I want to talk to her.'

'That's just it,' said Rob dully. Shelby gripped the phone tightly, instantly angry and impatient with her son-in-law's vagueness. 'What do you mean? That's just what?' she demanded sharply.

For a moment he was silent, and Shelby felt her fury rising, mushrooming, filling her chest, squeezing her lungs, crushing her heart. It was easy to be angry. Easier than to acknowledge the fear that was trickling, like a tiny stream of melting ice, down her back. 'What, Rob?'

'Chloe is . . . missing.'

THREE

Shelby's extremities were numb, as if she had spent the night outside. 'I don't understand,' she said.

Rob cleared his throat. His voice sounded tinny and his words came in a rush. 'Believe me, neither do I. Last night I was in a sports trivia contest. I was on a team and . . . oh, it doesn't matter. Anyway, Chloe got a little . . . restless, and she left. She said she was going to . . . find something else to do. When I got back to our state room, after the contest . . . she wasn't there. I went back out on deck and I looked for her, but I had no luck. No one had seen her. Finally, I . . . alerted one of the stewards who called the captain and they searched the ship. They didn't have any more luck than I did. Now we're heading back to the nearest port. Which is St Thomas.'

'I don't understand? How could she get to St Thomas?'

Rob was silent.

'Rob,' Shelby demanded furiously. 'Where is Chloe? Where did she go?'

'They said . . . they think she must have gone . . . overboard.'

For a moment, Shelby felt her vision narrowing, growing darker.

'Shelby, are you still there?' Rob asked.

'Overboard?' she whispered.

'The captain called the police in St Thomas, and the Coast Guard has been searching for several hours now. That's the droning sound you hear. The planes and the helicopters are searching these waters.'

'Overboard? Into the ocean?'

'Yes. That's what they're afraid of.'

Shelby had the sudden, impossible wish that she had never picked up the phone, that she could rewind time back to before she had heard this news. Shelby started to shake from head to toe.

'I don't know any more than that right now, Shelby. I'm sorry. If I find out anything I'll let you know.'

Shelby could tell by the distracted tone in his voice that he was finished with her, that he was about to hang up. '*No,*' Shelby shouted into the phone. 'No. Wait a minute.'

'Take it easy. I'm still here,' said Rob.

'No.' Shelby was shaking her head. She stood up, clenching the phone in her hand, and started pacing the room.

'No, what?' Rob asked wearily.

Shelby was shaking her head, trying to collect her thoughts. 'No, I don't understand any of this. Chloe . . .'

'I don't either. Look, I promise I will call you back as soon as I know anything,' Rob insisted.

'No,' said Shelby stubbornly.

'I have to go,' said Rob. 'Just sit tight. I'll be in touch.'

'Oh no you don't. You can't just brush me off like this.'

'I'm not doing that, Shelby,' said Rob in a strangled tone of voice.

'Well, I'm sorry, but I'm not just gonna sit here and wait for the phone to ring . . .'

Rob did not reply.

Shelby made up her mind. 'I'm coming down there,' she said.

'Shelby, you can't. I need you to stay there. To take care of Jeremy.'

'I don't care what you need,' Shelby cried. She could feel her own heart beating wildly in her chest. 'Chloe is my . . . baby. I can't . . . I won't . . . I have to be there.'

'What about your grandson?'

Shelby thought of Jeremy, fast asleep in his bed, and her heart felt as if it were being sawed apart. 'Just tell me where he can stay. Do you have any friends who can take care of him?'

'It's so complicated . . .' Rob said.

'Complicated?' Shelby cried. 'I'm sorry but my daughter is missing and I am coming down there. Don't try to argue with me. Just tell me who I can get to watch Jeremy.'

Rob sighed. 'Call Lianna,' he said. 'She and Harris won't mind. And Molly will watch over him. She adores him.'

'Are you sure they'll do it?' Shelby asked.

'I don't know. You were supposed to do it,' Rob protested.

'You were supposed to take care of my daughter,' Shelby cried.

Rob was silent.

'Look, Rob. I need to be there.'

'I guess you do,' said Rob, miserably. 'Give Lianna a call. I'm sure they will mind Jeremy.'

'I'll handle it,' Shelby said. Before he had a chance to protest or rethink his decision, she said, 'I'll get Jeremy situated and then I'm coming. If they find her in the meantime . . .'

'I'll call you, of course,' said Rob dully.

Shelby ended the call, and tried not to think of what the worst could be. Right now, she had to find a safe place for Jeremy to stay, buy a plane ticket – whatever the cost – and go. And not think. Try not to think.

As she stared at Chloe's emergency numbers, written in Chloe's sweet, familiar hand and posted on the refrigerator, Shelby's finger hovered over the keypad of the phone. It was too early to call anyone, but Harris Janssen was a doctor. They would probably be used to calls at all hours. And even if she had to wake the house, it didn't matter. What she needed could not wait. She hesitated for another moment, and then dialed the number. A man's voice answered gruffly.

'I'm sorry to call so early. Is Lianna there?' Shelby asked bluntly.

'Just a minute,' the man said, sounding more curious than annoyed.

A woman's voice in the background asked if it was the hospital calling.

'No,' the man said, turning away from the phone. 'It's for you.'

'For me?' Shelby heard the woman ask, surprised. There were clunking sounds as the receiver was exchanged. Then, a woman spoke warily to her caller: 'Yes?'

'Lianna, you don't know me,' said Shelby hurriedly, her voice wobbling. 'I'm so sorry to bother you at this hour. My name is Shelby Sloan. My daughter, Chloe, is married to Rob.'

'Oh sure,' said Lianna. Then she hesitated. 'What's wrong?' she asked.

'I just got a call from Rob—'

'They're on a cruise,' said Lianna.

'Yes. And . . . well, apparently, it seems that Chloe has gone missing. They think she may have . . . fallen overboard.'

'Oh my God,' Lianna cried.

Shelby could hear her husband in the background, asking what was wrong. Lianna turned away from the phone. Shelby could hear her muffled voice say, 'Rob's wife is missing on that cruise. They think she went overboard.'

'Jesus,' Harris exclaimed.

Lianna returned to the phone. There was no hesitation in her brisk, businesslike tone. 'How can we help?' she asked.

Shelby felt relieved, at least for a moment. 'I hate to ask this of you, but Rob told me to call you. I want to go there right away. To St Thomas. The Coast Guard is searching for my daughter right now and I want to be there. But my grandson—'

'You've got Jeremy,' said Lianna.

'Yes,' said Shelby. 'I'm staying at their house with him.'

Lianna did not hesitate. 'Bring him over here. We'll take care of him.'

Lianna's words lifted a weight from Shelby's shoulders. 'Oh, that would be just great . . .' Shelby said.

'No problem,' said Lianna. 'Molly will be thrilled to have her brother here for a while. Do you know where we live?'

Before Shelby could reply, Lianna was giving her directions.

Shelby called the airlines, called the airport shuttle and packed up her overnight bag, worrying, as she did so, that she had no lightweight clothes with her. She didn't want to take the time to go to her own apartment. At the last minute she went to Chloe's bureau. She did not want to rifle through her daughter's things, but she needed a couple of T-shirts to wear in the Caribbean heat. She unhesitatingly reached for the handles on the second drawer from the top. It was the drawer where she kept her own T-shirts at home. She knew that Chloe would put them in the same place. As the drawer slid open, the faint scent of Chloe's shampoo and body lotion seemed to rise to her nostrils from the drawer. The pleasant, familiar smell made Shelby want to moan in pain, but she could not allow herself the indulgence right at this moment. She grabbed a couple of Chloe's less fitted T-shirts, which looked as if they would fit Shelby as well, and stuffed them into her bag. Then, she slid the drawer shut, left the bedroom and went downstairs.

In the laundry room she found a pile of Jeremy's clothes that she had already washed and folded. She put them in a bag. In the same bag she packed some of his toys from the playroom, and, in the kitchen, a woven grocery sack of his favorite foods. She worked quickly, trying to concentrate, trying not to think of why she was doing all of this. She waited until the last minute to go back upstairs and wake her slumbering grandson.

'Jeremy,' she whispered. 'Come on, honey. You have to get up.'

'No,' he protested.

'Yes. Come, come. Come on, Jeremy.'

Jeremy frowned, and blinked at her. 'Why?'

Shelby tried to make her voice sound cheerful, as if this were some wonderful adventure. 'You're going to go and stay at Molly's for a little while.'

A fleeting look of pleasure crossed his little face. And then he frowned again. 'Are you staying at Molly's, too?' he asked.

Shelby hesitated. 'No honey, I can't.'

'Why not? No. I want to stay with you, Shep,' he insisted.

Shelby pulled him close and hugged him. 'I want to stay with you too,' she said, trying to keep her voice steady. 'But I have to go.'

'Why?' he demanded, angrily this time.

She had already decided, as she packed up his things, that she was not going to tell him what had happened. She was not going to say that his mother was missing. How could she make him understand, when she didn't understand it herself? Besides, it was too soon. There was no need. It could all prove to be a horrible misunderstanding. 'Your mom and dad need my help,' she said, 'so I'm gonna go help them. And you have to help too, by going to Molly's and being a good boy. Can you do that?'

'No,' Jeremy protested.

'Please. Shep needs you to do this.'

Jeremy stuck out his lower lip and folded his pudgy arms over his chest.

'Please Jeremy. I'm really in a fix. Nobody can help me but you,' said Shelby.

Jeremy hesitated. 'OK,' he grumbled.

'That's my boy,' she said. 'Now quick, put some clothes on. Molly's waiting for us and we need to go.'

It turned out not to be a lie. When Shelby pulled into the driveway of the large, stone house in leafy, upscale Gladwyne, Molly was the first person she saw. The girl was standing in the doorway in shapeless sweat pants and a Jonas Brothers t-shirt, peering anxiously out at the driveway through purple-framed glasses. Her long, dark brown hair was twisted into a ponytail, and her round face, marred by acne, looked ashen. When Molly spotted them, she turned and called into the house behind her. Then she opened the door and started down the front steps. She was wearing large, furry green slippers that made her feet look like a clown's.

Shelby parked, and lifted Jeremy, who was dozing again,

out of his car seat. He fell against her chest, warm and completely relaxed. The young teenager came toward Shelby holding out her arms.

'Molly?' Shelby asked.

Molly nodded, as Shelby gently shifted Jeremy to her waiting arms. A couple appeared at the front door. Lianna was immediately recognizable from Chloe's descriptions of her. She was a slim, beautiful woman with fine features, huge dark eyes and black hair. She was barefoot, wearing a comfortable-looking bathrobe, and a worried, sympathetic gaze. Behind her, Harris Janssen, the neurologist who had stolen her away from Rob, was not at all what Shelby had expected. Knowing how good-looking Rob was, Shelby had pictured his rival as a lothario who looked like a movie star. Harris was a balding, stocky man of medium height with a round face and a gap between his front teeth. He was dressed in casual, Saturday clothes, a pair of baggy cords and an oatmeal-colored sweater. He looked like the sort of man women would confide in as a friend, while they slept with other guys. Of course, he was a doctor, Shelby thought. There was something very attractive about having an MD after one's name. And Chloe had always said, during the year she had worked in his office, that Dr Janssen was the soul of kindness. He was well known for his volunteer work, and Chloe had once told her that he often treated patients even if they had no insurance.

Harris was the first to offer his hand. 'You must be Chloe's mother. She's such a lovely girl.'

'Yes. Thank you,' said Shelby. 'She's always spoken highly of you.'

Lianna reached out her hands to accept the bag of toys and clothes that Shelby had lifted from the back seat of the car.

'There's a bag of his favorite foods too,' said Shelby. 'I'm sure I've forgotten things but if you need anything . . .'

'Molly has a key to the house,' said Lianna, shifting the bags in her arms. 'I'm sure we can find anything we need for him.'

'I'll take that,' Harris said, reaching for the bag of groceries.

'I can't thank you enough,' said Shelby. 'Rob doesn't want me to come, but I just have to be there.'

'Of course you do,' said Lianna, reaching out and briefly grasping Shelby's hand in her own. Shelby felt the warmth of her grasp, and her gaze. 'I'd do the same if it were Molly.

Don't worry about Jeremy. We'll take good care of him. Just let us know – you know. I'm sure it will be all right.'

Shelby pressed her lips together, blinking back tears.

'Do you need a ride to the airport?' Harris asked.

'I've got a taxi picking me up at the house in about half an hour,' said Shelby. 'I'm too rattled to try and drive there.'

'Because I can drive you,' said Harris.

'No. I'm covered. But thank you so much,' said Shelby.

'Don't worry about Jeremy,' said Lianna.

Shelby nodded. She turned to Molly who was still holding Jeremy.

'He weighs a ton,' Molly said. Then she nodded to Shelby. 'I've got him though.'

'Thank you, Molly.' Shelby bent over her sleeping grandson, inhaled his scent, and kissed him. Before her tears could splash on him, she turned away and got back in the car. The family in the driveway, their arms full of Jeremy and his belongings, frowned as they watched her go.

FOUR

S helby consulted the airline callboards and made her way quickly to security. As she edged along patiently in the line, she felt grateful that she had the habit, from her job, of carrying her passport with her. She flew so often out of this airport on buying trips that it had been second nature to keep it zipped in a special compartment in the large, leather sack she always carried. She showed it now, along with the boarding pass she had printed on Rob's printer, and easily passed through the gauntlet of bored security officers. She put her shoes back on and headed to her gate. The lounge at the gate was filled with passengers, young and old, wearing jeans and sneakers and sandals, chattering happily about their upcoming vacations.

Shelby walked over to a newsstand across from the gate and glanced at the collection of newspapers. She half expected to see Chloe's picture splashed across the front page, under a huge headline about her being missing, being overboard. But there were no pictures of Chloe in sight. Shelby bought a couple of newspapers and sat down far from the other waiting passengers. She began to thumb through the papers impatiently. Nothing. She stopped looking for a moment and tried to think why this was not on the front page. Perhaps the news hadn't reached the newspaper yet. No, that's stupid, she thought. News was instant on the internet. Perhaps the newspaper had been printed before Chloe disappeared. Almost to reassure herself, she glanced up at the overhead TV in the lounge that was tuned to CNN. If there were any news, it would be there, on CNN. She stared at the screen, one story scrolling after another, but there was no mention of her missing daughter. Shelby felt indignant on Chloe's behalf; indignant that the news media was being so dismissive of her disappearance. Maybe that meant she was fine, Shelby told herself. Maybe that meant she had been found.

The ticket agent announced the boarding of the flight, and Shelby got up to join the line, shuffling toward the jetway. She found her seat on the plane and prepared to wait it out. The woman in the next seat tried to make conversation but Shelby remained monosyllabic, and discouraged any questions.

Although the trip was amazingly uncomplicated, to Shelby, it was one of the most torturous days of her life. A thousand times she wanted to call Rob, but she resisted the temptation. Once the plane landed in St Thomas she called his cell and he told her to take a cab to the police station. When she began to ask about the search he said, 'We'll talk when you get here.'

Before Shelby could protest, he hung up.

Shelby clutched her phone as she made her way through the crowded airport, just in case he wanted to call her with news. She needed all her strength just to get to her destination. She stepped out of the air-conditioned airport and was smacked by the sultry, tropical air of the Caribbean. The sky was somewhat overcast, the humidity high, as if rain were imminent. She threaded her way to the taxi stand. A large black woman in a lavender blouse and oiled, skinned-back hair was the dispatcher. She glanced at Shelby's overnight bag and pointed impassively to an approaching driver.

'Which hotel?' the woman asked in a lilting accent, checking a clipboard to see who she could place along with Shelby in the cab.

Shelby realized that she had not given a thought to a hotel, or where she was going to sleep, in part because she could not imagine herself sleeping – not while Chloe was missing.

The dispatcher was looking at her impatiently. Shelby felt the sudden, urgent need to tell someone. 'My daughter is missing,' said Shelby. Tears filled her eyes.

The woman's severe gaze softened. 'Where are you going, ma'am?' she asked more gently.

'The police station,' said Shelby. Her voice was faint, but the woman caught her words. She looked at the expression on Shelby's face and frowned, shaking her head. Then, she summoned a driver and spoke to him. The man insisted on gently wresting Shelby's bag from her, and putting it in his trunk. Shelby sat down in the taxi, and the man pulled away from the curb without another word. His radio was on, tuned to a Christian station where a preacher exhorted his listeners to give their lives to God.

The traffic out of town was almost at a standstill, but the driver found narrow streets where he could zip up and away from the road leading past the harbor. Shelby caught sight of several enormous cruise ships docked there, and her heart stood still. Which was their ship? Which one of those monstrous boats had Chloe been on? The people on board seemed to be the size of ants, and the drop from the jutting decks to the turquoise waters of the harbor looked steeper than a snow-covered glacier. The taxi climbed a hillside and Shelby was almost glad when the ships in the harbor were hidden from view. She could see how beautiful and picturesque the streets were with their colorful, shuttered buildings, cascading flowers and palm trees. It was an elegant, tropical paradise. The cab left the charming streets of the downtown and drove back down to the harbor road, pulling up in front of a modern concrete building painted in buff and salmon, with lots of hermetically sealed windows. The cab stopped. Shelby could see dark-skinned men and women in suits, or in crisp police uniforms, coming and going from the building. 'This is it, ma'am,' the driver said carefully in accented English. 'Courthouse on the right, police station on the left. Up those steps.'

Shelby asked him the fare, and as she counted out the bills the driver went around to the trunk and pulled out her bag. He handed it to her gravely as she paid him. 'I'm very sorry for your trouble, ma'am,' he said. 'I'll pray for you.'

For a moment she was taken aback, wondering how he knew, and then she remembered the taxi dispatcher at the airport. She must have told him. Shelby wanted to thank him for his kindness but the words caught in her throat. She nodded, and pressed her lips together to hold back her tears as he got back into his cab and pulled away from the curb. Then, her knees shaking, she turned, hoisted her bag over her shoulder, and climbed the steps to the police station.

A receptionist rose from her desk the moment Shelby identified herself and led her down a bustling hallway and through a closed door to a room at the rear of the modern-looking police station. At the door, a burly man in a police uniform, sat at a desk, blocking the entry.

'This is the missing girl's mother . . .' the receptionist said to him.

Immediately the guard's stern expression softened. He stood up and gestured to her. 'Come through,' he said to Shelby. Still clutching her overnight bag, she followed the man through the doorway.

If she had doubted the urgency of the investigation, the sight of the room she entered was both reassuring and terrifying. The room was abuzz with groups of officers and men dressed in street clothes conferring, clustered at desks, maps, bulletin boards, and lightboxes.

The lightboxes were devastating. Photos of Chloe in her summery yellow cotton dress had been enlarged and posted. Shelby gasped at the sight of them. They had clearly been taken on board the ship and seemed professional in quality. Chloe's skin was slightly tanned, her long hair windblown. Shelby covered her mouth with her hands to stifle a cry as she stared at these images of her daughter. Chloe's companion had been cropped from the photo, and all you could see of Rob was his hand, draped over her shoulder, the wedding ring on his finger.

'Shelby.'

Shelby jumped at the sound of her own name. She turned and saw her son-in-law.

His face was ashen under the fluorescent lights, his beard stubbly. His large, light eyes were dull with exhaustion and red with weeping. He set down a paper coffee cup on a nearby desktop.

'Rob,' she cried out. She asked him the only important question with her eyes, but she knew the answer before he could reply.

'Nothing,' he said, shaking his head. Suddenly, his chin began to tremble, and his blue eyes filled with tears. 'I'm sorry.'

He reached to embrace her, but Shelby drew back and stiffened

'I'm so sorry,' he said miserably. 'I should have been with her.'

Shelby suddenly found the sight of Rob's hapless expression infuriating. 'That doesn't explain anything,' she said. 'How could she have fallen overboard? Rob, people don't just fall overboard.'

'There was a balcony outside our bedroom,' he said.

Shelby recalled the brochures, remembered choosing the nicest cabin for them. She had pictured them eating breakfast on their balcony. Watching the sunset from their private little deck.

'They think she fell from the balcony. They found her sandal on the awning below it,' he said.

Shelby felt as if she could not draw in a breath. She knew instantly that the image of that single sandal, flung off in flight, would haunt her days forever.

'You should sit down,' said Rob.

A dark-skinned, middle-aged man in a short-sleeved police uniform approached them. 'Is this your wife's mother?' the man asked.

Rob turned and looked around. 'Yes,' he said. He turned back to Shelby. 'She just arrived. Shelby, this is the Chief of Police here in St Thomas, Chief Giroux. This is my mother-in-law, Shelby Sloan.'

'Please,' said the policeman. 'Mrs Sloan, I'd like to speak to you in my office.'

'Shall I come?' Rob asked.

'No, why don't you wait out here.' It was an order, not a question. The police chief guided Shelby by her forearm, as if she were blind. They walked into a spacious, light-filled office where two other men were seated, talking quietly. There were three pots of shiny-leafed, tropical plants on the window sill, and on the walls was an assortment of framed diplomas and citations. The other men stood up as Shelby was led into the room.

'Mrs Sloan, let me present to you Mr Warren DeWitt from the FBI, and Captain Fredericks, the ship's captain.'

Captain Fredericks took off his hat and turned it nervously in his hands as he gave her a brief nod. Agent DeWitt extended a hand to her and Shelby shook it. Then she gripped the back of the chair in front of her, feeling suddenly faint.

'Mrs Sloan, please sit down,' said Chief Giroux.

Shelby seated herself carefully in the chair he offered.

Chief Giroux bent down and spoke to her kindly. 'Can one of my officers get you something to drink? You've had a terrible shock and a long trip. Something hot? Tea perhaps? Or a cold drink?'

'No, I'm fine,' Shelby whispered.

The FBI agent and the ship's captain resumed their seats. Captain Fredericks fiddled with the brim of his hat.

Shelby looked at Agent DeWitt, a beefy man with a beard, wearing a jacket and tie. 'Why is the FBI here?' she said in a small, frightened voice.

DeWitt leaned forward in his chair. 'It's standard procedure, Mrs Sloan. St Thomas, being a US possession, is in our jurisdiction. Captain Fredericks contacted Chief Giroux when it became clear that your daughter was no longer on board the ship. Chief Giroux contacted the Bureau, as well as the Coast Guard, for help.'

Shelby stared at him. Her lips were so dry that they felt like they were made of paper. She could barely raise her voice above a whisper. 'I don't understand. Was there . . . a crime?'

'We don't know that,' said Agent DeWitt. 'It was, most likely, an accident.'

'You talk as if she was . . . as if Chloe . . .' She couldn't bring herself to finish the sentence.

'The search is ongoing,' Chief Giroux said kindly. Shelby grasped at the word 'search' as at a life preserver. 'Yes, the search . . .'

She looked hopefully at Captain Fredericks, a tanned, wiry, white-haired man dressed in a white uniform. He started when she met his gaze. Then he cleared his throat. 'The Coast Guard,' the captain explained, 'sent an HU-25 Falcon jet to the scene as well as a Dolphin helicopter, and two Coast Guard cutters.

They have been looking for her ever since I alerted them to your daughter's disappearance.'

'In addition,' said Chief Giroux, 'we have many local fishermen and boaters who have volunteered to aid in the search.'

'How long has it been?' Shelby whispered.

Agent DeWitt frowned, and looked at the captain. 'Well, we received notification at about five thirty this morning.'

'That's when my son-in-law called me,' said Shelby.

'But we surmise, from the evidence now available, that she fell overboard somewhere between eleven and twelve midnight,' said Agent DeWitt.

Shelby gasped as if they had punched her. The men exchanged grim glances.

Warren DeWitt cleared his throat. 'According to your son-in-law, he got back to the room around midnight. When he realized that your daughter wasn't there, he went looking for her. He then asked a steward for help, and, when they both couldn't find her, they went to the captain. Captain Fredericks ordered a search of the boat.'

'You went back the way you came, looking for her?' Shelby said hopefully to the captain.

The ship's captain nodded. 'When the search was completed, yes, we turned around and headed back,' said Fredericks.

It took a moment for the import of his words to dawn on Shelby. 'When the search was completed? How long did that take?'

The captain tapped anxiously on the crown of his hat. 'It took approximately three hours to search the ship.'

Shelby covered her mouth with her hands and stared at him. Finally, she said, 'You left my daughter in the ocean and kept going? For three hours?'

The captain did not flinch. 'We don't stop the ship and turn back when a passenger is reported missing, unless someone actually saw the person going overboard. We couldn't. We'd never be able to adhere to our schedule. These ships are enormous, and people are often reported missing when they are actually somewhere else on board. This is an official policy of the company.'

The hopelessness of it all suddenly struck Shelby like a sack of concrete. Chloe had been missing now since last night. Even in these warm waters, to be alone, in the vast ocean.

Her next thought made her feel sick to her stomach. 'Are there sharks . . . ?'

Fredericks' gaze flickered. 'The Coast Guard is still searching. It's possible they will find her. I'm terribly sorry . . .'

'Sorry?' Shelby cried. 'That's not enough.'

FBI agent DeWitt interrupted. 'Mrs Sloan, Chief Giroux has very kindly set me up in a room across the hall. And I need to ask you a few questions. Could I prevail upon you to come with me for a few minutes, please?'

Shelby hesitated, looking from the captain to the FBI agent. Both of them wore identical, impassive expressions.

'What is he going to do?' she demanded of Chief Giroux, looking, all the while, at Captain Fredericks.

'I need to speak to some people at our corporate head-quarters. They've asked me to keep them updated on the situation,' Fredericks said.

'Mrs Sloan?' DeWitt repeated. 'Could you come now?'

'Yes, all right,' Shelby mumbled.

'It's just outside and down the hallway,' he said, rising to his feet. 'We can speak privately. If you wouldn't mind.'

'Yes,' Shelby said. 'All right.' She got to her feet and followed the FBI agent. They left the chief's office and entered a wide hallway with cubicles along the right hand wall. The hallway was crowded with people milling around, sitting on the industrial carpeting, or leaning against the wall. They were clearly Americans, judging by their sporty, casual clothing. Most everyone, men and women both, were sunburned, and wearing shorts and fanny packs, hats and, often, sunglasses. Others, similarly dressed, were already seated in the cubicles, talking across desks to policemen. Shelby glanced at Agent DeWitt.

He answered her unspoken query. 'Chief Giroux and his team are still questioning people from the ship. They're talking to passengers as well as crew. Anyone who might know some-thing, or have seen what happened,' he said.

Shelby nodded and followed him into a small, bare office. He closed the door behind him. Suddenly it was quiet.

The agent sat down at the desk opposite her and folded his hands in front of him. 'I know this is very difficult,' he said. 'I understand if this becomes too much for you, but we really need your cooperation.'

'I'll do my best,' said Shelby.

Agent DeWitt nodded. 'All right. Good. Now, did you speak to your daughter in the last few days? Did she call you from the boat?'

'Yes, she called a couple of times. She has a son. A four-year-old. Jeremy,' Shelby whispered. 'She never left him before. She liked to talk to him.'

'How did she sound to you?' the agent asked.

Shelby closed her eyes and tried to remember. 'She sounded . . . normal.'

'Cheerful?' he asked. 'Having a good time?'

Shelby opened her eyes and gazed at him. 'Do you think my daughter is . . . dead?' she asked.

The agent would not be drawn into speculation. 'They're still searching,' he said.

'How long can someone survive in the water like that?' Shelby asked, pressing the palms of her hands on the desktop.

'I'm no expert on the water,' said DeWitt. 'You'd have to ask someone from the marine unit about that.'

'I'd like to do that, right now,' Shelby said.

Agent DeWitt's expression was opaque. 'When we're done here. First, let's get back to the phone calls. You said she sounded normal . . .'

Shelby could feel her eyes filling with tears.

'Mrs Sloan, I know you want to help your daughter,' he reminded her. 'This is the best way for you to help.'

Shelby nodded and wiped the tears away with the side of her hand.

'Normal,' he repeated. 'Nothing out of the ordinary.'

'No. Why?'

'How about her husband?'

Shelby frowned at him. 'What about him?'

'Were they getting along?' Agent DeWitt asked.

Shelby frowned. 'Chloe and Rob? Yes. Wait a minute. Wait a minute. Why are you asking me about Rob?'

'It . . . it has to be asked.'

'Why?' And then she understood. 'Oh no. You don't think . . .'

'We don't have any reason to suspect your son-in-law. To be clear, we have surveillance tapes which show him at the sports trivia contest where he said he was.'

Shelby shook her head. 'So . . . ?'

'Right now we are leaning toward the theory that this was an accident.'

'But it just doesn't make any sense,' Shelby cried. 'How can someone accidentally fall overboard?'

'It's not that difficult,' said Agent DeWitt grimly. 'Not if a person is inebriated.'

For a moment Shelby stared at him in disbelief. 'Inebriated? You mean drunk? You think my daughter was drunk?' Shelby let out a mirthless laugh and shook her head.

'She wouldn't be the first person . . .' he said.

'I'm sorry. I don't mean to laugh, but you don't know my Chloe. She's a health nut,' said Shelby. 'She was worried that I was going to give her son junk food while she was gone.'

Agent DeWitt held her in his steady gaze without speaking.

Shelby rattled on. 'I'm not saying that my Chloe never took a drink. I mean, it's possible that she had a drink or two. But how drunk would you have to be to fall overboard?'

Agent DeWitt sighed slightly, and picked up a paper that was lying on the desk in front of him. He frowned at it. 'Probably very drunk.'

Shelby spoke firmly. 'Obviously.'

'Mrs Sloan, are you aware that your daughter had a problem with alcohol?'

Shelby was stunned. She felt as if he had smacked her across the face. 'That's a complete lie,' Shelby cried. 'That's just not true.'

Agent DeWitt was stone-faced. 'We have surveillance video of your daughter playing bingo that evening. At one point, she passes out at the table and falls off her chair.'

'No,' Shelby scoffed. 'Maybe she was ill. Seasick.'

The agent looked at her steadily. 'Two other couples at the table had to help her back to her room. She couldn't walk unaided.'

'No, no that's not possible,' said Shelby. She was trying to picture Chloe – trying to imagine her falling-down drunk. The only image which came to her mind was of her own mother, passed out on the bathroom floor, and Shelby calling out, trying to rouse her, pushing the door up against her, trying to force it open. Chloe? No. That wasn't Chloe. 'No. Wait a minute. What you're saying . . . I don't . . . no. I mean, it's possible to get a little high without meaning to . . . that could happen to anyone . . .'

Agent DeWitt sighed and tapped his forefinger on the pile of papers on the desk. 'I have a statement here from a bartender on the boat. Apparently she ordered seven double-vodka tonics that night.'

Shelby stared at him.

Agent DeWitt smoothed down the papers on the desk. 'This was not an isolated incident. She repeated this behavior every night that she was on board the ship.'

Shelby's face flamed.

'You didn't know,' he said. It was not a question.

FIVE

'**M**y Chloe?'

'You didn't know about her . . . problem.'

'Her problem?' Shelby repeated, stunned and bewildered.

'She never mentioned this to you.'

'No.' Shelby tried to align this news in her head with her fixed image of her daughter. A girl who worked for a doctor, who was ever vigilant about her health, her tidy home, her orderly needlework. Chloe? A drinking problem? No. A drinking problem was her own mother, forgetting to wear underwear to a block party and lifting her skirt to scratch her thigh. Kids laughing. Howling. Not Chloe. Never. Shelby doubled over, as if she had taken a blow to the stomach.

Agent DeWitt watched her patiently.

'I don't understand,' Shelby wailed.

'Were you close to your daughter?' Agent DeWitt asked.

Shelby knew what he was thinking. She must be the worst mother who had ever lived not to know this. 'Yes. She was my whole world,' Shelby said.

'She may have wanted to spare you,' he said.

Dimly, Shelby knew that it could be true. If Shelby ever noticed that she seemed irritable, or in a blue mood, Chloe denied it. 'But why? Why would she get drunk? She was happy with her life,' Shelby cried.

Agent DeWitt shrugged. 'It's a disease.'

Shelby stared ahead, her face flaming. How many times had she scoffed when people tried to excuse Estelle Winter's behavior as a disease? Shelby had always seen it as a choice. Diseases were something you couldn't help getting. Something genetic. An inheritance. Something her mother might have passed down to her granddaughter. Her mother who had never remembered Shelby's birthday and had spent her children's lunch money to buy another bottle. But Chloe was not anything like her grandmother. Not in any way. 'You don't understand. My Chloe has a son. She's the most devoted mother. Ask my son-in-law. She would never—'

'I'm afraid, it's your son-in-law who informed us.'

'Rob?'

DeWitt nodded.

Shelby's frantic gaze met his cool, hazel eyes. 'What did Rob say?'

Agent DeWitt shook his head, as if to say that he was not going to share that information. 'You can ask him about it. It's not as if we are basing our conclusions solely on what he said. As I told you, we have sworn statements from a number of people who saw her drinking heavily during the course of the cruise.

'I think we have to proceed on the assumption that her . . . fall . . . was the result of her diminished capacity. She was extremely intoxicated, and perhaps she became disoriented when she was alone in her cabin. Her judgment was impaired. We are surmising that she may have stepped outside on to the balcony, leaned over too far and lost her balance. Now, we're still questioning people, hoping to find an actual witness. But even without a witness, it seems pretty clear what occurred.'

Slowly, Shelby rose to her feet. 'I have to talk to my son-in-law,' she said.

'I have a few more questions,' said Agent DeWitt.

'No,' said Shelby, holding up a hand to stay him. 'I can't.' She walked through the doorway and stepped into the crowded hall.

'Hey,' one of the passengers, a paunchy, sunburned man in a t-shirt, long basketball shorts and sandals, a madras bucket hat covering his head, said in a loud voice, 'how much longer are we going to be stuck here?'

'We're going to get this done as quickly as possible,

people,' said Agent DeWitt. 'I want to thank you all for your patience.'

'This is my vacation,' the man called after him. 'We want to get back on the damn boat and get moving again.'

Some of the other passengers grumbled agreement, while others tried to shush the irate passenger.

Shelby's face flamed and she lowered her head. She blinked away the hot tears in her eyes and tried to thread her way through the crowd.

'Hey, what did he ask you about in there?' demanded the man in the t-shirt.

'They're trying to find a witness,' Shelby said in a shaky voice, avoiding his impatient gaze.

The man raised his voice and looked at the bedraggled crowd. 'Listen, if anybody here saw that dame go overboard, do us all a favor and speak up, will ya? So we can all get out of here.'

Shelby looked up at him, her cheeks flaming. 'That dame is my daughter,' said Shelby.

The complaining man looked startled. 'Sorry,' he said gruffly. His expression was grumpy, but he was clearly reddening from embarrassment.

Shelby turned away from him. The people in the crowded corridor parted, creating room for her to pass through. They watched her warily.

As Shelby hurried through the crowd, a woman reached out a hand and stayed her. Shelby looked up and saw a dried-out stick of a woman with lifeless brown hair and kind eyes. She was wearing a sprigged blouse, a pale blue A-line skirt and shiny white sneakers. A man in a plaid, short-sleeved shirt, who could have been her twin brother, stood nearby, looking sympathetically at Shelby. 'You're Chloe's mother?' the woman asked.

The sound of her daughter's name from this stranger's lips caught her by surprise. Shelby nodded, wiping away her tears.

'Don't mind that guy. Some people ought to be ashamed of themselves. This is a tragic situation. Don't they know what's important?'

'Darn right,' said the man standing beside her.

'My name is Virgie Mathers, and this is my husband, Don. We're on this cruise for our fiftieth anniversary. We played bingo with your Chloe. And she was a real nice gal. She was sweet as could be. Told us all about her son. And her quilting. Right, Peg? Peggy and Bud were there too.'

The old woman indicated a stocky, balding, middle-aged man. The pudgy, sweet-faced woman who was holding his arm and leaning on a metal cane nodded enthusiastically. 'Very nice girl,' said Peggy stoutly. 'She was just having a good time.'

Bud raised his eyebrows. 'She was pretty wasted.'

'Bud, hush. You don't know that. She might have been feeling sick is all,' said Peg. 'You got a little sick yourself on this boat.'

'That's true.' Bud admitted.

'Are you the people who tried to help her?' Shelby asked.

Don gallantly shrugged off the suggestion. 'We didn't do much. We walked her back to her room. She kept saying she was sorry, but it wasn't necessary. We were happy to help her.'

'That's for sure,' his wife, Virgie, agreed.

'It's just awful what happened to her,' said Peggy, 'A young girl like that. With a husband, and a little child. Got her whole life ahead of her.'

Peggy's husband, Bud, nodded solemnly in agreement. 'Terrible thing.'

Despite her middle age and obvious infirmity, Peggy had a soft, unlined face, and pink cheeks. 'The poor thing,' she said gently, and, for a moment, Shelby felt grateful if these people were the last her daughter had seen.

Virgie wrapped her cold, bony fingers around Shelby's hand. 'Now, don't you give up just yet. They still might find her. I was reading somewhere that people have been known to survive a fall from a ship like this. Don was in the Navy. He would know. Isn't that true, Don?'

Don winced. 'I don't know about that . . .'

'Mr and Mrs Ridley,' Agent DeWitt called out. He was gesturing to Bud and Peg.

'He wants to talk to us,' said Bud anxiously. 'We better go.'

'I'm sorry about all this,' said Shelby.

'Oh, heavens, don't you be sorry,' said Peg. 'We're just sorry this happened.'

All the others murmured agreement.

Shelby felt hot tears spring to her eyes again at their kindness. But their recounting, however downplayed, of Chloe's last evening on the ship had closed around her heart like cold fingers.

'Thank you for your kindness,' said Shelby to the couple as Bud cleared a path for his wife who dragged one leg as she walked and leaned on her cane.

'We'll keep your Chloe in our prayers,' Peggy called back.

Virgie reached out her hand and patted Shelby's forearm consolingly. 'And you too.'

'That's right,' Don agreed, and the pity in his eyes was so genuine that Shelby could not bear to look at him.

'Thank you,' she mumbled. She lowered her head and hurried away from them. She was intercepted by Chief Giroux as she reentered the incident room.

'I want to speak to my son-in-law,' Shelby said.

'Right now, that's not going to be possible,' said the chief. 'He's being questioned.'

Shelby looked around for a vacant chair. 'I can wait,' she said. 'I just need a chair.'

Chief Giroux looked pained. 'Mrs Sloan,' he said. 'You'll pardon me for saying so, but you look exhausted.'

'I'm all right,' said Shelby.

Chief Giroux ignored her protestations. 'And you've probably not had a bite to eat. We have arranged for you and your son-in-law to have rooms at a guesthouse here in town tonight. You can have some dinner there and get a bit of rest.'

'No,' said Shelby, shaking her head. 'I'm fine. I want to stay here.' Tears leaked from her eyes and ran down her face.

The chief's voice was firm. 'I will call your cell phone if there's any news.

'I promise you. If there's anything at all, I will contact you. It's not five minutes from here.'

Shelby looked at him helplessly. Did she have to go, she wondered? Could he force her to leave? In this strange, exotic place, she did not know the rules. She appealed to him the only way she knew how. 'It's my daughter,' she pleaded.

Chief Giroux took her hand and held it briefly. The warmth of his grip made her aware of the coldness of her own hand. For a moment she felt lightheaded, as if she was going to faint. She gripped his wrist with her own hand to steady herself.

'I understand,' Chief Giroux said. 'I have a daughter myself, ma'am. Believe me. You don't need to be in this room to remind me of the importance of all this. I will do my very best for your daughter. But right now, you should go.' Without giving her a chance to protest, the chief summoned one of his officers, a light-skinned young man with pale green eyes.

'Darrell, drive Mrs Sloan to the Maison,' he said. 'Christophe is expecting her.' Then, he turned back to Shelby. 'When we are finished talking with your son-in-law, I will send him along. And I will see you both in the morning. First thing. Now, you go with Darrell and he will take you to the guesthouse. Go on, now. It's best if you do.'

The young officer nodded and indicated that they would be heading to the door.

Numbly, Shelby picked up her bag and followed him.

SIX

S helby sat in the back seat of the police car and stared out the window. The young officer drove slowly, waving and calling out occasionally to people he passed on the street. Though it was evening, the sunset lingered. On the waterfront the sea was silver, the sky layered with violet and blood orange over the low, dark hills that ringed the harbor. On the darkening streets, between the tall graceful trunks of palm trees, Shelby saw elegant boutiques with wrought-iron fences and restaurants glowing from within, shoulder to shoulder with modest, shuttered gingerbread cottages.

Darrell pulled over to a curb in front of a wooden house with a café on the first floor, and the floors above encircled by white railings with flowerboxes trailing exotic, brilliant blooms. A sign above the café read, Maison sur la Mer. Darrell got out of the car, and retrieved Shelby's bag from the trunk of the car. Then he opened the door for her.

'This is it,' said the young officer.

A tall, mocha-skinned man with dreadlocks came out of the front door and greeted Darrell. He had a broad face, even features, and fuzzy traces of gray around his hairline.

'Christophe, this is Mrs Sloan.'

Christophe's smile was so kind and solicitous that Shelby had to look away to keep herself from bursting into tears. 'Your room is ready for you,' he said.

'Thank you,' Shelby whispered.

She turned and thanked the officer as well. Then she picked up her bag and followed her host into the cool foyer of the guesthouse.

Christophe nodded at the doors of the off the lobby café. 'We have a restaurant if you're hungry.'

Shelby shook her head. 'I couldn't eat,' she said.

'As you wish.' Christophe went behind the desk, and handed her a key. 'Second floor,' he said. 'Room 204. Do you need help with your bag?'

Shelby shook her head and took the key from him.

'If you need anything . . .' he said.

Shelby nodded, and began her climb up the dimly lit staircase to the floor above.

The room was cell-like, with roughly surfaced walls painted the color of sunflowers. A narrow bed was covered with a Provençal quilt in a red and mustard print. Beside it, on an end table, sat a pottery lamp, and, against the opposite wall along with a small chest, a spindly desk and a chair, on which Shelby placed her bag. On the desk, a bud vase held an exotic, fresh bloom. Shelby turned on the bedside lamp and went to the French double doors that took up most of the far wall, pulling them open. A balcony, only large enough for two small chairs and a tiny round table between them, looked out on the street below. Through the palm fronds of the tree in front of the building, Shelby could see people moving lazily along the gas-lit street, calling out to one another, or quarreling or laughing.

Shelby felt the tropic breeze envelop her and she felt a sudden longing for someone to lean on. She thought that she was used to being alone. She had lived alone ever since Chloe moved out, and in some ways she enjoyed her solitude. But she had never in her life felt as alone as she did this night. Through the spaces between the buildings across the street she could see the twinkling lights along the harbor and the blackness of the sea beyond. Somewhere, in that sea, her only child was lost.

Shelby began to shiver, although the night was warm. She had rushed to get to this island in the grip of a superstitious agitation that her presence on the scene would somehow rescue

Chloe from peril. It was irrational, of course, but it was part of being a mother – the belief that you could protect your child if only you could reach them. It didn't matter how many mothers could testify that this was untrue and that fate was implacable. The belief persisted. Though she was no sailor, there was a part of Shelby that wanted to flee from this narrow room, and run to the harbor. She wanted to hire a boat, clamber in, and set out to sea. She imagined herself in the prow, calling Chloe's name. Somehow, her voice would drown out the sound of the motor, and the trade winds, and reach to the middle of the vast sea, to where Chloe floated, waiting for rescue. Shelby could almost picture Chloe there, bobbing impatiently on the shifting waves, wondering what was taking her mother so long. The image made her smile, and then her smile faded and the image dissolved. Chloe was not suspended there awaiting her, safe from the elements, the creatures of the sea. She was gone.

Shelby turned her back on the open window. She could not bear to look out at the lights of St Thomas's capital: Charlotte Amalie. The sight of them made her feel short of breath, as if she could feel her daughter's panic. Shelby's stomach heaved as she imagined Chloe falling overboard, hurtling into the water. Despite what everyone had told her, she continued to wonder if perhaps Chloe had survived the plunge from the deck to the water. And then . . . what? Had she struggled to the surface only to see the huge ship, unaware of her plight, steaming on its way to the next port, deaf to her cries? Perhaps, frightened and desperate, Chloe saw those faraway lights of the harbor and tried to swim towards them, barefoot in her yellow dress, her curly hair streaming behind her. Did the hopelessness of her situation dawn on her as she swam, her arms weary, her heart heavy, as she made little progress? Was she full of regret, like a mermaid who realized too late that she had foolishly traded her tail for the dream of love with an indifferent mortal? At the thought of it, Shelby's soul could not contain her anguish, and she let out an unearthly groan of pain and misery.

A rap on her door turned her groan to a cry, and she stared fearfully at the door.

'Mrs Sloan?'

Shelby walked to the door and opened it. The innkeeper,

Christophe, stood at her door holding a tray. There was a bowl of fragrant soup, a glass of wine and a basket with some bread.

'But, I didn't . . .'

'Chief Giroux said to make sure you had something to eat,' said Christophe firmly. He did not ask if he could come in, but simply walked past her, crossed through the room and set the tray down on the small table on the balcony.

'There,' he said. 'It's soup. It will go down easily.'

Shelby looked around, flustered, for her purse. She didn't know whether to offer the man a tip or not.

Christophe understood what she was doing and strode past her into the hallway. 'Please,' he said. 'Accept our hospitality. This is a terrible day for you. Perhaps when you eat you'll feel a bit better.'

The smell of the soup caused a twisting of hunger in her stomach. Shelby hung her head. 'Thank you. You're very kind.'

Christophe waved away her thanks and began to descend the stairs to the first floor. 'If you need anything, call the desk,' he said.

Shelby closed the door and went out on to the balcony. She sat down in the chair and looked at the simple, lovely tray in front of her. She felt tears rising to her eyes again. Like a dam once breeched, tears trembled at the surface and seemed to spill over at will. Shelby took a deep breath, broke off a golden crust of the bread and dipped it into the soup. After the first bite, she picked up the spoon and began to eat and take a few sips of the wine.

There was another tentative knock on her door. She turned in her chair.

'Shelby, are you there?' asked a familiar voice. 'It's Rob. Can I come in?'

She hesitated, then walked over to the door and opened it. Her son-in-law, pale, disheveled and with a heavy five o'clock shadow, seemed to be propping himself up against the door-frame with one arm.

'Is there any news?' she said.

Rob shook his head.

Shelby turned away from the door, leaving it open behind her. She walked back out to the tiny balcony and sat down in her chair. Rob hesitated a moment, and then came into the room, closing the door behind him. He walked out to the balcony also and put a hand on the back of the other chair. 'May I?' he asked.

Shelby nodded, but said nothing.

Rob sat down gingerly on the small chair and looked at her tray of food.

'Have you eaten?' she asked.

Rob shrugged. 'Someone at the station got me a sandwich.'

Shelby nodded, and broke off another corner of bread. She stared at it, wondering if she had the strength to chew it. 'Did they say anything more?'

Rob shook his head 'Nobody is stating it outright, but I think they're ready to rule it an accident. They think that Chloe fell over the railing . . .'

Shelby glared at him. 'Because you said she had a drinking problem.'

Rob took a deep breath. 'I know it's upsetting to you, but it's true,' he insisted. 'I'm sorry, but it is'

'I don't believe you,' Shelby hissed. 'My Chloe?'

'Yes. Your Chloe.'

'You made it up,' Shelby said.

Rob did not bristle at her accusation. 'You don't have to take my word for it. They have a record of the drinks she bought. They have film of her on the boat, buying them. Drinking them. Ask Chief Giroux.'

'I heard all that.'

'Then you know it's true.'

'A couple of drinks on vacation is not a drinking problem,' Shelby snapped. 'You implied that she was a problem drinker before you even went on this trip.'

'She was,' said Rob. 'Well, actually I thought she'd stopped. She was attending AA meetings. But obviously she slipped.'

'How you can sit there and say this to me? Chloe's not in AA. She would have told me.'

'I'm sorry, but she was. Her drinking was out of control.'

'No,' Shelby insisted. 'That is not Chloe. She doesn't do anything sloppy. She likes everything to be just perfect.'

'That was an illusion. An illusion that was too hard for her to keep up.'

'I don't believe you,' Shelby insisted.

'Believe what you want,' he said wearily.

They sat in angry, uneasy silence.

Rob sighed. 'I know it's a shock, Shelby. Believe me, it was for me, too, when I found out.'

Shelby glared at him.

Rob did not seem to notice. Or perhaps, he didn't care. 'I'd had my suspicions for a while,' he said, 'but . . . there was nothing specific. Then, oh, about a year ago, she went to pick up Jeremy at a play date and she didn't come home,' said Rob. 'It was snowy and I was worried, so I called and she didn't answer her phone. I went looking for her. I found the car jumped up on the curb in front of a vacant lot. Chloe was passed out behind the wheel. Jeremy was crying in the back seat.'

'You said it was snowy,' Shelby cried. 'Maybe the car skidded and she hit her head.'

'She was drunk,' said Rob firmly.

Shelby's eyes blazed. 'With Jeremy in the car? No. Not Chloe. I don't believe it. She never . . . she would never do anything that might hurt that child.'

Rob's eyes filled with tears. 'Don't you think I know that? That's how I realized how bad it was.' He began to sob. Shelby looked at him wonderingly.

Finally he sniffed and wiped his tears away with the back of his hand. 'I confronted her and it all came out. She was hiding vodka in water bottles. She was drinking at work and while Jeremy was at preschool. It's a miracle something worse didn't happen. For a long time I wouldn't let her take him in the car after that. But she joined AA. And she swore she was sober. She promised me . . . over and over. Swore she had stopped . . .'

'Why didn't she tell me?' Shelby cried.

Rob shook his head. 'She was so ashamed. She wouldn't tell anyone. Except for the people at AA, I guess. And she made it a point to go to a meeting far from home. She used to go down to some church in Old City. So she wouldn't . . . I don't know, run into someone she knew. I tried to explain to her that it wasn't a sign of weakness to ask for help. But she was ashamed. She made me swear.'

Tears filled Shelby's eyes, and ran down her face. 'Why?' she wailed. 'Why would she do that?'

'Do what?' Rob asked wearily. 'Keep it from you? She knew how you felt about your mother's drinking. Chloe wanted your approval. Don't you know that? She always worried that you wouldn't think well of her.'

'I loved her,' Shelby protested.

Rob shrugged. 'She didn't want you to think she was weak.'

Shelby shook her head, trying to shake off the truth of what he was saying. If she was honest with herself, she knew there was always a sadness in Chloe that nothing could assuage. But she couldn't bear to imagine her daughter worrying about being judged. Fearing her disapproval. It was too painful to think about. Not now. Not ever.

'She wasn't weak,' Shelby insisted. 'She was strong. I mean, you know how strong she was. She was always so disciplined. So fit. In fact, I am thinking that she might have survived the fall from the ship. People have jumped off the Golden Gate Bridge and survived. Chloe might have survived. I've been thinking about this. Tomorrow I'm going to go on board the cruise ship and see where it happened for myself.'

Rob shook his head.

'They can't stop me,' she said. 'Just let them try.'

Rob put his head in his hands.

His defeated look made her suddenly furious. 'What? Why are you doing that?'

'The ship is gone,' he said.

Shelby stared at him. 'What?'

'It's gone. They're underway to their next port of call.'

Shelby felt stunned. 'They can't be,' she whispered.

'They are. They have a lot of passengers who've paid a lot of money.'

'That's more important than Chloe's life?' Shelby cried.

Rob did not reply.

'Well?' she demanded. 'And you just let them go?'

'They didn't have to ask my permission,' said Rob coldly. 'It's what they do. It's perfectly legal. Captain Fredericks explained it to me.'

Shelby felt a sudden fury in her heart at his matter-of-fact tone, at his words that sounded so clinical. 'So, that's fine with you? You don't even care that she's gone, do you?' Shelby accused him. 'You're glad that she's gone. And who can blame you? You're rid of your alcoholic wife.'

As soon as the words were out of her mouth she regretted them.

Rob sat for a moment without speaking, and then he stood up. 'I need some sleep,' he said. 'Tomorrow's going to be a long day.'

Shelby felt ashamed of herself. 'Rob, I'm sorry. That was unfair,' she said.

'Doesn't matter. There's nothing fair about any of this. My world is in pieces.' On that last word, his voice broke.

Shelby began to weep openly. 'I shouldn't have blamed you, Rob.'

'I blame myself,' he said. 'I didn't keep her safe. I feel like it is my fault.'

'Oh God. And Jeremy.'

'I know,' he said.

Shelby shook her head. 'Maybe tomorrow something will happen,' she said hopelessly.

'I'll knock on your door in the morning and we'll go back to the police station.'

'If you hear anything during the night . . .'

'Of course,' he said.

'I feel so helpless,' she said.

'We are helpless.'

Their bruised gazes met for a moment. 'I'll see you in the morning,' he said.

She closed the door behind him, and heard his footsteps in the hallway, the sound of him opening the door of his room. She locked her door and went back out to the balcony. She sat back down and stared into the night. In the street below she could hear a young girl singing as she went by on the street. Lighthearted. Untroubled. Her song wafted up through the palm tree fronds.

Shelby buried her face in her hands. Tears seeped through her fingers and dripped from her chin. As the singer disappeared down the street, the sound of her voice became muffled, and then, little by little, it drifted away.

SEVEN

The next morning they arrived at the police station early and found Chief Giroux deep in conversation with Agent DeWitt. As Shelby and Rob entered the large common room where half a dozen officers were working, chatting, and drinking tea, the room fell silent. Everyone stared at them for a moment, and then resumed their work in a quieter fashion.

'How was the Maison?' Chief Giroux asked. 'Did Christophe make you comfortable?'

'Yes, thank you,' Shelby said dully.

'He runs a very nice place. My father and Christophe's father came here from Martinique when they were young men. Our mothers are sisters. So, we are more like brothers than cousins,' he said.

Shelby and Rob did not reply. The only family they could think about was their own.

The Chief did not bother to ask them how they had slept. It was obvious from their rumpled clothes and the blue circles under their puffy, reddened eyes, that the night had been long and grim. 'We have a few things we need to discuss with you,' he said.

'If you both would come with us,' said Agent DeWitt.

Chief Giroux indicated one of the open interrogation rooms and they all filed in. Agent DeWitt closed the door. On a table at the front of the room was a computer monitor, humming, but blank. Chief Giroux offered them all a seat. Rob refused. Shelby took it gratefully. Chief Giroux's dark skin made his shirt look almost blindingly white. He clasped his hands behind his back and spoke to them gently but firmly. 'First of all, Mr Kendricks, Mrs Sloan, It's my sad duty to tell you that the search for Chloe is no longer a rescue mission. The Coast Guard has suspended all operations . . .'

'Oh no,' Rob groaned.

'What?' Shelby cried.

The Chief continued speaking as if they had not spoken. 'Now, it's officially considered a recovery mission. We don't need the Coast Guard for that. That can be carried out by the local police.'

Shelby stared at him through eyes grainy from weeping. 'What does that mean?'

Agent DeWitt toyed with the end of his tie. 'Simply put, it means that we no longer have the expectation that your daughter can still be alive. We base this on all our knowledge of the sea, the body's susceptibility to hypothermia, the ocean predators. In fact, there was little chance that she was alive when she went into the water after a fall like that. But by now, the chances are . . . negligible really.'

'No,' Shelby protested. 'You can't just give up.'

Chief Giroux sighed. 'Mrs Sloan. I know it's terribly difficult, but you must understand that your daughter is not going to be found alive. She probably won't be found at all.'

'She certainly won't be found if you stop looking,' Shelby retorted.

Rob did not protest, but he slumped down into the nearest chair. His face was white as chalk. The police chief simply shook his head and crossed his arms over his chest. Shelby turned to Agent DeWitt. 'Can't you do something? You're from the government. Tell them they have to continue.'

Agent DeWitt frowned at her, his gaze sympathetic, but immovable.

'So, that's it?' said Shelby in disbelief. She turned to Rob. 'Are you just going to sit there? You have to do something.'

Rob's eyes flashed with anger. 'I'm not a magician, Shelby. If I could bring her back I would.'

Shelby ignored him, hating him. 'What if we were to hire searchers of our own? Maybe you could suggest someone. People who know these waters . . . I can pay for it. I'll gladly pay for it.'

'Mrs Sloan,' said the chief, his eyes filled with concern. 'I cannot stop you if that is what you want to do. But she went overboard nearly thirty-six hours ago. Short of a miracle . . .'

'Yes,' Shelby said hopefully. 'A miracle. It could be—'

'I would be lying to you if I agreed with you. It's impossible to survive that long in the water. Especially after a fall like the one she took from the boat,' said the chief. 'I cannot encourage you to throw your money away.'

'It's my money. If I want to hire someone—'

'See here,' said the chief. 'I will arrange it for you, all right. I will arrange for several boats to continue the search, for as many days as you authorize.'

'I don't want just anybody,' Shelby insisted. 'I want helicopters too. And qualified people. Boaters who know these waters.'

'I understand. And all this can be arranged.' he said soothingly. 'Independent contractors. I warn you, it will be at great expense. But, I can contact these people for you, if that is what you wish.'

'Then do,' said Shelby.

'I have to advise you against this,' said Agent DeWitt. 'It makes no sense. This is a waste of your resources. The Coast Guard used aircraft – both helicopters and a long-range surveillance plane. They used their own cutters, and they thoroughly searched an area of approximately 800 square miles. They scanned it repeatedly with the most sophisticated equipment available.'

'Still . . .' Shelby said stubbornly.

Chief Giroux and Agent DeWitt exchanged a glance. 'You don't have to decide right this minute,' said the chief. 'Think it over and you can call me. If you decide that's what you want, it won't take any time at all to put this plan into operation.'

'And furthermore, I'm not at all satisfied with your conclusions. You don't even know how she came to be in that water. It's not good enough to say she was drunk and she fell overboard. I don't accept that,' Shelby insisted.

'That's one reason we brought you in here. I want to show you something,' said the chief. He approached the computer that was sitting on a desk at the front of the room. 'Mr Kendricks saw these yesterday. I wanted you to see them. Look here.' He began to key in some commands, and the computer screen raced from one image to another. The chief halted at the one he wanted.

Shelby leaned forward and watched the video that was on the screen. The film was shot from above, from a fixed location. The people on the film were strolling in front of a café. It took Shelby a moment to recognize the young woman with long, wavy hair, wearing a sundress, leaning against the bar.

'Chloe,' Shelby yelped, automatically reaching for the screen. 'Where is she? Where did you get that?'

'It's film from the security camera on the Lido deck of the ship,' said Agent DeWitt. 'Watch what she does.'

Shelby watched as Chloe, looking all around her guiltily, placed an order. The bartender pulled a bottle off the shelf behind him and made her a drink. Chloe handed him her card and gulped the drink down. He had no sooner swiped her card than she indicated that she wanted another. The bartender complied.

'So, she had something to drink,' said Shelby dismissively.

'If you like, we can watch her drink two more of these,' said Agent DeWitt with a hint of sarcasm.

Shelby felt her face redden.

'Now,' said Chief Giroux, aiming a remote at the keyboard. Another image arose, this one of tables with many people seated, talking and consulting the cards in front of them. It was easy to spot Chloe. She sat stiffly at a table near the back of the room, a numbered card on the table in front of her. The camera that caught her was also positioned near the back of the room, so Shelby was able to have a clear view of her daughter. She was a few seats down from the other people. A woman leaned over to talk to her, and Shelby recognized Virgie and Don, the fiftieth anniversary couple who had talked to her in the hallway yesterday. They were clearly trying to engage Chloe in conversation. Shelby watched as Chloe replied, gesturing vaguely.

The other couple Shelby had met, Bud and Peggy, joined the table, and Peggy leaned her metal cane against it. The conversation continued. Chloe's eyelids drooped and, while she was talking, she made an expansive gesture that knocked the cane over and it clattered to the floor. Chloe looked chagrined, and got unsteadily to her feet. She bent over to try to retrieve the cane, but couldn't seem to grasp it. The lame woman's husband came around and picked it up. Chloe clearly was apologizing but he shook his head as if to say it didn't matter. This time, he placed the cane far out of Chloe's reach.

The bingo game proceeded and all were marking their cards except Chloe, who was staring into her drink, and occasionally making some comments to no one in particular. Her head would begin to nod, and then she would force herself awake, like a sleepy driver at the wheel of a car. Finally, she could resist her condition no more. Her eyes closed, and her head hit the table, her arms splayed out across the table, sending bingo cards skidding across the table's surface, and markers fluttering to the floor. Her cheek was mashed against the tabletop. Her eyes were closed. People from the other tables turned to stare. The people at Chloe's table looked at her, and then at one another worriedly. The old woman began to shake Chloe's shoulder and speak directly into her ear. Chloe shook her head but did not lift it from the table.

Shelby averted her gaze from the screen. 'Enough,' said Shelby.

The chief turned it off. 'We have a lot more footage,' said the chief with a sigh. 'We have footage of her being helped to her room, these people carrying her shoes and pocket-book, and she cannot even stand up. Of course there is no footage from inside the cabins – that's private space – but we can surmise that after these nice people left her alone in the room . . .'

'All right,' Shelby cried. 'All right.'

Rob sat, stone-faced, staring at the blank screen.

The chief and Agent DeWitt exchanged a glance.

'What now?' Shelby whispered.

'You go back home and remember her in happier times,' Giroux advised.

'I can't,' Shelby wailed.

Shelby wanted to cling to her chair, to refuse to move like a stubborn child, but when she looked at her son-in-law's face she knew that he had given up the fight. He had accepted it; his wife had fallen overboard in a drunken accident.

'I wish there was more we could do,' said Chief Giroux.

'I understand,' said Rob. He shook hands with him. 'Thank you,' he said. 'Thank you for everything. Thank you for trying.'

Chief Giroux nodded gravely. Shelby got up from her chair. She felt too disoriented and outraged to offer the police chief her hand. But, at the last moment, as Rob urged her toward the door, she turned to the chief and Agent DeWitt. 'Yes,' she said humbly. 'Thank you.'

'We're terribly sorry for your great loss,' said the chief, nodding slightly. 'One of my officers will take you back to the hotel. You can wait for him in the lobby.'

Stiffly, they walked down to the vestibule. But as if by common consent, they both decided to step outside. Rob stood in the narrow street as Shelby leaned against the building, feeling woozy from the tropical heat.

'So you're not in favor of continuing the search,' she said to him in an accusing tone.

Rob shook his head but did not look at her. 'I'd do it myself if I had that kind of money. I suppose I could sell the house or whatever. But I have to think of the kids. Of their future. That's what Chloe would want.'

'You're so . . . passive. You're so resigned to it,' Shelby said angrily.

'Well, I've been here a bit longer than you,' Rob retorted. 'Reality has begun to set in,' he said.

The officer pulled up in front of the Justice Center, and they got into the car. They returned to the hotel in silence, and, upon arrival at the Maison sur la Mer, they went their separate ways without speaking.

Shelby lay on the bed, the fan revolving over her head, her hands covering her eyes, and thought about mounting her own search. She knew they were not lying to her. It was probably hopeless. And it would be expensive. Although she had some money, she was far from rich. But there was a brokerage account that she could cash out. It was her money for a rainy day. And she had money saved for her retirement. After a while she got up off the bed and rang the police station. The chief answered her call immediately.

'I want to start the search again. A helicopter. And boats.'

'This could cost tens of thousands of dollars,' the chief warned.

'Please arrange it for me,' Shelby said. 'I'll pay for it. Shall I come down to the station? You must have papers you'll want me to sign.'

'Well, yes, as a matter of fact. I will need proof that you have the funds available to pay for this,' said the chief.

'I'll come down there before my flight back. I'll give you my bank references.'

'I'll waste no time having them checked, and we'll get the search underway.'

'Thank you,' said Shelby.

'Then you can go back home and see about your grandson. I promise I will keep you informed.'

'I'd appreciate that,' said Shelby.

While Rob was on the phone trying to make travel arrangements, Shelby went downstairs and asked Christophe to prepare their bills.

'You're leaving?' Christophe said.

Shelby nodded. 'They think it's hopeless.'

Christophe winced, as if he could imagine the pain of that verdict. 'I'm so sorry.'

'You've been very nice,' said Shelby without feeling.

'What will you do when you get back?' Christophe asked.

Shelby shook her head. 'I don't know. Go home I suppose. Try to . . . I don't know. I was going to say "start again" but I . . . well . . .'

Christophe nodded. 'I wish you well. I hope you find your peace of mind.'

Shelby thanked him and returned to her room. She opened the bureau drawer and took out the clothes. She packed her few things, including Chloe's t-shirts that she had brought to wear herself. Just folding them into the suitcase made her feel as if she was going to collapse from the pain. It felt so wrong to leave. Even though, she reminded herself, she was spending all her savings for the search to continue, she felt that by leaving she was agreeing to give up on Chloe. Chloe, whom she had worked for, struggled for, dreamed about. Now, the meaning of her life was gone – lost beneath the glimmering waves.

For a moment, Shelby thought that she would stay right here in St Thomas. She sat down beside the open suitcase and considered the possibility. Why not, she thought? Why not let everything else go except her slim bit of hope? She could question every boat's captain as he returned from the search. Remain vigilant. If she did, she would eventually go mad sitting by the harbor, staring out at the blinding surface of the pale jade sea, still hoping after all hope was gone. But so what? What did it matter if she went mad? Why go on?

But one image flickered persistently in her heart. It was the face of a small boy who was about to be dealt an unimaginable loss. Jeremy was Chloe's son, and he would need her to put her own sorrow aside and come to his aid. Chloe would want her to go – to be with Jeremy. To help him through it. She knew it was true. So, that decided it. She rose from the chair to finish her meager packing. She would go. At least for the moment, she would leave it to the searchers, and go.

Shelby and Rob were booked on the same flights home, first a small plane to Miami, and then a later flight back to Philadelphia. They were not seated near one another, but Rob waited dutifully for her after the first leg of the flight, and they sat in silence together in an airport bar in Miami.

'Did you talk to Jeremy?' Shelby finally asked him as she clinked the ice cubes in her limeade. 'Does he know yet?'

Rob shook his head. 'No. Not yet. I honestly don't know how I'm going to break it to him.'

Shelby nodded. She glanced over at her son-in-law resting his head in his hands. She thought about all the cruel accusations she had leveled at him. It was true that he had been more passive in the face of this disaster than she would have wished. But looking at him now, it was clear what a toll the loss of Chloe was taking. His skin was ashen and his eyes were red-rimmed and sunken. He seemed to have aged about twenty years in the last week. She had been thinking about something that she hesitated to say. Finally, she decided to just blurt it out. 'You know, Rob,' she said, 'I've been thinking. This is all going to be so hard on Jeremy . . .'

Rob nodded and spoke absently. 'No kidding.'

'The last thing I want to do is to make things more difficult. But I was just wondering,' said Shelby, 'if it might be best for Jeremy, if I stayed with you. Just for a little while. Just till he gets used to the idea that his mother is . . . isn't coming back.'

Rob looked at her warily 'You mean . . . at our house?' he said.

'Just for a few days. Of course, I realize that I may not be welcome with Chloe gone.'

'No, it's not that,' he said.

'What?' she asked.

'Nothing. It's just that I know you're busy. I mean, Chloe was telling me about your new boss and all. She said you were worried about it.'

Shelby thought about her job. The man who had hired her, groomed her, and repeatedly promoted her, Albert Markson, had died suddenly last month. His nephew, Elliott, a younger, less approachable man, had taken over, and made it clear that every employee and every position was going to be reevaluated. 'I feel like none of it matters any more,' she said.

'I know what you mean,' Rob agreed. Then, he sighed. 'But you don't want to lose your job.'

'The job can wait. Of course, if you think I would be in your way,' Shelby said, feeling the awkwardness between them.

Rob avoided her gaze and said nothing to contradict her. A voice on the loudspeaker was making a preliminary boarding call for their flight to Philly. 'That's us,' said Rob, standing up.

Shelby stood up and pulled out the handle of her bag. She had not expected wild enthusiasm for her idea, but did feel as if he could have at least been polite about it.

'All right,' he said.

Shelby looked at him uncertainly. 'All right I should stay?'

Rob shrugged. 'For Jeremy,' he said.

'I think it's what Chloe would want me to do,' she said.

Rob did not reply. He rolled his bag out around her chair, and, avoiding her gaze, headed for the door.

EIGHT

They barely spoke on the drive back from the airport. When they arrived at the house, all the parking spots along the curb were taken. Rob pulled his pick-up truck beside a parked car and held his foot on the brake. 'You can get out,' he said. 'I may have to park up the block.'

Shelby gazed at her daughter's home. Winter pansies bloomed in Chloe's carefully tended windowboxes. It was only a week ago, Shelby thought, that she had pulled up and seen her daughter waiting for her in front of that gray stone row home. It seemed like an eternity. 'I'm dreading going in,' she said.

Exhaustion and impatience were written all over Rob's face. 'You can wait outside if you want,' he said.

'No, I only meant . . . Never mind. I'll go in. I have my key.' Slowly, painfully, as if all her joints were frozen, Shelby forced herself to get out of the truck's cab. She lifted her bag out of the truck bed and walked up to the front door, rolling her suitcase along behind her as Rob pulled away from the curb.

Shelby unlocked the slate-blue front door and it swung open into the cool darkness of the vestibule. She walked in and stood still, overwhelmed by her memories of Chloe.

Rob followed in a few minutes, dragging the suitcases. I better put this stuff away, he said. 'Jeremy will be home any minute.'

'Any minute?' Shelby asked. 'What do you mean? Aren't we going to go and pick him up?'

Rob answered without looking at her. 'I called Lianna when we landed in Philly. She offered to bring him over.'

Shelby's stomach churned at the thought of Jeremy's imminent arrival. She wasn't ready. She didn't want to hear Rob tell this small boy that his mother was gone forever. 'Maybe you should call Lianna back and tell her we'll come and get him.'

'What for?' Rob said. 'They can bring him.'

'I know. I understand,' said Shelby. 'I just thought—'

She was interrupted by a knock at the front door. 'Probably them,' said Rob. He went to the door and opened it. Two men in jackets and ties stood on the front step. They both displayed their police shields.

Rob stared at them. 'Yes?' he said.

'Sir, I'm Detective Ortega. This is my partner, Detective McMillen. Can we trouble you for a minute?'

'What for?' Rob demanded.

'Rob,' Shelby protested. She knew that he was fed up with police, but his attitude was rude. 'Please, come in,' she said.

The two officers entered the living room. 'Just back from a trip?' said the younger one.

Rob and Shelby exchanged a glance. 'Yes,' said Shelby.

'This won't take long. We wondered if you would mind looking at this picture for us.' He held out a photo of a man with short hair and vacant eyes. It was the sort of photo that hung on the post office wall – full face and profile. 'Do you recognize this man?'

'No. Who is he? What's this got to do with us?' Rob demanded.

'His name's Norman Cook. He recently escaped from a prison road crew out near Lancaster. He hijacked a car that just turned up in a municipal lot where it had been towed. When we found it, it had a parking ticket from this block on it. We're canvassing the block to see if anyone knows this guy and can help us to find him. He could be very dangerous.'

Rob frowned and looked at the drawing more closely. 'No. Can't say that I've ever seen this guy.' The officer showed it to Shelby.

Shelby shook her head. 'Sorry. No.'

'OK,' said Detective Ortega. 'Keep an eye peeled. If he does have a connection to someone on this block, he may return to the neighborhood. If you see him, please, give us a call. He's a violent felon.'

'Will do,' said Rob.

The officers left and went on to the next house, although their black and white cruiser remained parked in a no parking zone across the street, its lights flashing.

Rob sighed. 'All right. I'd better put these suitcases away before Jeremy sees them.'

'We need more time,' Shelby fretted.

Rob frowned at her. 'Putting it off isn't going to make it any easier,' he said.

Shelby knew that he was right. She realized that she would have put it off forever, if only she could. To be useful, to stop herself from thinking, she took her bag back up to Molly's room.

While she was unpacking, she heard the front door open, and a young voice called out 'Dad?'

Shelby went to the top of the stairs and looked down.

Molly, dressed in a baggy sweatshirt and jeans, stood there uncertainly. She looked up and saw Shelby, and the teenager's eyes widened behind her glasses. Without a word to Shelby she disappeared into the vestibule. As Shelby started down the stairs, she heard Molly calling out the front door to her mother. 'Mom. Hurry up.'

Shelby followed her into the vestibule. 'Come on in,' Shelby said.

Molly avoided looking at Shelby, as if fearful she might be

stricken by a curse if she met Shelby's gaze. Molly edged past her into the living room. Rob came down the stairs and saw his daughter. He opened his arms and Molly flung herself against him, her cheek flattened against his shirt.

'I'm sorry, Dad,' she said, her voice muffled.

Rob stroked her unkempt hair tenderly, his gaze faraway. 'Thanks, sweetheart. I know you are.'

Shelby walked out on to the front step and peered into the darkness. Lianna was leaning into the back seat of the car, which was double-parked in front of the house. The car's flashers were blinking. Harris got out of the driver's seat and waved to Shelby. He indicated the police car, its lights still flashing, parked illegally across the street, and frowned.

Shelby walked out to the curb. 'Some escaped convict got a parking ticket on this block,' she explained. 'The police are looking for anyone who saw him.'

Harris grimaced. 'That's comforting,' he said, shaking his head. 'Welcome home.'

'Life in the big city,' said Shelby, trying to force a smile. 'Thanks for bringing Jeremy home. We could have come for him.'

Lianna stood up and regarded Shelby frankly, her keen, gray eyes looking pained. 'We were glad to do it. How are you holding up? You and Rob?'

Shelby shook her head. 'Surviving.'

Lianna gazed at Shelby with genuine sympathy. 'I swear, I don't know how. I am so sorry,' she said.

Shelby felt her tears well up, and she didn't try to stop them. 'Thank you,' she said. She wiped her tears on her sleeve and took a deep breath. 'I want to thank you so much for keeping Jeremy,' she said, 'so I could be there.'

'We were glad to do it.' Lianna frowned in the direction of the open car door and stepped away from it. She lowered her voice to almost a whisper. 'About Jeremy. I think you should know . . .'

Shelby could see Jeremy's legs inside the car, kicking into the back of the front seat. Harris came around and wedged himself into the space between the front and back seats. 'Hey buddy,' Harris said, as he reached down to unbuckle the car seat. 'You're home.' He lifted the boy out, cradling him against his chest.

Jeremy looked over Harris's shoulder at Shelby and blinked as if he could not believe his eyes.

'Hi sweetie.' Shelby reached up for her grandson, but Jeremy reared back, kicking his chubby leg at her.

'No, Shep, I don't want you. I don't want you. I want Mommy,' the child yelled, his face red.

'Hey, slugger,' Harris cajoled him. 'Stop that now. Say hi to your grandmom.'

Jeremy began to scream. 'No Shep. I want Mommy, I want Mommy, I want Mommy.' Tears spurted from his eyes and he clutched Harris's jacket with his fists. Harris kept a firm grip on the child.

Lianna spoke quietly to Shelby in her low, husky voice. 'I'm so sorry. This is what I wanted to tell you. Some volunteer at that church school he goes to told him about Chloe. Some old biddy who helps out in the classroom. I don't know what she was thinking. She said she was afraid the kids would tell him that his mother was drowned in the ocean and she had to explain it to him.'

Jeremy had buried his face against Harris's shoulder. 'Hey there buddy,' Harris murmured. 'Everybody wants to see you.'

'NO. I won't,' Jeremy insisted.

'He's just upset,' said Harris to Shelby. 'Let me carry him inside.'

Shelby glanced back at the row house. Rob was in the doorway, comforting Molly. Shelby took a deep breath. 'I'll do it,' she said. As Shelby reached for him, Jeremy began to strike at her with his little, balled-up fists. His face was as red as a tomato. Ignoring Jeremy's angry blows, his kicking, sneakered feet, Shelby lifted her grandson from Harris's arms.

'Put me down,' Jeremy insisted.

'Maybe he wants to walk,' Lianna suggested as Jeremy continued to kick and punch his grandmother. A teenage driver in a low-slung car with a loud boom box pulled up behind Harris's late model sedan. Between the illegally parked police cruiser and Harris's doubleparked Lexus, there was no room to get by.

'Molly,' Shelby called out to the girl who was still huddled beneath her father's arm in the front doorway, 'can you get Jeremy's stuff for me?'

Molly nodded and hurried down to the car. Harris opened the trunk and began to hand Molly her brother's belongings.

Lianna wrapped her arms around her own, slightly expanded waist and walked up to Rob. They spoke awkwardly. Shelby could see that Rob was saying something to his ex-wife, and she was nodding, staring at the ground.

The teenager honked his horn.

Harris turned and glared at the young driver. 'Keep your pants on,' he said to him. Then he turned back to Shelby. 'Are you sure you don't want me to carry him?' Harris asked.

Shelby shook her head. She thought of all the times as a young mother when she had been flummoxed by Chloe's angry outbursts. Inexperienced with children, inexperienced with life, she would try to placate Chloe, which only served to make the child more furious. Shelby felt none of that uncertainty with her grandson. She knew that he was suffering. She held the flailing child close as he pummeled her. 'It's not necessary. I've got him.'

Molly emerged from the trunk carrying Jeremy's bags of clothes and toys. 'Hey, Jeremy, you want to keep some toys for the next time you come over?' Molly asked her brother gently.

'No,' Jeremy retorted. 'Leave me alone.'

'You come see us again soon,' Harris said kindly to Jeremy.

'NO,' Jeremy shouted.

'We love you, Jeremy,' Molly said in a small voice.

'Thank you, Molly,' said Shelby. 'Thank you both. For everything.'

The teenage driver leaned on his horn again, and Harris shook his head.

'Go on. You go ahead,' said Shelby.

'Are you sure you're all right?' asked Harris.

'We'll be all right,' said Shelby in a determined voice.

Jeremy bellowed in protest and twisted furiously, trying to escape from her arms.

'Jeremy, I'm not going to let you go,' Shelby whispered, but it was a promise, not a threat. 'Shep's here now. And Daddy. Daddy has missed you so much. And listen. Your Dad and I are gonna stay right here with you. We're gonna take care of everything. You'll see. It's gonna be all right.' She was not sure if that was true. But she knew that she had to try and make him believe it.

Lianna and Molly got back into the car. Harris gave the teenage driver behind him a disgusted glance, as if daring him to honk again. Then he slid into the driver's seat and turned off the flashers. Lianna and Molly waved as he pulled away from the curb. 'Bye Jeremy,' Lianna called out sadly. 'Bye honey.'

Jeremy suddenly stopped struggling and stiffened. He watched the car's disappearing taillights longingly. Then he gasped, and began to sob anew. 'I want M . . . mommy,' he wailed. Shelby pulled him close, and felt his wet tears against her ear, in her hair. She could feel his small heart beating frantically, close to hers, and his grieving cry pierced Shelby's heart like an arrow. She felt the warmth of his feverish little body radiating against hers.

Rob appeared at her side, and reached for his son. Jeremy reared back and turned his wrathful gaze on his father. 'Why is Mommy gone? How come Mommy fell in the water?' he demanded, pointing a pudgy finger at him.

'I don't know, son,' Rob said, opening his arms to the boy.

Jeremy turned his back on his father and huddled against Shelby. 'You didn't bring her home. You shoulda brought her home.'

Shelby's heart was beating fast, and she couldn't bring herself to look at Rob.

'I should have,' Rob said. 'I know.'

NINE

The next few days they were inundated with calls and visits from friends and neighbors. Most people's intentions were only the best. Members of Rob's church arrived and brought covered dishes. Chloe's co-workers at Dr Cliburn's stopped by with a flowering plant. Darcie, Jeremy's preschool teacher, came by with brownies and a favorite book, which she read to Jeremy, several times over.

'Thinking of you' bouquets arrived and filled up every surface of the house. There was one from the Markson stores, with a card signed by her colleagues. When she called to say that she was going to stay a while with her son-in-law and grandson, Elliott Markson was said to be too busy to take the call. Shelby suspected that, unlike his Uncle Albert, who was a consummate family man, Elliott did not believe that family came before business. Shelby's determination did not waver. In fact, she was amazed at how little she cared. If Elliott Markson didn't understand what she was doing, that was his problem. She would try to explain it to him when she returned to work.

Shelby knew that going back to work was inevitable. In a little over a week the search had exhausted half her savings, and still no trace of Chloe. Chief Giroux sent her an email urging her most strenuously to call it off. Shelby hesitated, frightened by the mounting expenses he had listed, and then insisted they continue a little longer.

Talia called, complaining that their mother was almost in-coherent now, slipping in and out of consciousness. It took Shelby a few moments to realize that her sister was completely ignorant of Chloe's disappearance. When Shelby explained what had happened, Talia hung up abruptly, as if insulted. Two days later, a sympathy card arrived in the mail, signed 'From Talia and mother.' There was no word from Glen.

Rob went back to his job, coming and going like a zombie. If people were questioning him at work about Chloe's disappearance, he did not mention it.

Shelby let Jeremy stay home for a few days, and then, at Rob's insistence, she sent him back to preschool. She knew that Rob was right. At home there were too many reminders of Chloe, and Jeremy needed distraction, not reminding. Shelby dropped him off, worrying at the sight of him trudging into school, listless, quiet, and unsmiling. But when she came to pick him up, he seemed better – wrestling and trading snacks with a friend. His gloom returned when he saw Shelby. Apparently he had forgotten for a moment that it would not be his mother picking him up.

The Saturday after they arrived back the phone rang. Rob had taken Jeremy to a softball game at the field by the elementary school. Shelby looked at the area code on the caller ID and did not recognize it. She answered the phone warily, afraid that it might be a reporter. Rob insisted that they avoid all contact with curious local reporters.

'Mrs Sloan?'

It took Shelby a moment to recognize the voice at the other end. Then, she was flooded with relief. 'Franny!' she cried, greeting Chloe's childhood friend. After years of helping out in her parents' pizzeria, Franny had graduated from culinary school and moved to Los Angeles where she was now a sous-chef at an upscale trattoria. Despite the distance between them, Franny and Chloe had remained friends all their lives and saw each other whenever Franny came home to Philadelphia.

'Mrs Sloan, I'm so sorry about Chloe. I should have called sooner,' Franny said in a rush. 'I didn't know what to say. I can't even really believe it's true.'

'How did you find out?'

'My mom called me. She read about it in the Philly paper. She said it was only a little item – she almost missed it.'

'I should have called you,' Shelby admitted.

'Oh no, not at all. I was just afraid to pick up the phone and hear your voice. I know how much you loved Chloe.'

'Thank you. That means a lot,' said Shelby. She could picture Franny's round face, her shiny, black hair.

'Is there going to be a . . . memorial or something? If there is, I will definitely be there. I mean, I feel like it isn't real somehow. Maybe if there were a service . . .'

Shelby hesitated. When the minister from Rob's church paid a call and mentioned the possibility of a memorial service, Shelby bristled at the suggestion. 'We don't know for sure that she's dead,' Shelby insisted. Rob had frowned at her, but Shelby stuck out her chin defiantly. Of course, she knew – she was just trying to avoid the final pronouncement.

'We don't have anything planned,' Shelby said. 'They never found her.'

'Oh no,' Franny moaned. Shelby heard the thickness of tears in her voice. 'Oh it's too terrible.'

'The Coast Guard mounted a search with boats and helicopters but they finally gave up,' said Shelby. 'I've hired people to continue searching for her but . . . so far . . . nothing.'

Franny sniffled, and then collected herself. 'Do they know how it actually happened?'

Shelby didn't even want to speak the words aloud. But then she thought, if anyone would be likely to know about Chloe's drinking problem, it would be Franny. She decided to be blunt and gauge Franny's reaction.

'They said that it appeared that Chloe was drinking, and accidentally fell overboard.'

'My mom said that was in the paper,' Franny admitted, 'I can't believe it.'

Shelby's appreciated her indignation. 'Me neither. But Rob said that . . .'

'What?'

'He said that she had developed a problem with alcohol.'

'No way,' Franny protested. 'Since when?'

'Well, I don't know. When was the last time you saw her?'

Franny thought for a minute. 'Last time I was home. It was about a month ago. I came over for dinner. In fact, we were talking about the cruise. I was trying to tempt Chloe with this great bottle of wine I brought, but she said she didn't want any. Now that I think about it . . .'

'What?' Shelby asked.

'I actually remember wondering if she was pregnant again. Or trying to get pregnant. It never occurred to me that she might be . . .'

'An alcoholic,' said Shelby.

'Never,' Franny insisted.

'Apparently she was going to AA.'

'No way! God, I had no idea.'

'I thought if she would talk to anybody, it would be you,' said Shelby.

Franny sighed. 'I thought I knew her better than anybody.'

They were both silent for a moment, thinking their own thoughts. Then Shelby said, 'How did she seem to you when you were here?'

'Oh well, you know Chloe. A little anxious.'

'Anxious about what?' Shelby asked.

Franny hesitated. 'I don't know. Sometimes she would borrow trouble.'

'How? What do you mean?' Shelby asked.

'Well, she was always comparing herself to Lianna. She would always say how beautiful Lianna was. And she mentioned that Lianna was pregnant. I thought she might be a little . . . jealous.'

Shelby's heart ached. In that instant she remembered

Chloe with tears in her eyes, insisting that there was nothing wrong in her marriage. 'Do you think that she and Rob had problems?' Shelby asked.

'I don't think so. I mean, he may have been upset about the drinking. Rob's such a straight arrow. But if he said she'd stopped . . .'

'Well, he said she went to AA. You have to be sober to go to those meetings,' said Shelby, ruminating aloud. 'But I got the feeling that he didn't really trust her. Chloe must have known that.'

'You know how Chloe is. She isn't the most . . . self-confident . . .'

'I know. She gets down on herself . . .'

They both realized at once that they were talking about Chloe in the present tense.

'I just can't believe this,' said Franny miserably. 'Any of it.'

The back door of the house slammed and Shelby heard Rob call out, 'We're back.' She heard the sound of Jeremy's feet thundering up the stairs as he yelled out 'Shep!' Jeremy ran into the room, his eyes alight for the first time, it seemed, since they had arrived back. He held up a grimy softball and offered it to her. 'I caught it, Shep,' he cried.

Shelby took the proffered ball. 'That's great,' she said to the beaming child. 'Franny, Jeremy just got back from the park, and he's here with me so I'm going to have to go.'

'OK. You'll let me know if there's any news? How long are you going to be there with Rob and Jeremy?'

'I'm not sure yet.'

'You'll let me know if you decide about a service?'

'Of course. I will,' said Shelby. 'And thanks.'

Rob came into the room, looking grimy but cheerful. 'Jeremy show you the ball he caught?'

Shelby hung up the phone carefully. 'Yes,' she said. 'And I want to hear all about it.'

'Who was that?' Rob asked.

'A friend,' she said.

'It was Aunt Franny,' Jeremy piped up.

Shelby's face reddened and Rob raised his eyebrows. 'Oh really?' he said coolly. 'That's nice. How is Franny?'

'She's grieving. Of course,' Shelby snapped, before she could stop herself.

Jeremy looked warily from his grandmother to his father and back.

'Sorry,' she mumbled. 'That was a difficult call.' Before Rob could reply, Shelby sat down on the sofa and pulled Jeremy up on to the cushion beside her. 'All right,' she said. 'Now, let's get to the important stuff. I want to hear all about this catch of yours.'

Later in the afternoon, as Shelby was staring into the refrigerator, trying to figure out what to make for supper, Rob came into the kitchen and announced that he was taking Jeremy, Molly, and Molly's friend, Sara, to Pizza Hut and the new Disney movie.

Shelby looked at him in surprise. 'Really? I wouldn't think thirteen-year-old girls would be interested in that.'

'Actually,' said Rob, 'they wanted to see the new teen vampire movie, but I wanted to include Jeremy. When I called Molly to explain the problem, she was the one who suggested the Disney movie. She still loves her animation.'

'That was thoughtful of her,' Shelby said.

'She's a good kid,' said Rob. 'And she adores her brother. Chloe never understood that.'

'What does that mean?' Shelby asked.

'Nothing,' said Rob defensively. 'She just couldn't seem to grasp that they were brother and sister. I mean Jeremy was hers, and Molly . . . just didn't belong in the picture.'

Shelby felt stung by his complaint. How can you speak ill of Chloe, she wanted to say? Is that really all you can remember about her? 'It's not easy to become a stepparent.'

'I don't mean it as a criticism,' Rob said stubbornly. 'That's just the way it was. I just kept hoping she would adjust.'

Shelby was not placated, but she kept her thoughts to herself as she helped Jeremy to get ready. Rob asked her politely if she wanted to come along, but Shelby insisted that she would enjoy an evening to herself. She waved goodbye at the door, trying to smile as they pulled away. But once they were gone, she turned back to the house with a feeling of despair. Alone in the house with Chloe's quilts and her magnetized photos on the refrigerator, and her careful arrangements of her cupboards, Shelby suddenly felt overwhelmed by her loss. She did not belong here and she knew it. So far, Rob had been tolerant of her presence. He had even thanked her for helping him with Jeremy.

But Shelby had no illusions about her role here. Jeremy was her grandson, but he had his father and his sister as well. And she had no one. It seemed to her now, without Chloe, that she had nothing. Rob and Jeremy would go on with their lives and, without Chloe to remind them, would forget to call her, to keep in touch. For a few more years Jeremy would welcome her attentions and then, he would have less and less time for his grandmother. Shelby felt her spirits sinking and recognized the imminent onset of another crying jag.

You need to get out of this house, she thought. These walls are closing in.

Do something. Get in your car and drive to Center City, she thought. Call Jen for dinner. Relax in your own space. But even as she toyed with the idea and went up to Molly's room to put on some makeup, she felt a paralyzing inertia, and knew she wouldn't do it.

She was staring at herself in the mirror uncertain of how or where to escape the misery of her own heart when the doorbell rang. Shelby went to the top of the stairs and waited, hoping that whoever it was would go away. The doorbell rang again. With a sigh, Shelby descended the stairs and opened the door. She saw a complete stranger standing there. It was a woman about her own age, although this woman had a wan, deeply lined face and seemed careless of her appearance. She had graying, frizzy hair, and wore a shapeless canvas coat.

'Mrs Sloan?' the woman asked.

Shelby stared at her suspiciously. 'Yes.'

'My name is Janice Pryor. I'm not from around here. I live in New York.'

Shelby frowned at her, and did not reply.

'I'm here about your daughter,' Janice said.

Shelby's heart skidded. 'What about her?'

'Well, I wanted to talk to you about what happened to her.'

Shelby's heart began to hammer. 'Were you on the same cruise with her?' she asked.

'No. But I know a lot about these cruise ship accidents and I think you may have been misled. Could I come in so we could talk about this?'

Every warning bell went off in Shelby's head. This woman

was some kind of crackpot. She began to close the door. 'Look, I'm sorry,' she said. 'I'm busy.'

'Please,' said Janice Pryor. 'Hear me out. Just hear me out. I drove all the way down here tonight to talk to you. Believe me, it's important.'

Shelby recoiled from the woman's earnest, anxious gaze. 'Well, that's too bad. I'm sorry you wasted your time.' Before Shelby could shut the door in her face the woman blurted out, 'My daughter disappeared on a Sunset Cruise ship too.'

Shelby gripped the doorknob and stared at the woman standing on the step.

Janice Pryor gazed into Shelby's wide eyes, and took in her stunned expression with a satisfied nod. 'May I come in?' she asked.

TEN

'These quilts are beautiful,' Janice Pryor said, as she settled herself into a chair in the living room, and gazed at the colorful array of patterned needlework that hung from horizontal poles, decorating the walls.

Shelby was still standing by the door. 'My daughter made them.'

Janice looked sympathetically at Shelby. 'She had a wonderful eye for color.'

Shelby gazed at the quilts. The pain of her loss was a crushing weight on her heart.

'Do you think I could have something to drink?' Janice asked. 'A soft drink maybe?'

'There's herbal iced tea,' said Shelby.

'That would be fine,' said Janice.

Shelby went out into the kitchen and prepared a glass of tea while her mind raced. Now that she had let Janice Pryor into the house, she wondered if she had made a terrible mistake. This was a complete stranger who must have found Shelby through news reports. It could be that she was a little bit unbalanced. But the thought that Janice's daughter had died in the same way as Chloe made Shelby painfully curious, in spite of her misgivings. She carried the glass out to the living room, the ice cubes clinking, and handed it to her visitor.

Janice took a sip and then set the glass down. Shelby remained standing.

'Please. Sit down,' said Janice. 'I know how tired you must be.'

Suddenly, Shelby was keenly aware of her exhaustion, which normally hovered somewhere at the edge of her consciousness. 'I am tired,' she said. 'I've been helping out with my grandson.'

'Taking care of kids. It's the hardest work there is,' said Janice amiably.

'His father took him out to the movies tonight.'

'Yes, I know. I saw them go,' said Janice, taking a sip of her tea.

Shelby was taken aback. 'What do you mean you saw them go?' she cried. 'Were you spying on us?'

'No. Nothing like that,' Janice protested.

'Well, what then?' Shelby demanded.

'Please, Shelby . . . can I call you Shelby? It's nothing sinister. I promise you. I've followed the details of your daughter's story. I know about your son-in-law and your grandson. I just wanted to wait and speak to you alone,' said Janice calmly. 'Mother to mother.'

Shelby was not placated. 'Look,' she said, 'I'm really sorry that you lost your daughter the same way I did, but that really doesn't mean we're linked together somehow. I mean, I appreciate your . . . interest, but perhaps it would be better if you just . . .'

'I know you're probably thinking that I'm some kind of a nut, but I promise you, I'm anything but. Please.' Janice indicated the sofa.

Shelby hesitated and then perched stiffly down on the edge of the couch cushion, tensed to flee.

Janice looked at Shelby almost tenderly. 'I read that your daughter, Chloe, was twenty-four years old.'

'That's . . . that's right,' said Shelby.

Janice reached into her pocketbook and pulled out a framed photo. Janice gazed at it fondly, and then offered it to Shelby. It was a picture of a young girl, blonde-headed and bright-eyed. 'My Elise was seventeen. She went on the cruise with her senior class. It was a small class. A Catholic girl's school. She disappeared overboard on the third night of the cruise. That was ten years ago.'

Shelby hung her head, imagining a pain that never lessened. 'I'm sorry,' she whispered.

'Do you know what they told me happened to her?' Janice asked indignantly. She did not wait for Shelby to respond. 'They told me that she got drunk and accidentally fell overboard.'

Shelby looked up at her in surprise.

'That's what they told you about Chloe, wasn't it?' Janice demanded.

Shelby frowned. 'Yes, as a matter of fact.'

Janice nodded. 'That's what they always say.'

Shelby, initially stunned by this similarity, didn't know how to respond. 'It's probably just a coincidence,' Shelby protested faintly. 'I'm, afraid . . . well, I didn't know it but apparently my daughter had a drinking problem.'

'Who told you that?'

Shelby deflected the question. 'It seems that she'd had this problem for some time.'

Janice folded her arms over her chest. 'The cruise line wanted me to think that my daughter had a drinking problem. But Elise never touched alcohol.'

'Kids do try things sometimes when they're away from their parents,' said Shelby. 'You know, they experiment.'

Janice shook her head. 'Not Elise. She hated the taste of alcohol. She always said that it made her sick to her stomach.'

'Well, tropical places . . .' Shelby demurred. 'They make those fruit drinks that are so sweet. You can't even taste the alcohol in it.'

'NO.' Janice slammed her open palm down on the arm of the chair. 'That is not what happened. That is just the excuse they came up with to try to avoid responsibility. My daughter was murdered by one of their employees.'

Once again Shelby felt a mushrooming alarm that she had let a crazy person into the house. 'Really?' she said skeptically.

'I'm not just guessing about this, Shelby. This really happened. They hired a convicted sexual predator without looking into his background.'

Shelby frowned. She wished, fleetingly, that she had not agreed to let this woman call her by her first name. It made her uneasy. 'How do you know that?'

Janice shook her head. 'Not because the cruise line admitted it. Oh no. My husband spent all his time looking into it. Night and day. He ended up losing his job. Then he had a stroke. Now he's in a nursing home. Possibly for the rest of his life. But he found out the truth. That he did do.'

'A sexual predator.'

'Three arrests. One conviction,' said Janice flatly. 'All with young adolescents.'

'So . . . they got this guy for killing your daughter?' Shelby asked.

Janice held up her hands, as if in surrender. 'Not exactly. Look. I'm not here to talk about Elise.' She rummaged in her large pocketbook and pulled out a sheaf of pages. 'Here. I printed these up for you. They're not about Elise. Not entirely, anyway.' She thrust the papers at Shelby, who reluctantly accepted them.

'Just glance through that stuff,' said Janice.

Shelby frowned at the pile of papers. She began to leaf through them. Each stapled set had a heading that read 'Overboard.' Each set of papers concerned a different person, and the story of how they were lost at sea.

'What is this?' Shelby asked.

'Overboard is the name of our organization. These are some of the cases you can read about when you visit the website. We are the survivors of people who disappeared or died on a cruise ship,' said Janice.

'There are a lot of them,' said Shelby wonderingly.

'Those are just a few,' said Janice grimly. 'There are many others.'

Shelby scanned a few of the cases, making a special note of the outcome. She shook her head. 'Suicides. Accidents.'

'The cruise ships don't want bad publicity. They'll do almost anything to avoid it. They don't want people to know the truth.'

Shelby could feel the outrage emanating from Janice – and from pages of the survivor's accounts. 'I don't understand,' said Shelby. She frowned at Janice. 'What truth?'

'That throwing someone off a cruise ship is the perfect crime,' said Janice.

'What?'

'It is. As long as no one sees you do it, it's foolproof.'

Shelby shuddered and shook her head. 'Now, wait a minute—'

Janice leaned forward, her weary eyes suddenly fiery. 'Just think about it. How long was it before the ship stopped, and headed back to search for your daughter?'

Shelby sighed. 'Hours,' she admitted.

Janice cradled her large pocketbook on her lap, and nodded sharply. 'Exactly,' she said. 'People think those boats stop and search for people. But unless someone actually sees it happen, it always takes hours before they even turn back. By that time, your loved one is long gone. The bodies are never recovered.'

'Don't say that,' Shelby protested.

'Sorry. I forgot. You're still hoping.'

Shelby could hear the pity, bordering on scorn, in the other woman's voice. She blinked at her and then looked away.

'Look, I know this is a lot to take in,' said Janice gently.

'What do you want from me?' asked Shelby.

'First of all, I want you to know that you are not alone. That's number one.'

'Well, thank you,' said Shelby without conviction.

'And secondly, I want you to join us. I want you to look at our website. Read the other people's stories. You'll see what I mean. It doesn't cost anything. We are just people who were blindsided by a sudden loss. We had our loved ones stolen from us. Their deaths have gone unavenged for far too long.'

Shelby looked at her suspiciously. 'You want vengeance,' said Shelby.

Janice grimaced at the word. 'I prefer the word justice. But we don't even hope for justice because there is none. We are hoping that there will be power in numbers so we can exert some influence.'

Shelby studied her skeptically. 'Influence on what?'

'Well, for one thing, on the way these incidents are investigated. It's a disgrace the way they respond. As if a person going overboard were a minor annoyance. Where is the urgency to continue the cruise?'

Shelby recognized the painful truth in that question. She had wondered the exact same thing. 'The captain told me that there are a lot of false alarms on these ships,' she offered halfheartedly.

'Yes,' said Janice. 'But they are indifferent when it turns out to be an actual disappearance. I'll tell you why: the cruise lines don't want anyone to know that people have died on these cruises. It's bad for their image. You hardly see a thing about these disappearances in the papers.'

'I noticed that with Chloe,' Shelby admitted.

'And you won't,' Janice insisted. 'The cruise lines make sure of that. Their PR departments go into overdrive white-washing these things.'

Shelby nodded slowly. 'Looking at these stories . . . it's so upsetting.'

'We want to hold them accountable for what happens on these ships. For their lack of security and their inadequate response when a crime is committed. Of course, it's difficult, because no one is ever prosecuted for these crimes. No body, no crime. No prosecution,' said Janice.

'I don't see what you hope to accomplish,' said Shelby.

'We want to attack them where it hurts: in the pocketbook. We want to mount a class-action lawsuit against these giant cruise lines.'

Shelby recoiled. 'Oh,' she said. At last she understood. Albert Markson once said that suing was the way that Americans grieved. 'Well, I'm not interested in suing anybody. I mean, if you can find a way to profit from your loss, all well and good—'

'Profit from my loss! My husband needs constant care in a nursing home for the stroke he had. And it's all because of what happened to our daughter on that ship,' Janice protested. 'If that's your idea of *profiting* from something—'

'Mrs Pryor, please,' she said, standing up. 'I didn't mean to say that in an offensive way. I understand that you've suffered. Believe me. I guess I'm just not thinking in terms of liability at this point.'

Janice leaned forward, her forearms resting on her purse. 'Do you think these cruise lines should be allowed to get away with this?'

'Look, it would be a comfort if there was someone else to blame. But if there's anyone to blame for my daughter's death, it's me,' said Shelby earnestly. 'I gave her and her husband the cruise as a present. If it weren't for me, they never would have been on that ship. And if that weren't enough, I saw my daughter on a regular basis and never knew that she had a drinking problem. But she did. Apparently, she did. She drank too much and she fell overboard. Blaming the cruise ship line is not going to bring her back. Or bring me any satisfaction. All I want is to be left alone with my grief.'

Janice sighed, and stood up as well. She looked at Shelby sadly. 'Once you read what is on our website you may change your mind. And you should feel free to contact me. My information is all there.'

'Yes, fine,' said Shelby.

'Just one more thing,' Janice said. 'You might not want to mention this visit to your son-in-law.'

'Why not?' Shelby demanded.

'Well, he was there on that boat with Chloe. It's possible that he could be . . . involved.'

At first Shelby was baffled and then, in the next moment, she was furious. Who was this stranger to accuse Rob? She might have had her own, fleeting doubts about her son-in-law, but she had heard him at night, in this house, weeping, when he thought that everyone else was asleep. 'All right, that's enough,' said Shelby. 'I won't listen to this.'

Janice stood at the door for a moment. 'I'm not going to say that you'll thank me for this visit,' she said. 'But I hope you can stop blaming yourself and Chloe, and figure out where the blame really belongs.'

'Good night, Mrs Pryor,' said Shelby, closing the door behind the departing woman and leaning against it. She waited until she heard the woman's footsteps fading, and then she peeked out the front window to be sure she was gone.

Once the car was out of sight, she angrily picked up the sheaf of papers that Janice Pryor had left on the chair and carried them through the house to the recycling bin where she dumped them. She emptied the ice cubes out of Janice Pryor's glass, and put the glass out of sight in the dishwasher. She felt as if she wanted to remove any trace of the woman and her dismal visit.

Shelby was shaking from head to toe, freezing, despite the mildness of the night. She felt ready to weep, and dirty all over, as if she had been splattered with filth. She had not eaten and now she couldn't eat because her stomach was in a knot. She couldn't watch television because she wouldn't be able to concentrate on a show. Why did I ever open that door, she thought?

There was only one thing she could think of that she wanted to do. She would take a long hot shower. In the shower, she could weep as loudly and as long as she wanted. Even if Rob and Jeremy came home early they wouldn't hear her. Shelby locked the front door, and the back. But even as she jiggled the handle, to be sure that she was safe, she admitted to herself with a shudder that locking the door was no guarantee of safety. If someone evil wanted to get through, she thought, they could always find a way.

ELEVEN

S helby, in her robe and pajamas, went down to the kitchen. She glanced at the clock and realized that Rob and Jeremy might soon be on their way home from the movie theater. She ate some cheese and crackers and went back up to Molly's room to try to find something distracting to watch on television in the meantime.

But even as she flipped through the channels with the remote she was thinking about Janice Pryor's visit. Forget about it, she chided herself. Forget that Janice Pryor ever barged into your life. But it was no use. When Chloe disappeared from that ship, Shelby became a de facto member of the Overboard group – whether she cared to admit it or not. These were the people on this earth, she thought, with whom she now had the most in common. These were all people who had wished their loved ones a cheery 'bon voyage', or 'good night', or 'enjoy your jog around the deck', never to set eyes on them again. How could she expect herself to resist their stories?

Finally, she climbed off the bed, went to her computer notebook, and punched in the word 'Overboard.' The website sprang up before her eyes. In spite of her better judgment, she began to read. After about half an hour, she heard the front door open downstairs and the sound of Rob and Jeremy's voices in the house.

Shelby stayed very still, listening to snippets of their conversation as they wondered aloud if she were asleep and debated about waking her. Rob finally prevailed upon Jeremy to brush his teeth and get ready for bed.

'But Shep has her light on,' Jeremy protested.

'She probably fell asleep with the light on,' Rob reasoned.

'Can we turn it off?' Jeremy asked.

'No. We might disturb her. Let her sleep. Shep is very tired,' said Rob.

Shelby wasn't sure why she didn't go to the door and call out to them. It wasn't as if she didn't want to see them or hear about the movie. But when she thought about it, she had to admit that she didn't want to tear herself away from the website. She wanted to continue poring over every story recounted there. At the same time, she was a little bit reluctant for them to know what she was doing. So she stayed silent.

Their voices grew fainter as Jeremy, distracted from thoughts of his grandmother, enthusiastically recalled his favorite parts of the movie while Rob murmured in response.

Once she could no longer hear them, Shelby resumed her reading. The fascination she felt for these stories was akin to rubbernecking at the sight of an accident. In this case, Shelby felt as if she were both rubbernecker and victim.

If the people who told their stories on the site were planning a lawsuit, it was not evident from the testimonies they gave. Instead, their stories were filled with frustration, grief, and disbelief.

There were a couple of cases where, Shelby thought, people just did not want to face facts about the missing person. There were stories of people who went on cruises to try to alleviate depression, and ended up leaving all their belongings in their cabin in a neat pile topped with a note of farewell. There were other cases that seemed to cry out for a criminal investigation. One victim was a middle-aged woman who did not approve of her son's wealthy, dissolute admirer. She accepted an invitation to go on the cruise with them, at the expense of said admirer, and disappeared from the boat, never to be seen again.

One of the strangest cases was, as it turned out, the disappearance of Elise Pryor. Rejecting the official version of events, Janice Pryor and her husband had updated the account repeatedly as they sought out, and found, answers. There was, indeed, a convicted sex offender working as a steward on Elise's ship. His history linked him to previous assaults on teenage girls. After Janice's husband brought this fact to the attention of the cruise line, the steward was eventually dismissed, and his cabin was searched. Wedged between his bunk and the wall they found a bikini swimsuit top that had belonged to Elise Pryor. The police investigated, but finally insisted that this was not enough evidence to bring charges against the man. The steward was fired from his job for lying on his application, and he was put off the ship in Miami. After that, he disappeared.

Reading this account, Shelby felt a mounting fury on the Pryors' behalf. She also felt guilty for having dismissed the bereaved mother out of hand. No one could understand how the Pryors felt the way that Shelby did. She had suffered the same loss, and been told the same lie. Yes, Shelby thought. The same lie. Now that she thought back on those terrible days in St Thomas, it did seem as if their first concern was to make this problem of Chloe's disappearance go away. How better to make that happen than to blame it on the victim? To say that she tripped and fell in a drunken stupor. It was possible that Chloe had met with foul play. A cruise line that had hired one sexual predator might have hired others.

Shelby felt adrenalin coursing through her veins. Stunned by the revelation of Chloe's drinking, she had accepted what the officials told her. Now, she felt ashamed for having agreed, on so little information, to blame her own daughter for her own demise. No, she thought. I need to find out if there was something else going on. But how, she wondered? There was no use in trying to explain this all to the Philadelphia police. The police in St Thomas and the FBI were satisfied with the existing explanation. She couldn't investigate it herself – she wouldn't know where to begin. She needed someone else – someone who would know how to proceed.

The thought of trying to hire a private detective filled her with a sense of futility. All she knew about private eyes was what she had seen on television, or read about in mystery novels. In fiction they were always rumpled guys who smoked and had problems with women and were barely able to stay sober long enough to solve the crime. It was almost laughable to imagine paying someone like that to help. In real life she imagined they were much less colorful. But she had no personal experience to go on. What was she supposed to do, pick a name out of the phone book?

And then, feeling a little thrill of hope, another thought occurred to her. She did know a detective. She knew one very well. Perry Wilcox, the head of security for the Markson stores, was a soft-spoken man who had been, for fifteen years, a homicide detective for the city of Philadelphia. But his daughter became ill with severe diabetes and Perry was often needed at home. He was no longer able to put in late and irregular hours on the job. He signed up for a course on computer crimes and surveillance techniques and found that he was interested in these burgeoning areas of security. He decided to opt out of police work and take a job in the private sector. He was hired by Albert Markson and had worked in the Markson stores for eight years, making sure that the security system was state of the art.

Perry can tell me what to do, Shelby thought. If he can't do it for me, he can tell me about someone who could. Someone I could trust. She quickly scanned her own list of contacts and found Perry's email address. It took her a while to compose what she wanted to say in her message. No more than a few moments after she pressed 'Send', she had a reply and an appointment to meet Perry at his office on Monday morning. 'I'm not sure if I can help you,' he wrote, and Shelby could picture his grave, dignified expression, 'but I will certainly try.' It was enough for now, she thought, as she returned to the Overboard website, and began to surf its grim, hopeless pages. It was a start.

The next morning, Shelby was having coffee and reading the Philadelphia Inquirer at the dining room table when Rob and Jeremy returned home from church. Jeremy ran to her and buried his face against her side.

Shelby looked up at Rob, alarmed.

'Lot of questions about his mom. People don't mean to be rude,' he said.

Shelby rubbed Jeremy's back and murmured soothingly. 'How was the movie last night?' she asked, hoping to distract him.

Jeremy mumbled something unintelligible, his face buried in Shelby's sweatshirt.

Rob poured himself a cup of coffee. 'The kids enjoyed it. Molly was wishing she could come back home with us and stay over but I dropped them off at Sara's house after the movie.'

Shelby heard the implication in his words; with her continued presence here she was getting in the way. Jeremy had pushed off from her and now interrupted her thoughts in loud voice. 'We saw a kitten,' he announced.

'Really?' Shelby asked. 'Where?'

Jeremy nodded. 'He ran between the houses. Out to the back.'

'Maybe he's out in the garden,' Shelby says. 'Why don't you have a look?'

'I'm gonna go have a look, Dad,' Jeremy said to Rob.

'OK. But stay in the garden.'

Jeremy headed to the back door, reached up and opened it. Shelby watched him head out into their tiny backyard. With Jeremy outside, it seemed an opportunity to mention her plans. 'I'm going home to my apartment tonight. I have to go into work tomorrow,' she said casually.

'Really?' he said, making no effort to conceal the fact that he welcomed this news. 'Great.'

'It's just for tomorrow,' said Shelby, carefully folding the paper. 'Then I'm coming back. Can you find someone to watch Jeremy after school tomorrow?'

His face fell visibly, but he quickly recovered. 'Sure,' he said. 'I'll ask his teacher, Darcie. She offered to help any way she could.'

'Good,' said Shelby.

She studied him for a moment. She had no intention of telling him about her plans to have Perry Wilcox investigate Chloe's disappearance. She didn't want to think too hard about why she was avoiding that conversation. But she did feel that she had to mention the uneasiness between them.

'Look, I know I'm probably wearing out my welcome here,' she said. 'But I don't think Jeremy is quite ready for me to leave yet.'

Rob shrugged. 'Whatever you think.' He put down his coffee mug and picked up the paper.

Shelby stood up. 'I think I'll stay a while longer. I'd better go out and explain to him about tomorrow.'

Rob did not lower his paper. 'If you say so,' he said.

TWELVE

Shelby had not been home to her condo since she went to Chloe's house to fill in while they were on the cruise. She was blindsided by the desolation she felt when she walked in. Everything was in order. Her friend Jen, as promised, had collected her mail and watered her plants. The apartment, with its river view twinkling in the night, was neat and elegant as ever. But as she entered the front hall, she wondered automatically if there would be a message on her machine from Chloe. And it was then that it hit her – there would be no message. Not now. Not ever.

As she walked around, turning on the lights, she thought that no one but the doorman knew that she had returned, or cared. She felt ashamed of her own loneliness, as if she had failed to make herself a meaningful life. She went to her computer and checked her mail. There was a message from Chief Giroux and her heart leapt with hope until she read his words. 'There is no point in continuing the search. All hope is gone.' Shelby read it several times, tears running down her face, before she replied. Then, she poured herself a glass of wine, sat on her sleek gray sofa and looked out at the swags of lights on the Ben Franklin Bridge.

In the darkness, beneath the Ben Franklin, the Delaware River flowed to the Bay. And the Bay, she knew, emptied, at the tip of New Jersey, into the Atlantic. And the Atlantic, far away to the south, merged with the Caribbean. And in the Caribbean, on its white sand floor, Chloe. The shell that was Chloe's living body, now drowned, was somewhere snagged on a reef or entangled in the sea grass. All the water is connected, she thought. Merged and connected. She stared at the sparkling onyx surface of the river, and felt a glacial chill trickling through her veins.

She slept badly and the next morning Shelby was up early and dressed long before it was time for her to leave. She arrived at the Markson's Store about half an hour before her appointment with Perry, rode the elevator to the fifth floor and entered her old office. Her assistant, Rosellen, a brown-skinned Wharton grad with shoulder-length cornrows in her hair, was hunched over her computer entering figures into a program. She looked up from her work and, to Shelby's relief, a look of genuine pleasure and surprise crossed the girl's face as she recognized her boss.

'Shelby,' she cried. 'I didn't know you were coming in.' Rosellen got up from her desk, came around and gave her boss an unrestrained hug. 'I am so sorry about Chloe,' she said.

Shelby thanked her.

'You should have let me know you were coming in,' Rosellen chided her. 'I've got a list a mile long of people who want to see you.'

Shelby had not realized, until that moment, how unready she was to get back to work. She glanced into her office and saw piles of folders and photos on her desk and racks of clothing, tags dangling from the sleeves, hanging against the wall. Normally, the sight of those unfinished tasks filled her with energy and determination. Today, she just wanted to avert her eyes. 'As far as those people are concerned, I'm not here,' said Shelby. 'I'm only in because I have an appointment with Perry Wilcox.'

Rosellen frowned. 'The security guy?'

Shelby nodded and decided not to explain. 'How's it going around here? Managing all right without me?'

'It's a madhouse,' Rosellen admitted, sitting down beside Shelby on the low sofa that took up one wall of the office. The coffee table in front of it was piled high with fashion magazines. 'Elliott Markson has been . . . hands on, shall we say.'

'I'm sorry,' said Shelby.

'Don't worry about it,' Rosellen said stoutly. 'I can handle him. You don't need to be worrying about anything around here. Not until you're ready.'

Shelby stood up. 'Thanks. I'd better get over to Perry's office.' She waved and went out into the hallway and down the corridor to the security office. Perry Wilcox was waiting for her, looking calm and well-groomed as usual. Perry was not yet sixty, but he had an avuncular air, and the bearing of an older man. His thinning hair was neatly combed back, and he wore silver-rimmed glasses. Perry offered her a chair in the inner office and closed the door.

'I have not been idle,' Perry said, 'since I received your email, Shelby. I don't personally have a lot of experience with this area of investigation, but I made some phone calls and talked to several colleagues who were helpful.'

'What did they suggest?' she asked.

Perry sat down behind his desk and folded his hands on his immaculate blotter. 'First of all, I want to do a background check on all the staff of the ship.'

'Yes, absolutely,' said Shelby.

'And I'll request copies of the security tapes.'

'I saw them,' Shelby said. 'The police showed them to me in St Thomas.'

'With all due respect, you were in no condition to know what to look for. I'm also going to ask the cruise line for a copy of Chloe's charge card and that of her husband. These will show what they bought, where they went on board, and when they came and went from their room.'

'OK,' said Shelby.

'One investigator whom I spoke to suggested that you may want to post a reward for information.'

'But the police talked to everyone on the ship. I mean, if anyone had had information, wouldn't they have said so?'

'Shelby, these ships can have upwards of 2500 passengers,' Perry said patiently. 'It is not possible that they talked to everyone on the ship. And nothing loosens the tongue like the opportunity for a little financial gain.'

Shelby nodded grimly. 'I'm sure that's true. Where do we post it?'

'Well, ideally we would want to email every passenger on the ship's manifest,' he said.

'Manifest?'

'That's the list of all passengers and their addresses. This would be useful to have for another reason. You could examine it and see if anyone on board that ship might have had a personal connection to your daughter. We need to know if there was anyone on that boat who had a disagreement with her or wished her ill. Other than her husband, of course.'

Shelby stared at him. 'You suspect him,' she said flatly.

'I mean,' said Perry, 'obviously her husband was the only person, that we know of, who might have wanted to harm her. That's why we need the list. To see if there might be anyone else. Any name that rings a bell.'

'That makes sense,' Shelby agreed. 'Can we do that?'

'Well, it's difficult. The cruise ship line will probably refuse to give it to us. They'll cite privacy reasons. One attorney I spoke to told me that, in a similar matter, he was able to get a subpoena, and all the cruise line produced was a list of passengers with no contact information.'

'That's so unfair.'

'It's bad publicity. They want it to go away,' Perry said.

'So you're saying we can't get it,' Shelby said dejectedly.

'The police in St Thomas may have requested and received the manifest. I'll check with them.'

Shelby nodded. 'Chief Giroux was very nice. He tried to be helpful.' Shelby recalled the words in the chief's email. 'All hope is gone,' he had written. She knew that he was telling her this for her own good. It was time to face it. In her reply, she had sorrowfully, reluctantly agreed to end the search.

Perry unfolded his hands and wrote a note on a pad on his desk. 'G-I-?'

'R-O-U-X.' Shelby finished the spelling. 'Anything else?'

Perry hesitated. 'I have to ask. Does your daughter's husband know that you wish to reopen this investigation?' Shelby avoided his gaze. 'I haven't mentioned it to him,' she said.

Perry nodded, a knowing expression in his eyes. 'Are you aware of whether your son-in-law took a polygraph test in St Thomas?'

Shelby's eyes widened. 'No, I don't know.'

Perry nodded. 'I will ask Chief Giroux when I speak to him.'

Part of Shelby wanted to pursue his question. Part of her did not want to hear what he was thinking. 'Is there any hope at all of finding out what really happened to Chloe?'

Perry nodded. 'Of course there's hope. That's why you got in touch with me, right? Now, try not to worry.' He stood up. 'I will let you know as soon as I know anything.'

Shelby reached into her purse and fished out her check-book. 'All right. That's good enough for me. Let me just give you a check now and then, at the end, you can make me out a bill . . .'

Perry raised a hand. 'No, no,' he said. He shook his head. 'No payment necessary. I'm going to treat this as company business. You're a valued employee here at Markson's. It's what Mr Markson would have wanted.'

Albert Markson, Shelby thought. She wasn't sure at all that Elliott would feel the same way. 'Are you sure? I'd be glad to pay you, Perry.'

Perry shook his head. 'I don't want it to seem like I'm moonlighting,' he said. 'Let's just keep this between us, shall we?'

Shelby stood up. They shook hands.

'You'll hear from me, soon,' he said.

'I can't thank you enough,' said Shelby.

'You lost your only child,' Perry said. 'It's the least I can do.'

THIRTEEN

The balance of her day passed in a blur. She left Markson's and did a multitude of errands in Center City. Her last stop of the day was at the office of Dr Cliburn, where Chloe had worked. Shelby had been avoiding the task of picking up Chloe's belongings and having to come face to face with Chloe's co-workers. But all of the young women who had worked with Chloe treated Shelby gently, fully aware of the difficulty of her errand. One of them had placed Chloe's belongings in a shiny, sky-blue shopping bag. Shelby glanced in at the contents and saw a pair of clogs, a coffee mug, a cardigan sweater, and a framed photo all neatly packed. Dr Cliburn, a big, gruff man in his fifties, came out of his office and offered his condolences. Shelby felt claustrophobic under their sympathetic scrutiny. She couldn't wait to flee the cheery office full of parenting magazines and baby photos on the wall. She felt a headache beginning to form over her eye, and all she wanted was to escape their kind wishes and solicitous glances. A text from Talia arrived just as she was getting back into her car. 'GLEN HOME,' it read. 'CALL.'

Glen, she thought wearily. Was he in trouble again, she wondered? Glen was the youngest of the three Winter siblings, and the only one of the three who, despite his keen intelligence, had never seemed to have any goal in life other than to get high and avoid responsibility. He worked sporadically, stayed with friends and acquaintances, and eschewed all entangling emotional alliances. He had frequent skirmishes with the law, which usually resulted in an indignant rant against the police. His visits home were infrequent. Mother must be worse, Shelby thought. Glen wasn't visiting for a social call. Shelby wished she could block the whole problem out, but there was no avoiding it. No use pretending that she hadn't seen the text.

The only thing more unsatisfactory than a face-to-face conversation with Talia was texting her or trying to talk to her on the phone. Shelby was in her car and already near the college. She decided to go directly to Talia's lab and get an update directly from her sister.

The parking lot at Franklin University was full of cars and Shelby had to park far from the computer lab. The façade of the lab building was mostly glass. The staircases and hallways were industrial pipe and pressed metal walkways that contrasted with the warmth of the interior brick walls. The building seemed to glow in the twilight as she walked toward it. She entered the building and descended the stairs to the computer lab and Talia's office.

A thin, pleasant-looking woman with a shaggy haircut was seated at a computer desk, frowning at her monitor. Shelby tapped on the open door.

The woman looked up. 'Yes?'

'Faith?'

'Yes,' the woman said, surprised, her eyes widening.

'I'm Shelby. Dr Winter's sister.'

Faith smiled. 'Oh hi. Come on in.' She indicated a chair by the desk, and Shelby sat down.

'Is she in there?' Shelby asked.

Faith glanced at the computer monitor. 'She should be along any minute now,' she said. 'This is her early night.'

'You look like you're involved in something,' said Shelby.

'I am. I have to finish this research. But I never have enough time. My husband and I are renovating our house ourselves. Going home is almost worse than being at work,' she said with a good-natured smile.

'Don't let me interrupt you,' said Shelby. 'I can wait in the hall.'

'No, wait right there,' said Faith. 'It doesn't bother me. She'll stop in on her way into the lab.'

Shelby nodded and watched the hallway as students carrying laptops came and went. Her headache began to throb. She knew that a visit home was unavoidable. If Glen was there, that would make it more tolerable. Despite his shortcomings, Shelby still liked seeing her brother. But she dreaded seeing her mother in the throes of her terminal condition. And the house itself was encumbered with their dismal family history. She almost envied her mother the fact that she was losing her ability to remember it.

Just then, Talia came around the corner wearing pants with a stretchy waist, a cardigan, and rubber-soled shoes. The frown lines in her face were permanent. Shelby stood up.

Talia looked startled, and reached out a hand to her sister, as if to shake it. Or was it to push her away? Shelby stared at her sister's hand in confusion. Talia wiped her hand on her pants.

'I got your text,' said Shelby. 'About Glen. What's going on? Is mother worse?'

'About the same,' said Talia. 'But when he called the other night I told him he better get himself over to see her. Before it's too late. You better go over there too. I'm tired of telling you.'

Shelby sighed. 'Why don't you come with me?'

'When I'm done. Right now, I have work to do.'

'I haven't seen either one of you . . . since Chloe . . .' Shelby stopped speaking.

A look of annoyance crossed Talia's face. 'I can't just drop everything like that. These programs have to be run.'

'Can't it wait?'

Talia shook her head. 'The world does not revolve around your schedule.'

Shelby knocked on the door of the home where she had grown up. Their neighborhood was an anomaly in the city – block upon block of free-standing houses. When their father was alive and teaching algebra at a city high school, this neighborhood had seemed idyllic to young families who could afford to buy there. In the years since he died, the area had been colonized by Russian immigrants, and the street signs were now written in both English and Russian. In her childhood it had been a neighborhood of families with kids in the local school and a playground across the street. She supposed that it still was, except that now the families were poorer, the cooking smells were denser, and, if you closed your eyes, it might sound as if you were in Moscow. Talia did the minimum of upkeep on the family home, none of it cosmetic, so the place looked much bleaker and more run-down than it actually was.

Glen opened the door. He was still in his thirties, just barely, but his thick hair was graying. He was dressed in layer upon layer of t-shirts and flannel. His jeans were faded and full of holes. 'Shelby,' he cried. He held his arms open and pulled her in. She could hear his muffled voice in her ear. 'I'm so sorry about Chloe. I just couldn't believe it when I heard. That child was an angel.'

Shelby could barely conceal her surprise. For a moment she wondered if Talia had told him. 'Thanks, Glen. How did you know?'

'I do read the paper from time to time,' he said. He leaned back and looked her in the eye. 'You know I loved her. She meant the world to me.'

Shelby sighed. He had never remembered Chloe's birthday, or attended any of her school events, but he would occasionally arrive, unannounced, on the doorstep with some book he had stolen from a library, or some toy he had picked up at Goodwill. In his own way, she supposed, he meant it when he said he loved Chloe. 'I know,' she said.

Glen looked over her shoulder into the quiet street. 'Where's Dr No?' he asked playfully.

'Still in the lab,' said Shelby, smiling in spite of herself.

'Quick. Get in here before she swoops in on her broom. I got us a bottle of wine. And food.'

'You bought food?' Shelby said in amazement.

'I did.' Glen led the way through the dark house. The drapes were drawn over the picture window in the living room. The dining room had been turned into Talia's office, with computer equipment as well as piles of papers and folders on every surface. They went into the kitchen, which had the same counters, the same scuffed linoleum it had had in their childhood. On the counter was an open bottle of wine and a hunk of cheddar cheese still in its plastic wrapper, along with a box of saltines.

Shelby sat down on the stool opposite her younger brother and smiled as he poured out the wine into juice glasses and opened the cheese to slice it.

'How's mother?' said Shelby, accepting a piece of cheese on a cracker with the realization that she was very hungry.

'Asleep,' he said.

Shelby could picture her mother's old bedroom, dimly lit, smelling of sweaty clothes and beer. 'Talia said she's pretty bad.'

Glen shrugged. 'Talia got her painkillers, so she's washed them down with gin and she's feeling fine. Just the way she likes it.'

They had survived their childhood with the aid of gallows humor. There was no reason to change that now. 'Nirvana,' said Shelby. 'So what brings you here?'

'What brings me here?' he asked. 'This is a family crisis.'

'Mother's condition?'

'Mother's condition is her own doing. Sad, but . . . hey. I meant Chloe's death, of course,' he said.

Shelby smiled wryly. 'Thanks. For a minute I thought maybe Talia had contacted you about it but then I realized . . .'

'Nah,' he said. 'For quite a few reasons.'

'She sent me a sympathy card,' said Shelby. 'I couldn't believe that. A sympathy card.'

Glen shook his head. 'She's fucked up.'

'So is everything OK with you?' Shelby asked, grimacing as she waited for the answer.

'Everything is the same with me,' he said. 'But we're not here to talk about me. I want to know about Chloe.'

'I don't know how much you already know,' she said.

'I read that she was drinking and fell overboard,' he said bluntly.

Shelby recoiled from the indictment. 'Geez, Glen.'

'Hey, it was in the news,' he said.

'Well, that was the official version. But I've asked the head of security at Markson's to look into it,' said Shelby.

Glen looked at her in surprise. 'Really?'

Shelby told him briefly about Janice Pryor's visit and the Overboard website.

'It just seems wrong to accept this unquestioningly.'

'I agree,' said Glen. 'But why the security chief at Markson's?'

'He used to be a homicide detective here in Philly,' said Shelby.

'Well, that doesn't make him an expert,' said Glen derisively.

His contempt for the police was well known to Shelby. Years of living on the razor's edge of the law, protesting one drug or DUI arrest after another, he had come to see himself as a victim, and the police as an organized entity out to get him.

Shelby short-circuited the familiar rant. 'There are no guarantees, of course. In the end, I may have to accept the official version of events. But I need to know for sure.'

Glen frowned. 'Did you know that Chloe was drinking?'

'No. Apparently she didn't want anyone to know. Including me. Even Rob didn't know it until she had an accident with Jeremy in the car. She drove off the road and up on to a curb. Fortunately they weren't hurt.'

'Did anyone report it to the cops?' asked Glen, swilling the wine in his glass and pouring himself another.

'No. Luckily Rob got to them before the police could get involved. But she promised him she would stop drinking after that.'

'That's what Rob told you.' He shook his head.

Shelby frowned at him. 'Yes. Why are you shaking your head?'

'Hey, if nobody reported it, that means there was no police report,' said Glen. 'No breathalyzer. No hearing. Believe me, I know what happens when you get caught drunk driving.'

Glen spoke, Shelby knew, with the voice of authority on this one. 'I suppose you're right,' Shelby said.

'Of course I'm right. Chloe didn't lose her license. There's no proof that it ever even happened the way he said,' he persisted.

'Well, whatever happened, it was enough to make her go to AA.'

'He says,' said Glen, waving a knife with a pale hunk of cheese in the air.

'What do you mean?' Shelby asked.

'I mean how do we know she went to AA? It's anonymous.'

Shelby frowned at him. 'Well, why would he say that?'

Glen shrugged. 'Is it possible that it's not true? That she didn't have a drinking problem? That he just wanted you, and the police, to think that she did?'

'Glen, that's paranoid. Rob wouldn't just make that up. Besides, I saw a security video of Chloe on the boat at the bar, ordering drinks. They have video of her passing out at the bingo table, for heaven's sakes.'

'You saw her ordering something at the bar,' Glen said. 'It could have been a soft drink.'

'No. *No*. The bartender told the police it was vodka.'

'Maybe the bartender was lying. Maybe someone paid him to spike her drink. To make her appear inebriated.'

'No,' said Shelby, trying to remember the video. 'Why would anyone . . . Look, Glen, this is bad enough without one of your conspiracy theories,' Shelby said impatiently.

Glen lifted his hands. 'Hey. You can believe what you want to believe. I'm just saying. Her husband said she's a drinker. But you have no proof of that. Frankly, I don't see why you're taking his word for it. Anybody could have slipped a drug into her drink so that it would be easy to toss her over the side.'

Shelby blanched. ' No,' she protested. 'Why? You're just . . . No, it's impossible. If drugs were involved they would know that from the . . .'

'How? From the autopsy?' Glen asked triumphantly. He shook his head. 'Think about it, Shel. There was no autopsy. They don't have her body. There's no way to ever know.'

'That's true,' Shelby whispered. She set her wineglass down on the table because her hands had begun to shake.

FOURTEEN

Shelby did her best to enter the house quietly, taking off her shoes and leaving them in the vestibule. But she had no sooner crossed through the living room when she heard a voice from the top of the stairs. 'Shelby, is that you?'

'Yes,' said Shelby, striving to keep a light and friendly tone in her voice. 'Sorry to disturb you.'

Rob came down a few steps and leaned over the banister. 'I wasn't asleep. How did it go today?' he asked.

'Exhausting,' she said truthfully. 'Jeremy asleep?'

'Oh yeah, he's out.'

Shelby nodded and avoided his gaze. 'Well, good. It's the best thing for him.'

'Good night,' said Rob. He did not wait for her reply. He turned and headed back up the steps.

Shelby walked through to the kitchen, and poured herself a glass of water. Then she sat down on one of the kitchen chairs and looked around the room. If I were Chloe, she thought, where would I write it down? Chloe's gadgetry was minimal. Unlike her mother, she didn't have a BlackBerry or an iPhone. She was nostalgic for simpler times, as evidenced by her quilting.

Shelby tried to put herself into her daughter's head. Rob had said that she deliberately chose an AA meeting that was far from their neighborhood, at some church in Old City, so that no one would recognize her. But which church? And how did she choose it? Shelby wasn't about to ask Rob. She could not forget the shudder that ran through her when Glen suggested that perhaps it was a story designed to make Chloe look like an alcoholic. That perhaps, in reality, she was being drugged. Was it possible? Shelby couldn't stand to think about what that would mean about Rob. What reason could he have for doing such a thing? It would mean that he was a monster. She didn't want to think about it.

There was a calendar hanging on the wall with dates and times scribbled on it. Shelby carefully pulled out the pushpins that held it to the wall and leafed through the months past. Everything was abbreviated. She was able to discern some of Chloe's shorthand. Q was clearly for quilting evenings. J – no preS. was pretty simple. But there was no AA anywhere in evidence. She looked for a pattern of repeated times without any other abbreviations, and noted that she often had 12:30 a.m. written on the calendar. But nothing else.

Shelby looked around the kitchen. Everything was in its place. Chloe was something of a neat freak. The only place where she wasn't . . .

Shelby felt suddenly galvanized. The only place was her car. Was it possible that she had left some sign in the car of which AA meetings she attended? *If* she attended them.

Shelby was tempted to find a flashlight and go out on the street to look in the car right now. But as sure as she did that, someone would probably call the cops. A person rooting around in a parked car with a flashlight would alarm everyone on the block. No. She would have to wait until morning to look. After she took Jeremy to preschool, she would begin her search. She had to find out. She would start in the morning, with the car.

Jeremy was mopey in the morning, and made it clear that he had not appreciated her being gone all the previous day. Shelby cajoled and indulged him, giving him extra kisses and cookies in his lunch. As soon as she dropped him off, she drove to the playground near Chloe's house and parked the car between a trash can and a recycling bin. She didn't want to park on the street. Neighbors might ask questions if they saw her rummaging through the car, even in broad daylight. Here, at the park, she could sift through the detritus in Chloe's automobile without attracting attention.

A knot-like headache was forming in Shelby's forehead. She had to get started, no matter how frustrating the task. Shelby drew in a deep breath and climbed out of the car. She took out with her an armful of empty plastic water bottles that she dumped into the recycling can. Then, leaning into the back seat, she began to sort through the trash accumulated on the floor. There were notices from Jeremy's school, and bags with a few rice crackers still left in them. Shelby tossed them out after looking them over. She put the scattered change into her pockets, and collected a couple of Jeremy's socks for the wash.

The more trash she threw out, the more she thought this might be a hopeless quest. There was no way she could check out every AA meeting at churches in the Old City of Philadelphia. She had searched the internet last night and found a listing for AA meetings almost every hour of the day in one church or another.

Maybe, she thought, as she moved up to the front seats, the reason she was not finding anything was because there was nothing to find. Perhaps Glen was right and there was no AA meeting. That would certainly make her task impossible, she thought, as she lifted the driver's side floor mat. There, folded underneath the dusty mat was a church bulletin. This was not a bulletin from Rob and Chloe's church. This came from a Methodist church in Old City.

Shelby felt a fleeting thrill of discovery. She leaned against the car, and examined the bulletin. It was an ordinary Sunday bulletin. Hymns to be sung, numbers of readings. There was also a list of services provided by the church. A food closet, rummage sales, church retreats and, on the back page, the notice she was seeking. A discreet announcement that the parish hall hosted a chapter of AA, and a phone number. Shelby's heart started to pound when she saw that the number was underlined in ink. Shelby pulled her phone from her bag and called. The church secretary answered, and assured her that AA did indeed have a twelve thirty meeting and all were welcome.

Shelby looked at the time on her phone. She could make it in plenty of time.

The Old City of Philadelphia was a neighborhood where one could see the layers of time written in bizarre architectural juxtapositions, the old jostling the new and nothing quite fitting together. Grimy industrial buildings coexisted on the same streets with discount stores and historical brick homes. Within a block, one could buy custom-made canvas awnings or an orange update of the zoot suit and matching shoes, or a tenderly buffed Noguchi wooden table, too beautiful to use.

Shelby had always liked the Old City. When she was a teenager, the Old City was a kind of bohemian mecca, dangerous and artistic. In recent years it had become chic, the result of having spacious lofts ripe for renovating, and an abundance of tin-ceilinged, tile-floored bars and restaurants. Shelby parked in front of one such bar, not yet open for the day, and walked back down the block to the Methodist church, a red-brick bastion of historic days in Old City. She pulled open the heavy, white wooden doors, and slipped inside.

The interior of the church was painted a soft tint of robin's egg blue, the moldings eggshell white. There was no one visible in the nave as Shelby glanced inside. A makeshift sign in the lobby pointed to a stairwell and proclaimed that the AA meeting was being held in the basement. Shelby clutched to her chest a framed photo of Chloe, which she had taken from the house, and hurried down the stairs. The smell of fresh coffee wafted up the stairwell. At the bottom of the steps she rounded a corner and found herself in a large, open room filled with chairs and oblong tables. There was a stage at one end of the room that was flanked by desiccated velvet curtains and a window into a bright kitchen at the other end. About two dozen people were gathered there, talking in small groups. They were all adults, of varying ages. Several people were gathered around two brewed pots of coffee on a hot plate, carefully customizing their Styrofoam cups of steaming coffee with packets of sugar and a container of half and half. Halfway down the room an exit was propped open, letting in the spring sun, and the dissipating plumes of smoke from the cigarettes of those who were standing outside, having a few last drags before the meeting started.

Shelby felt conspicuous, standing on the periphery, clutching her photo. She was thinking of getting herself some coffee, just for something to do, although her stomach was far too knotted for her to have any hope of drinking it.

She edged toward the coffee drinkers. A tired-looking man in a tracksuit with a brown crew cut was talking to a tall, bony woman with a stringy gray braid, and a surgical gauze bandage over one eye. She had covered it with a silky black eyepatch. Her face was lined from too much sun, but her clothes were youthful. She wore jeans, a gray t-shirt and a black bomber jacket with paint-spattered sneakers. She was sporting about a dozen silver bracelets and large hoop earrings.

'What happened to you there?' the man was saying.

'Scratched my cornea. I was helping the block association clean up a vacant lot. No good deed goes unpunished, right?' She turned and smiled ruefully at Shelby.

'Hi,' she said. 'How are you doing?'

Shelby smiled. 'Fine. Well, I'm a little nervous,' she admitted.

'You're new here,' the woman said.

'I . . . haven't been,' Shelby said. She extended her hand. The woman shook it. 'I'm Shelby,' she said.

The woman nodded. 'Barbara,' she said. 'This is Ted.'

The man in the tracksuit nodded a greeting.

'You on your lunch break?' the woman said.

Shelby frowned. 'No. I'm off today.'

'At least you're working,' said Barbara. 'A lot of folks here have lost their jobs.'

'Including yours truly,' said Ted. 'I used to teach gym at a junior high.'

Shelby could easily imagine this man with a whistle around his neck. 'I'm sorry,' she said.

Ted shrugged. 'I'm doing some work as a personal trainer. The money's pretty good. If I could just get benefits . . .'

'No kidding,' said Shelby. 'It's hard to manage without benefits these days.'

'I've gone without benefits my whole life. I'm an artist,' said Barbara.

'What kind of art do you do?' Shelby asked.

'I paint.'

'So, you gotta pay for that out of your pocket?' asked Ted, pointing to Barbara's injured eye.

Barbara shrugged. 'Emergency Room at Dillworth. Wasn't too bad.' She turned to Shelby. 'Where do you work?'

'I'm a buyer for . . . a department store. I've been there for years.'

'I haven't seen you here before,' Barbara said.

Shelby suddenly felt uncomfortable and conscious that she was attending this meeting under false pretenses. She didn't want to start explaining about Chloe just yet. She needed the attention of the whole group, although there was something non-judgmental about Barbara that made Shelby want to confide in her. She resisted the temptation. 'It's my day off. I was in the neighborhood,' Shelby said.

Barbara clearly required no other explanation. 'It's nice out today. Good day to be off,' Barbara said, sipping from her steaming cup. 'Do you want some coffee?'

Shelby shook her head. 'I'm fine. Yes. I guess spring is coming at last.'

'Been a tough winter?' Ted asked.

Shelby almost had to smile. She had been thinking how tired and worn out he looked. Apparently, she looked the same. 'Yes, it has,' she said.

'Oh, we better sit,' said Barbara. 'Our fearless leader is calling the meeting to order.'

Shelby looked up and saw a red-faced middle-aged man with white hair, wearing a spiffy blue blazer, standing at the front of the room. 'Everyone,' he said. 'Can you sit down? We're going to get started.'

Barbara picked her way to a seat near the back. As Shelby watched her, she noticed that Barbara's silky black jacket was a Christian Audigier creation with the distinctive Ed Hardy tattoo-like images of skulls and hearts that shouted goth teenager. Expensive, and inappropriate, she thought, automatically thinking like the fashion buyer that she was in her work life.

Shelby turned and looked around the room. She wanted everyone to be able to see the picture when she held it up. She needed to be sure that anyone who might remember Chloe would have an unimpeded view. 'I'm going to sit up there,' Shelby said, pointing to a seat on the side, halfway to the front. She did not wait for Barbara to agree. She edged up to that seat and sat down, smiling anxiously at the man beside her. He gave a curt nod, and directed his attention to the meeting leader who was making some announcements at the front of the room.

'Now,' said the leader, who had identified himself as Harry. 'Would anyone like to share?'

The room was silent except for the sound of people clearing their throats. Finally, a man stood up and said, 'My name's Gene and I'm . . . uh . . . an alcoholic.'

'Hi Gene,' the crowd announced as one.

Gene, an overweight young man who was sweating profusely, began to tell about how many days he had been sober and working the program, and the difficulty he had encountered in the past week while looking for work. He admitted that he had nearly slipped, but that his sponsor had helped him through it. The people at the meeting listened with compassionate interest to what he said. Shelby was distracted and hardly heard him. She knew that she needed to stand up and speak. Normally, Shelby had little trouble with public speaking, but in this instance, she felt guilty, as if she were invading a secret society under false pretenses. The people here seemed to be eager to support one another, and she hoped that they would greet her question in that spirit, but she was not at all sure. Harry was thanking Gene, who sat down with visible relief.

'Anyone else care to share?' Harry asked.

Heart hammering, Shelby took a deep breath and stood up. Everybody swiveled in their chairs to look at her. 'My name is Shelby,' she said.

'Hi Shelby,' said the chorus of voices.

Shelby held out her framed photo of Chloe at arm's length and made a slow arc so that all could see it. 'This is my daughter, Chloe Kendricks. She was a wife, and a mother, and the best daughter you could ever . . .' Shelby choked up, and had to stop for a moment. The room was completely silent. 'Recently, while she was on a vacation, she . . . went missing. She was on a cruise and apparently she fell overboard.'

A shocked and sympathetic murmur ran through the group.

'I have since been told that Chloe was an alcoholic. I have reason to think that she might have been coming to this meeting. I'm just wondering if anyone here recognizes my daughter and can tell me if that's true. That she came here. That she belonged to AA,' Shelby said in a rush.

A disapproving hum seemed to vibrate in the room.

Harry, the leader of the meeting, did not hesitate. 'I'm sorry, Shelby, but the answer is no.'

Shelby looked up at him. 'You don't know her? You don't recognize my daughter?'

Harry shook his head impatiently. 'I mean, no. What you are asking is not possible. The anonymity of this group cannot be broken. Even if we did know your daughter, we wouldn't be able to say so.'

'Oh please,' said Shelby. 'All I need is a yes or no answer.

I don't want to know anything she said in a meeting or anything like that.'

Harry's red face seemed to get a little bit redder. 'You don't seem to understand. We cannot give you that information. Not even a yes or no answer. The anonymity of this group is absolute.'

'But my daughter is dead. You wouldn't be betraying her,' Shelby pleaded. 'And it may have some bearing on how, or why, she died.'

'Shelby,' said Harry in a tone that brooked no contradiction. 'I'm going to have to ask you to leave our meeting. I'm very sorry about your daughter, but these rules governing anonymity are the foundation of this organization. They still apply after death. There are no exceptions. Now please . . .' He gestured toward the exit.

Shelby looked from face to face, trying to glean some hint of an answer. Some sign of recognition. There were such a variety of expressions in the room that she could not get any coherent sense of their reaction. Some people looked shocked, and others seemed angry. Others still were wide-eyed and puzzled. Shelby looked back at Barbara, who averted her gaze and lowered her head. Was that a yes, Shelby wondered? There was no time to decide. Harry was walking toward her, repeating that she needed to leave.

She wondered for a moment if he was going to physically hustle her outside.

He stopped short of that, but his unsmiling gaze left no room for doubt. She pressed her lips together, and, clutching her photo to her chest, she hurried out of the meeting room. One of the men in the back row followed her to the stairway exit and closed the door behind her. She heard it slam as she started up the stairs.

FIFTEEN

'Shep?'

Shelby, who was making dinner while she mentally relived her failed visit to the AA meeting in the Old City, looked over at her grandson. 'What is it, honey?' she asked.

Jeremy was sitting at the kitchen table, laboring over a drawing of his favorite thing, a pirate ship. He did not look up at her. 'You live here now, right?' he said.

Shelby grimaced at the question. 'Well, for right now,' Shelby said. 'One of these days I will have to go back to my own house.'

'Why?' said Jeremy.

'Well, because that's where I have all my things. You know my house. Mommy brought you there lots of times. With the big windows over the river. And you'll come visit me there. And stay over.'

'No, Shep. Bring your things here. You don't leave,' Jeremy insisted.

'I'm not leaving now. I'm still right here, honey,' Shelby said.

Jeremy glowered. 'Not ever.'

'Let's not worry about it right now. There's plenty of time,' she said.

But it was too late. Jeremy pushed his markers off the table with an angry swipe of his arm and they clattered loudly to the floor. 'No,' he insisted. 'No, no.'

Shelby tried to soothe him. 'I can't stay forever, sweetie.'

'Why not?' he demanded.

'Well, Molly needs to get her room back, for one thing.'

Jeremy slid off the chair and stamped his foot. 'I don't want Molly. I want you.'

Rob had heard the racket and come into the kitchen. He scowled at Shelby as the boy burst into helpless tears. 'What did you say that for?' he demanded. He turned to the child. 'This is not about Molly,' Rob insisted as he tried to calm his furious son. 'Shep has her own house. And she has to go back to work. She'll be able to come and see you.'

Too late, Shelby realized that Rob was perfectly right. She should not have mentioned Molly. And she had miscalculated with Jeremy who, it had to be said, didn't require much provocation to erupt these days.

'Your dad's right,' said Shelby. 'I do have to go back to my own house. But I'm not going right this minute.'

Rob shook his head, as if her second effort had been no better than her first.

'I'll always be here for you Jeremy.' Shelby said. 'Anytime you need me.'

It was no use. The child was sobbing now, and not hearing a word she said.

Rob sat down beside him and pulled his son roughly on to his lap, rocking him despite his tearful, angry protests. 'It's all right, slugger,' he said. 'You're just missing Mommy. I understand. We all miss her so much.'

Shelby watched Rob trying to soothe his son. Do you, she wondered? Do you miss her? Or was this your plan? It had always seemed that Rob and Chloe had been building the life they both wanted. But was that just another illusion? What if he had another plan, that she knew nothing about. Did you say that Chloe was an alcoholic so that the police would believe that she fell, she wondered? So that you could get away with murder? No. No. It wasn't possible.

For a moment Shelby hated herself for even thinking such a thing. At that moment she wanted to confess to Rob that she had hired Perry to investigate Chloe's death.

But her nagging doubts stopped her, and she held her tongue.

Two days later, as she returned from dropping Jeremy off at preschool, her cell phone rang.

'Hello,' she said.

'Shelby, it's Perry. I have some information for you.'

Shelby sank down on to one of the kitchen chairs. 'Yes? What is it, Perry?' she asked.

'Well, as I predicted, Sunset Cruise Line refuses to give us the ship's manifest.'

Shelby shook her head angrily. 'I just don't get that. How is that fair?'

Perry did not attempt to answer her question. 'They were not completely oppositional. They sent me a record of the shipboard access cards that Rob and Chloe used. There's no question that Chloe was, indeed, buying alcoholic beverages on the cruise. They have her signature on the bills.'

'I see,' said Shelby, deflated, thinking of Glen's theory.

'And, Rob's card shows that he did not enter their state room until the hour he said. The security tapes confirm this. They were forwarded to my computer without delay. I looked at the tapes of the night in question. Rob can be seen leaving the salon where the sports trivia quiz was held. Not ten minutes later, he contacted a steward to ask for help.'

Shelby was silent, mulling this over, thinking that one could commit a deadly crime in ten minutes.

'I spoke to Chief Giroux in St Thomas. They did give him a lie detector test. At his own request.'

'I thought those weren't reliable,' Shelby said stubbornly.

'It depends on a lot of factors. Let's just say this: if he failed the test, we would certainly take it seriously.'

'But he didn't.'

'No,' said Perry. 'He passed.'

Shelby chewed the inside of her mouth. 'What else?'

'Apparently, on board ship, they have roving photographers who snap pictures which they sell to the passengers as souvenirs. It gives us a photographic record of just about all the people on the ship. They emailed those photos to me and I just forwarded them to your computer. Of course, you will have to look individually at every picture to see if there was a familiar face. There's really no other way.'

'I'll look at them,' she said.

'The reward has been posted. So far, no response.'

'I keep wondering . . .'

'What?' Perry asked.

'Do you think it's possible that she might have survived?' Shelby said. 'I mean, people have jumped off the Golden Gate Bridge and survived. I looked it up. Why not a cruise ship? It isn't even as high . . .'

Perry was silent for a moment. 'Is the search ongoing?' he asked.

'No,' Shelby admitted. 'I agreed to call it off. They said it was hopeless.'

'I think that's the logical conclusion,' Perry said. 'I'm afraid survival would be possible only if someone saw the fall. If they immediately began rescue operations.'

He did not need to remind her that Chloe had fallen, unseen, into the water. 'You agree that there's no chance,' said Shelby.

'I can't say that. I'm not the Almighty. All I'm saying is that I don't think her husband is lying about what happened. He clearly wasn't lying about her drinking. I think he has told the truth about the situation as he knows it.'

Shelby's eyes filled with tears of frustration. 'I guess I should be glad for that. He's my grandson's father. I wouldn't want to think that he was capable . . .'

'You need to look through the photos taken on the ship and see if any familiar faces jump out at you. And we may still get some information after people read about the reward.'

'I will,' said Shelby. But the familiar tide of hopelessness swept over her. Even though she had gotten out of bed only hours before, she felt unbelievably weary. She thanked Perry, and ended the call. Then, she trudged up the stairs to Molly's room, lay down on the bed, and pulled up the lovely quilt that Chloe had made. Curled into a fetal position, the sun shining brightly on her through the window, she soon fell asleep.

She was awakened by the sound of the front door opening. Shelby sat up, her heart pounding, feeling completely disoriented. She glanced at the clock. It wasn't someone bringing Jeremy. It wasn't time. She tried to get her bearings as she rolled off the bed, and hurried to the top of the stairs. She thought, for a moment, of those detectives who had come by the night they got back looking for an escaped felon. Maybe he was here. Maybe he had come back to the neighborhood. Stop it, she thought. Stop psyching yourself out. Get a grip. She tried to summon an authoritative tone.

'Who is it?' she demanded. Despite her best efforts, her voice quavered.

'It's me,' said Rob.

'Oh my God, you frightened me,' she said accusingly. She came down the stairs smoothing her hair with one hand.

Rob was standing in the living room with his arms crossed over his chest.

'What are you doing home from work?' Shelby asked.

'It's time you were leaving,' he said.

Shelby was taken aback, and somewhat insulted. 'Why? What's the matter?'

'I know what you're up to,' he said.

Shelby was perplexed. 'What I'm up to?'

Rob shook his head. 'Don't,' he said. 'Don't play dumb. I'm talking about your private detective,' he said.

Shelby reddened and did not reply.

'Oh, you're not going to deny it?' he asked in a taunting tone.

Shelby's temper flared. 'No. Why should I deny it?'

It was Rob's turn to be silent.

'I asked a friend to see if he could learn anything more about what happened to Chloe,' Shelby explained.

'You mean you asked him to find out if I pushed her overboard,' Rob said accusingly.

'No. I defended you,' she protested.

Rob's laugh was a cynical bark of disgust. 'Defended me?'

'No. I was thinking that maybe it was someone . . .' She started to recount her visit from Janice Pryor, but she could see in his eyes that he was not listening. 'How did you find out about this anyway?' she asked.

'I got a call at work today. From someone in public relations at Sunset Cruises. Your private detective had called demanding information, and they were calling me to threaten me, basically, to stop harassing them. Of course, it was news to me that there was a private detective involved.'

Shelby tried to control the tremor in her voice. 'I asked the head of security at Markson's to do some background checks on the crew. And to study the surveillance tapes. He also posted a reward for me, for information.'

Rob held up one hand as if to beg her to stop. 'I don't want to hear it,' he said. 'You think I'm to blame. Ever since it happened, I've known that. Don't think I didn't. But you've gone too far now.'

Shelby looked at him with narrowed eyes. 'We're talking about my daughter's death here. How far should I go? Pardon me for not accepting the official version of events without question. Come to think of it, how come you do?'

'I want you out of my house,' he said. 'I want you out now.'

Shelby suddenly realized that she might have to leave without saying goodbye to her grandson. 'What about Jeremy?' she demanded. 'He'll be very upset.'

'I'll explain it to Jeremy,' he insisted. 'Just go.'

Shelby didn't know whether to obey him or not. It was his house of course. He could forbid her to see Jeremy. He could cut off her visits with Jeremy, her last link to Chloe, if he wanted to.

'Look,' she said. 'Can we just talk this over?'

The expression in Rob's eyes was poisonous. 'Shelby, I never wanted you here in the first place. Out of respect for Chloe's memory – because I knew she would want me to – I let you stay. But that was before you hired a detective to go sifting through my life, looking for a reason why I killed my wife.'

'I should have told you,' she admitted. 'I thought it might upset you. I figured if he found out anything important, I would tell you then.'

Rob shook his head. 'At least be honest with yourself,' he said disgustedly. 'Admit you blame me for Chloe's death.'

'No,' Shelby insisted stubbornly. 'I just want to get to the truth.'

'I told you the truth. You just don't want to hear it. Chloe was an alcoholic. Just like your mother. She was doing her best to keep it in the road, but when she got on that ship with a bar every fifteen feet, and all the passengers drinking night and day, she lost it.'

'In other words, if you hadn't gone on the cruise . . .' Shelby exclaimed.

'We were fine. We were doing OK. But you wished she'd married some rich husband who could take her on cruises. When I couldn't afford that kind of nonsense, you gave her the cruise, just to make your point.'

Shelby shook her head. 'That is completely not true, Rob. I gave it to you because I remembered what it was like to have a small child and no money to spare. I just wanted you two to enjoy yourselves.'

Rob shook his head. 'Go pack.'

Shelby felt almost physically assaulted but she wasn't going to argue any more. She was not going to give him the satisfaction. She did not look at him as she started up the stairs to get her things.

His voice followed her up the stairs. 'If you're so busy looking for someone to blame, try looking in the mirror.'

SIXTEEN

Once seated in her car, Shelby had tried calling Glen at Talia's. Talia informed her that Glen had left again. Shelby knew from long experience that it was impossible to call Glen. He bought prepaid cell phones from time to time, but she never had his number. Talia did not ask what she wanted with Glen, or offer to help. Shelby wouldn't have asked for her sister's help anyway. She felt as if there was no one in the world she could talk to. No one who would understand.

She drove home to her apartment. Her hand was shaking so hard as she tried to unlock the door that her keys made a jangling noise. A door opened down the hall and a woman poked her head out. She frowned. 'Shelby.'

Shelby looked. 'Hi Jen,' she said weakly.

'You look terrible. What's the matter?'

Shelby sighed. 'It's a long story.'

'How about coming over for some dinner tonight,' Jennifer said. 'I'm going to try this new recipe and it makes enough for six people.'

Shelby almost said no, but then stopped herself. 'Thanks,' she said humbly. 'That would be great.'

She let herself in to the silent apartment, unpacked her bag, and ran herself a bath. After a long soak, she got dressed and went to her desk. The photos that Perry had forwarded to her in a file were on her computer. She began to go through them, searching in vain for a face she might recognize. She studied them until her neck ached and her lower back was cramped, and it was time for dinner.

She went gratefully down the hall to Jen's apartment, where she had a glass of wine, a complicated veal dish, and forced herself, no matter how Jen urged her to explain, to avoid talking about Chloe, Jeremy, or her son-in-law. Jen agreeably took up the slack, recounting her problems with a Main Line homeowner who wanted the best of everything and didn't want to pay for it. Shelby felt herself relaxing a little bit, just by being away from her own problems for an hour or two.

As she walked back into her apartment she heard the phone ringing. The message had just picked up, and she heard a breathless, frightened voice speaking to the voice mail.

'Shelby? This is Darcie.'

Darcie, she thought? Jeremy's teacher?

'I'm sorry to bother you but the police just called . . .'

Shelby grabbed up the phone. 'Darcie,' she said. 'It's me. I'm here. What happened? What's going on?'

Darcie swallowed hard, and when she spoke, her voice was shaking. 'I'm at Rob's house. He asked me to come over and babysit Jeremy tonight. He said he had to go somewhere. So I came over. When I got there Jeremy was already in bed, asleep—'

'Darcie, is it Jeremy?' Shelby cried impatiently. 'Has something happened to my grandson?'

'No, not Jeremy,' Darcie said miserably. 'It's Rob. The police just called. Rob's been in a terrible accident. He's at Dillworth Memorial.'

'Is he going to be all right?' Shelby demanded.

'I don't know. They wouldn't say too much because I'm not related to him. But apparently it's not good.'

'Oh my God. All right. I'm going to go over there,' said Shelby. 'Can you stay there with Jeremy a while longer?'

'Yes, of course,' said Darcie. 'As long as you need me.'

'Whatever you do, don't wake him up,' Shelby said. 'Let him sleep. He's had too many shocks already. I'll come over there as soon as I find out what is going on at the hospital and stay with Jeremy. But I don't want him to hear this until I'm there with him.'

'I understand,' said Darcie. 'Just let me know, OK?'

'I will,' said Shelby. 'As soon as I know.'

Shelby wove through the nighttime city traffic and arrived at Dillworth Memorial in record time. She parked haphazardly and rushed inside. As Shelby burst through the sliding doors into the subdued chaos of the hospital's emergency room, she realized that, in her haste to get here, she had committed a terrible oversight. Rob had more than one child. Molly needed to be told. Shelby pulled out her phone, ready to call, and then decided to wait, just until she had a little more information. She asked the receptionist where to find her son-in-law, and ran down the hall to the room where she had been directed.

Three uniformed policemen were conferring outside the room with an older man in a neat jacket and tie. They all looked up at her suspiciously as she approached.

'I'm looking for Rob Kendricks,' she said.

'He's in surgery,' said one of the uniformed cops. 'Who are you?'

'I'm his mother-in-law. My name is Shelby Sloan. What happened?'

'His mother-in-law?' the officer asked skeptically.

'I'm his closest relation, I guess. His parents are mission-aries in Southeast Asia. His wife, my daughter, just . . . she died recently. Will someone please tell me what happened?'

The man in the jacket and tie peered at Shelby. 'I'm Detective Camillo. How did you find out about this?'

'My grandson's babysitter called me after you called the house. I almost missed the call. I was having dinner with a friend.'

'Your friend will confirm that?' said Detective Camillo.

Shelby felt something tighten in her chest. 'Yes, of course.'

'What's his name?'

'Whose? My friend's?'

Camillo nodded.

'Her name is Jennifer Brandon. Why? What is going on?'

The detective exchanged a glance with one of the uniformed cops, who immediately turned away and began to make a call on his radio. Detective Camillo, whey-faced with dark circles under his eyes, looked back at Shelby. 'Your son-in-law was driving on the Schuylkill Expressway tonight. His pick-up truck was forced off the road and flipped over.'

'Oh my God.'

'He was ejected from the vehicle. He wasn't wearing a seat belt.'

'I can't believe this. I hate that road. Everybody speeds on it,' said Shelby. 'With all those huge trucks it's taking your life in your hands just to drive on it . . .'

Camillo shook his head. 'So far, we don't know what kind of vehicle it was. We're investigating that. It was dark, so the witnesses didn't see the plates or the make of the car. But we know it wasn't a truck. And we know it wasn't an accident.'

Shelby stared at him. 'It wasn't . . . What do you mean?'

'I mean,' said the detective. 'It was deliberate. Your son-in-law was forced off the road deliberately.'

Shelby shook her head, uncomprehending.

'It might have been road rage. Maybe he had a bumper sticker some idiot didn't like. It could be anything these days. Everybody's got their middle finger permanently at the ready.' Detective Camillo shook his head. 'Nothing surprises me anymore. There's no civility left. None at all.'

'Deliberate,' said Shelby.

Camillo shrugged. 'We need to know where he was immediately before this took place. He might have been in an argument with someone. At a bar or club, or whatever. Do you know where he went tonight?'

Shelby shook her head.

'You're looking a little green, ma'am.'

'I need to sit down,' said Shelby.

One of the officers stepped aside and offered her the chair behind him. Shelby sank down into it, trembling.

A doctor emerged from the nearby room and pulled his cap off his head. He spoke to the detectives, and then, when they pointed Shelby out to him, he came over to her.

Shelby looked up at him. 'How is he?'

'He has a lot of internal injuries.'

'But he'll be all right?'

'Well, I hope so. But, if there's any other family, you might want to get in touch with them,' he said.

'Is . . .' Shelby tried to wet her lips with her tongue. 'Is he . . . ?'

'Just a precaution.'

Shelby pulled out her phone and stared at it. She could still see Rob's angry eyes as he threw her out, furious that she had hired a detective to investigate Chloe's death. And now, someone had tried to kill Rob. Road rage? An accident? She had heard what the detective said, but what were the chances that it was all a coincidence? First Rob's wife. Now Rob. Both victims in such a short time. She wanted to call Perry and tell him. Ask him what he thought. But first, Molly. And Rob's parents. The church would know how to get in touch with them. She would call the church. First, Molly. She thought of calling Molly's cell phone, but then she decided, as she looked up her address book, to call Lianna instead. This was news that Molly needed to hear from her mother.

SEVENTEEN

Twenty minutes later Molly, wearing a jacket over her pajama pants and slippers, arrived, shepherded by Lianna. Molly was bleary-eyed, her face swollen from crying. Lianna was beautiful, even with no makeup and uncombed hair. She wore a trench coat pulled over her sweats.

'Where is he?' Molly demanded in raw voice. 'I want to see him.'

Shelby directed the distraught teenager to a nurse who was passing by. 'That's her father in there,' Shelby said.

The nurse nodded. 'Just for a few minutes. He's not awake. But he can probably hear your voice. He'll know you're there.'

'Do you want me to come with you, darling?' said Lianna putting a hand on her daughter's arm.

Molly shook off Lianna's hand and looked at her mother with malice in her eyes. 'No. Don't you dare.'

'It's one person at a time,' said the nurse.

'I'll be right here waiting for you,' said Lianna apologetically. Molly did not reply.

Shelby looked at Lianna questioningly.

'They never forgive you for a divorce,' she said with a shrug of embarrassment. 'At a time like this, it's all my fault.'

Shelby nodded knowingly. 'I suppose.'

Lianna sat down heavily on the chair next to Shelby. She pulled her trench coat tightly around her and looked at Shelby in disbelief. 'What happened?'

Shelby shook her head. 'The police don't know yet. Somebody ran him off the road. They're thinking it might have been road rage.'

Lianna peered at Shelby. 'You sound skeptical.'

Shelby looked back at her frankly. 'First my daughter. Now Rob.'

Lianna frowned and pulled at her plump upper lip with her index finger. 'It is bizarre.'

'It is to me,' said Shelby.

'You must be utterly wasted,' said Lianna.

'I am. I dread trying to explain this to Jeremy.'

'I can imagine,' Lianna agreed, shaking her head. 'This all so unreal. Molly is beside herself. She loves Rob. More than anything.'

'He's a good father,' said Shelby.

Lianna sighed. 'Yes. He is. I guess we'll be here for a while.'

'Well, now that you're here, I'm thinking I'll head back to their house,' said Shelby. 'Rob asked Jeremy's teacher to babysit and she's been there for hours. I should probably let her get home. Besides, much as I dread telling him, I don't want Jeremy to hear this from anyone but me.'

'I can understand that,' said Lianna.

Detective Camillo emerged from a room down the hall and walked up to where Shelby and Lianna were sitting.

'This is Detective Camillo,' said Shelby. 'He's investigating what happened.'

'You are . . . ?' he asked Lianna.

'I'm Rob's ex-wife,' said Lianna. 'Our daughter, Molly, is in there with him now. My husband is parking the car.'

'Where were you tonight, Mrs Kendricks?'

'Mrs Janssen. Well, I was home. With my family. My husband's a doctor. A neurologist, actually. He often operates at this hospital. Maybe you know him. Harris Janssen? Here he is now.'

Lianna waved to Harris, who was striding toward them, jingling his keys in his hand. Shelby noticed the glow in Lianna's eyes as she watched him approach.

Camillo seemed unimpressed. 'Did you and your ex-husband get along?'

Lianna raised her perfectly shaped eyebrows. 'As well as can be expected. For exes.'

'Not that well, then.'

'We each made a new life. And we share a daughter.' Lianna hesitated. 'We always will.'

Detective Camillo looked at her, unsmiling. 'I hope so, ma'am.'

Shelby drove back to Manayunk, and, luckily, found a space only half a block from the house. As she walked up to the front door, she saw Darcie holding back the curtain looking anxiously up and down the street. She waved, and Darcie's tense frame sagged with relief. Shelby let herself in.

'I'm back,' she said.

Darcie rushed up to greet her. 'How is he? How is Rob?'

'Well, there hasn't been much change,' said Shelby. 'I guess you could say that he's hanging in there.'

Darcie burst into tears.

Shelby looked at her in surprise.

Darcie shook her head and wiped her eyes on her sleeve. 'He's just such a great father. I can't bear the thought of anything happening to him. Of poor Jeremy, losing both his parents.'

Shelby looked at the large, sweet-faced young woman kindly. Darcie was in her twenties although she still had the wardrobe of a teenager. But despite her girlish clothes and soft features, she had a certain confidence that Shelby liked. The children in her class always seemed calm and happy at the end of a day with her. 'You've been such a big help to this family. I really, really appreciate it, Darcie. I know Rob does too.'

Darcie sniffed. 'I'm just glad I can help.'

'You have. But now you need to go home and get some rest. You're getting worn out. I assume you have school tomorrow.'

'I do,' Darcie admitted.

Shelby reached for her wallet. 'I don't know what Rob pays you.'

Darcie recoiled. 'No. Please. I couldn't accept anything. This was an emergency.'

Shelby hesitated, then realized she needed to accept the young woman's generosity. 'Thank you,' she said. 'I may have to call on you again.'

Darcie had recovered her self-possession. 'Call me anytime. Really. I want to help.'

Shelby followed her to the door and watched her walk up

the block. She only lived a few streets away. Darcie looked back and waved as she turned the corner, and Shelby waved back. Then she closed the door and locked it.

The house was utterly silent. She decided to go upstairs and check on Jeremy before she did anything else. She tiptoed up the stairs, and pushed open the door to his room. The light from the hall fell on the boy's curly hair, the lumpy covers and stuffed animals scattered about the bed. Shelby sighed at the sight of him.

The covers rustled, and then, before she could retreat, she saw Jeremy, squinting into the light. 'Mom?' he mumbled.

Shelby's heart ached to hear him call for Chloe. She slipped into the room and sat down on the edge of his bed, rubbing his shoulder and murmuring soothingly. 'It's me. It's Shep. Go back to sleep.'

'Shep?' he asked. And then he emerged from under the covers and buried his face in her side.

'Hi sweets,' she said. 'I'm here. You go back to sleep.'

'Where's Dad?'

'He's sleeping,' she said, trying to remain close to the truth. 'It's time for everybody to be sleeping.'

'Is the pirate still here?' he mumbled.

'No pirates,' said Shelby fondly. 'Just the sandman.'

Jeremy pushed away from her, and peered at her through sleepy eyes. 'No Shep, there was a pirate here. Before. A lady pirate.'

'A lady pirate,' said Shelby, smiling.

Jeremy nodded. 'I saw her. She was talking to Dad. Downstairs.'

'I'll bet you did.'

'I did. She had a coat with a skeleton. And big hoops in her ears. And one of them things on your eye. That goes on your eye? You know what I mean?'

'Glasses?' Shelby asked.

'Not glasses,' the child said wearily, as if he could barely tolerate his grandmother's ignorance. 'You know, it covers your eye when another pirate tears it out with a hook!' he cried, roaring, and clawing the air with a crooked arm.

Shelby suddenly felt a chill sweep through her. 'An eyepatch,' she said.

'YUP!' Jeremy cried.

In her mind's eye, Shelby saw it all. The Ed Hardy baseball jacket with the skull design on the back. The hoop earrings. The eyepatch.

'The pirate was here tonight?' she asked softly.

'Yeah. I got out of bed, but don't tell Dad. I heard them downstairs. Dad was yelling.'

'Was the pirate lady yelling too?' Shelby asked.

'Not pirate lady,' he corrected her. 'Lady pirate.'

'Sorry. Lady pirate. Was she yelling at Dad?'

'No. Well, a little bit. But mainly Dad.'

'What were they yelling about?' Shelby asked.

Jeremy yawned, and leaned against her side. 'I dunno,' he murmured. 'The treasure map, probably.'

'Most likely,' said Shelby.

'Maybe Dad knows where the treasure is hid,' Jeremy mumbled. His eyes were beginning to close, and it was getting more difficult for him to open them again.

'Maybe he does,' said Shelby.

'We'll ask him. Tomorrow,' said Jeremy.

Shelby gently smoothed his curls while her mind and her heart raced. 'Yes,' she said, as he drifted back to sleep. 'We need to know.'

EIGHTEEN

In the morning, she hedged the truth. She told Jeremy that Daddy had gotten hurt in the car, and had to go to the emergency room. Jeremy, whose playtime mishaps had landed him in the emergency room himself several times, found nothing to question in this. When he asked, 'Is he still there?' Shelby said that the doctors were making him stay a while until he got better.

When she deposited him at preschool Darcie asked, 'Does he know about the accident?'

'As little as possible,' said Shelby. 'Let's keep it that way for now.'

Darcie nodded agreement.

As soon as Shelby got back into the car, she phoned Perry at Markson's.

There was a slight delay, and then Perry got on the line.

'Perry,' she said breathlessly. 'A few things have happened that I think you should know about. There may be no connection—'

Before she could get any further, Perry cleared his throat and said, 'Shelby, listen . . .'

Shelby heard the apology in his tone. She frowned and waited.

'I am truly, truly sorry about this, but I am not going to be able to go any farther with this.'

'What do you mean?' Shelby asked. 'Why not?'

Perry hesitated. Then he said, 'Apparently the Sunset Cruise Line contacted Elliott Markson. Told him that his security chief had been asking questions about your daughter.'

'Oh no,' said Shelby.

'He blew up when he heard about it.'

'I was afraid of that when you said you would do this on company time.'

'Mr Markson would have wanted me to try to help you.'

Shelby sighed. 'Well, it's a new era. A new Markson. Look, Perry, I can pay you under the table. Can you continue on your own time?' she said.

There was a silence at Perry's end. He cleared his throat again. Then he sighed. 'He basically said that he doesn't want any trouble with the cruise lines. There may be corporate conflicts of interest.'

It was Shelby's turn to be silent.

'Shelby, I am really sorry. But I can't afford to lose my job over this. With my daughter's condition, we need the health insurance. And my hours here are flexible so I can help my wife to manage her care. Elliott Markson gave me a direct order to drop the matter. I'm afraid if I defy him . . .'

Shelby took a deep breath. 'I understand, Perry.'

'I can recommend some people to you who might be able to help.'

Shelby's heart was filled with outrage at this new management that had replaced Albert Markson's good manners and compassion with a flinty attitude of distrust and hostility. You could run a business and be decent to your employees at the same time. But then she forced herself to let it go. There is no time, she reminded herself, to worry about feeling angry or betrayed. 'That would be great,' she said, 'email them to me,' although she felt little optimism at the prospect of hiring another detective. It seemed as if she alone cared about the truth of what happened to Chloe. She couldn't think about it right now. Right now she had to find a lady pirate.

Shelby sat down on a bench under a tree across the street from the church, opened her newspaper and peeked out around it. She didn't want anyone leaving the church after the meeting to recognize her. After her ejection the other day, she felt certain that her face would be memorable. She pretended to read, and waited for the meeting to let out.

Just when she was beginning to wonder if today's meeting had been canceled, a few people began to straggle out and head in different directions down the street. There was no guarantee, of course, that on this particular day, at this particular meeting, everyone from the previous meeting would attend. She held her breath and waited, holding the paper open in front of her face and lowering it just enough to watch the people as they emerged from the church doors.

She saw Ted, the former gym teacher, coming down the steps. Instead of a tracksuit, today he was wearing chinos and a windbreaker. He loped across the street in her direction. Shelby frowned into the paper she was clutching in front of her face. Ted did not hesitate, but kept walking, entering the park behind her and heading off down one of the paths.

Shelby lowered the paper and glanced across the street just in time to see a gray braid above the Ed Hardy skull and hearts logo heading in the opposite direction. She jumped up from the bench, crossed the street and rushed after Barbara, who had turned at the corner. Shelby caught up with her as she was unlocking the door of an industrial-looking building on a street that was little more than an alleyway.

'Barbara,' she said.

The tall, lanky woman turned and looked at her, frowning. She was wearing a pair of sunglasses that covered her eyepatch.

'Chloe's mother,' Shelby reminded her.

Barbara grimaced and looked all around her, as if to be

sure there was no one in earshot. 'What? What do you want?'
she said irritably.

'I need to talk to you,' said Shelby.

'Look, I can't help you. I don't—'

'I know you went to see my son-in-law,' said Shelby flatly,
although she was only taking a stab in the dark.

Barbara sighed and glanced at her watch. 'I have work to
do,' she said vaguely.

'This won't take long,' said Shelby. 'Please.'

Barbara sighed and hunched her shoulders. 'I can't avoid
this, can I?'

Shelby shook her head.

Barbara pushed open the door and nodded for Shelby to
follow her. The foyer was dim, and the elevator looked like
it had not been serviced in a century. Shelby followed Barbara
inside and they rode to the fourth floor in silence.

Barbara unlocked a large door on the landing and pushed
it to the side. Behind the door was a loft space with a wall
of windows. There were paintings everywhere, on easels and
pushed up against the furniture. Shelby looked around with a
knowledgeable eye. The loft space was large and clearly a
valuable space. The paintings were plentiful, but ordinary and
uninteresting. Barbara was not paying for this loft space by
selling these paintings.

'This is my studio. And my home,' Barbara said proudly.

'What a fantastic space,' said Shelby.

'Yeah,' said Barbara. 'My dad owns the building.'

Shelby nodded, her suspicions confirmed. Barbara had to
be at least forty-five years old. How discouraging to still be
dependant, she thought.

'Sit,' said Barbara, perching on a kitchen stool by a stain-
less steel island.

Shelby sat down in a lipstick-red, art deco style armchair.

'So he told you,' said Barbara in a grumpy tone.

'I'm sorry?' Shelby asked.

'Your son-in-law. He told you about my visit? I asked him
specifically not to tell anyone.'

Shelby shook her head. 'No. My grandson saw you. He
described you to me. You're very distinctive-looking.'

Barbara took off her shades and set them down on the
island. She waved her long, narrow, paint-stained fingers

dismissively. 'I don't know why you're pestering me. If you want to know what we talked about, ask your son-in-law.'

'I can't ask him. His car was forced off the road last night. He's in the hospital, unconscious,' Shelby said bluntly.

'Oh my God. Sorry,' said Barbara.

'So I have to ask you. What did you tell him? And why?'

'I should never have gone over there,' said Barbara, shaking her head. 'I knew it, and I did it anyway. I broke every rule of AA. Everything that you hear at a meeting is supposed to stay in the meeting. No exceptions.'

Shelby watched her the way one might watch an exotic bird perched on a feeder – fearful of scaring it away with any sudden moves.

'I told myself it was wrong, and that I shouldn't go, but I did it anyway.'

'Why did you go there? How did you find him?' Shelby asked.

Barbara shrugged. 'It wasn't that difficult. After you showed up at the meeting with that picture of Chloe, and said her name was Kendricks, I just Googled her, and there was the whole story. About the cruise and all. I looked them up in the Philly phone book. They're listed. Address and phone number.'

'So what did you tell Rob that got him so upset? My grandson said you were arguing,' Shelby said grimly.

'We weren't arguing,' Barbara protested. Then she sighed again. 'I'm not going to get rid of you, am I?'

Shelby shook her head.

Barbara shook her head. 'Chloe used to come to our meeting. I can't believe I'm telling you this – if you ever breathe a word of this . . .' She pointed a finger at Shelby.

Shelby closed her eyes and shook her head to indicate that she would not.

'She and I just hit it off. She had a very artistic soul. I miss her. She came for a while. Must have been at least a year.'

Shelby registered the fact that now she knew. Chloe, her baby, had been an alcoholic. There was no doubt Rob had told the truth about that. She didn't have time to have any feelings about this news, other than to realize that she now had one answer, for certain. But at this moment, she just wanted to encourage her elusive witness and not scare her off. 'Yes, that's what I understand,' said Shelby cautiously.

'I knew they were going on the cruise. I warned her about those things. There's so much drinking on those boats. There's a bar every three feet. My parents took me with me with them once when I was a teenager.'

Shelby felt a stab of guilt. She had never even thought about that when she planned their gift. But she didn't ever dream it would be a problem for her daughter. Chloe had kept it a secret.

'She knew she was a little shaky, but she really wanted to go. She thought it would be good for her marriage. I think things were a little rocky.'

Shelby watched her cautiously.

'Anyhow, about a week before the trip, she came in and she was all agitated. She said she had a problem and she didn't know what to do. She wanted to tell me about it. Just me. Not the whole meeting. We would usually talk before the meeting. That's the beauty of it. Sometimes you can tell things to a stranger that you can't tell the people in your life.'

'Sure,' Shelby murmured encouragingly.

Barbara gave Shelby a disparaging glance, as if Shelby were to blame for her egregious breaking of the rules.

'What was it?' Shelby asked.

'She had found out somehow that her husband's ex-wife had been deceiving him. His daughter was not actually his. She was the child of another man.'

Shelby's mouth dropped open. 'Molly?'

Barbara shrugged. 'I don't know the kid's name.'

'It's Molly,' said Shelby. 'I can't believe it. What other man? How did Chloe know that?' But even as she asked, Shelby had an inkling. Dr Cliburn was Lianna's ob-gyn. It must have been in her records. Her confidential, medical records.

'I don't know,' said Barbara. 'I didn't ask. It's not important. The thing was, she knew she should tell Rob, but it was just before the cruise. She said if she told him, they'd have to cancel the cruise. He'd be all freaked out about it and he wouldn't want to go. So, she wanted to wait until they got back to tell him. But she didn't want to lie to him.'

'What did you say?' Shelby asked.

Barbara shrugged. 'I said it wasn't lying if she was going to tell him, after all. There was no harm in their having a nice vacation and then telling him after they got back. I think that's what she wanted to hear, because she decided that's what she

would do. I didn't think any more about it until you came to
the meeting with that picture of her and said that she died on
the cruise. And I thought, what the fuck happened?

'So, I decided to tell her husband myself,' said Barbara. 'I
figured he had a right to know. If Chloe wasn't going to be
able to tell him, I would.' Barbara made a fist and rapped it
on the cutting board built into the island.

'I had no idea,' said Shelby.

'And this is why you're supposed to keep your mouth shut
about what you hear at these meetings,' said Barbara. 'To
avoid a situation just like this one.'

Shelby forced her mind out of the tailspin it was in. She
looked squarely at Barbara. 'I know you feel guilty about
breaking the rules,' she said. 'But I really want to thank you
for doing it. And for caring so much about Chloe.'

Barbara was staring at the paint-spattered floor, her jaw
working as if she was trying not to cry. 'Maybe if she'd told
him right away, none of this would have happened.'

'Or maybe it wouldn't have made any difference at all,'
said Shelby.

'I don't know why anyone would take advice from me
anyway,' said Barbara. 'All my relationships have gone down
in flames. My life is so fucked up. How do I know what
someone should do?'

Shelby understood that Barbara was about to introduce her
own problems into the conversation. She also knew that she
owed it to this woman to listen. This woman had gone way
out of her way for Chloe. And now she wanted a little time,
a little empathy for herself. Shelby vowed to herself that
she would pay this debt off someday. But not today.

'There wasn't anything wrong with the advice you gave
her,' said Shelby, pushing herself up from the chair. 'It made
perfect sense, what you said to Chloe.'

Barbara looked up at her ruefully. 'Is that it?' she said.

'I can never thank you enough,' Shelby said.

'I should have kept my mouth shut,' said Barbara woefully.
'I never learn.'

NINETEEN

A spring day in Gladwyne was the definition of fair. Cherry blossoms floated on the trees and every curb and yard was planted with pink and yellow and violet-colored blooms. If Shelby hadn't been in such an agitated state, she might have stopped just to enjoy and be dazzled by the beauty of it. But flowers were the last thing on her mind. She had only been to Lianna and Harris's home once before, and that on a day when she was distraught, so she had to pay attention to her directions.

Shelby pulled into the Janssen's driveway behind a couple of other cars. As soon as she saw the other cars, all expensive, late-model sedans, she realized her mistake. She had not bothered to call first – she wanted to ambush Lianna with this accusation. She had not considered the possibility that perhaps Lianna was teaching a class. Well, she thought, this was more important.

She went up and tried knocking on the front door. As she expected, there was no answer. She went around the house to the carriage house that Lianna used as a yoga studio. She looked in the window and saw that there were, indeed, several women on their mats, and Lianna at the front of the room, svelte despite her slightly rounded belly, leading the group in a catlike stretch. Shelby opened the door to the studio and stood there, looking in, but not speaking.

Lianna looked up at her and frowned.

'I need to talk to you,' said Shelby, her voice jarring in the peaceful silence.

Lianna glanced at her students and then put up five fingers. 'Can you wait five minutes? Five minutes. We're cooling down.'

Shelby withdrew, unsmiling, and returned to her car. She opened the door and sat down in the front seat. While she waited she gazed at Lianna's garden. The yard was a dazzling tribute to Lianna's green thumb. She had her own gardening business when she first married Harris, but had apparently abandoned that in favor of teaching yoga classes. Obviously, she still practiced her gardening skills on her own yard. 'She's good at everything she does,' Chloe had said once, in utter discouragement. Shelby wasn't sure whether it was a tribute to Lianna's many gifts, or her inability to concentrate, that she seemed to have done a dozen different kinds of work between her marriage to Rob and to Harris. Then again, she wasn't feeling very kindly disposed toward Lianna at this particular moment.

The yoga students, all women over thirty, with expensive haircuts and watches, dressed in workout chic, began to emerge from the carriage house and disperse toward their expensive vehicles. The driveway was wide enough so that they could edge out past Shelby without her moving. Ordinarily, she might have backed out to make it easier. She did not feel cooperative at this particular moment.

Shelby walked back to the studio and opened the screen door. Lianna was pressing a towel to her arms and forehead. Unlike the other women, she wore a faded, stretched-out leotard, and pulled her hair up in a messy clip. Her perfect features were devoid of make up. 'Shelby,' she said. 'Is it Rob? Has anything happened?'

'Only in a manner of speaking,' said Shelby.

'I called the hospital this morning and they said he was holding his own.'

'There's no change. As far as I know.'

'I'm going to take Molly up there after school. She wants to spend every spare minute with him. Whew, I need a drink. Come over to the house,' she said in her engaging manner. As Shelby followed her across the lawn to the back door, she felt a sad sympathy for her own daughter, who had been so intimidated by this woman. There was something preternaturally graceful about her, as if she had never made an awkward move or a false step in her life. Of course, Shelby reminded herself, that was clearly not true.

Lianna went to the refrigerator and poured them each a glass of ice water. She took them out to a sunroom beyond the kitchen, indicating that Shelby should follow her. Lianna sat down in a wicker chair and pointed to the one opposite her.

Shelby shook her head. All the way over here, she had tried

to think about how she would phrase her accusation. She found it difficult to begin.

'What's the matter?' said Lianna.

'Was Rob here last night?' Shelby asked.

The expression in Lianna's eyes went from curious to vaguely guilty. 'Why do you ask?' she said stiffly.

'I want to know,' said Shelby. 'Did he come over here?'

Lianna pursed her lips and clinked the ice in her glass. 'Yes, he came over here,' she said. 'Who told you that?'

'Why didn't you tell the police?' Shelby demanded.

'They didn't ask me,' Lianna said. 'Not that it's any of your business.'

For a moment, Shelby hesitated, trying to remember if that was true. Then she dismissed it. Lianna was splitting hairs. 'He came over here to confront you about Molly, didn't he?'

Lianna flushed with anger. Shelby didn't care.

'I know that Molly is not Rob's daughter. And I know that he found out about it last night.'

Lianna looked at her coolly. 'Well. I guess there is no such thing as privacy.'

'My Chloe knew about it. She knew about it before she was killed.'

'Oh yes. She certainly did. And told her friends about it. Fun for everyone! I can only assume that she plundered my private medical records at the office where she works,' Lianna said indignantly.

Shelby ignored her accusation. She knew it was wrong, and completely unprofessional, for Chloe to do that, but it couldn't compare to Lianna's deception.

'You had a secret. You wanted to keep it a secret.'

'Yes, I had a secret. Now the whole world knows about it.'

'You didn't want Rob to know. You were desperate for him not to know. Desperate to keep Chloe from telling him.'

Lianna recoiled and shook her head. 'Desperate? Are you kidding? We're not even married anymore. Get a hold of yourself.'

'You never told him,' Shelby said accusingly.

'I wanted to spare him the unhappiness. And Molly. I wanted to spare them both.'

'How badly did you want to silence my daughter?'

Lianna's mouth dropped open. 'What the hell are you

saying?' She took a deep breath as if she were trying to control her response. 'Are you suggesting that I had something to do with Chloe's death? Because of this?'

Shelby stared back at her without replying.

'Look, Shelby, I know you're grieving, but get a grip. For one thing, I wasn't even on that cruise. I was here, as you well know. I took care of Jeremy for you, remember?'

'It's possible to hire someone.'

'Hire someone? You mean . . . a hit man? Yeah. I must have one or two of those in my phone book,' she said sarcastically.

'I'm not joking about this,' said Shelby.

'Neither am I,' said Lianna. 'This is about the most insulting accusation I've ever heard. Especially since your daughter was the one who violated my privacy, and my rights as a patient.'

Shelby didn't care if Lianna was insulted. 'What about Harris? Does he know about Molly? And Rob?'

'Yes. I told him long ago. He always wanted me to tell Rob. I kept thinking I would choose the right moment. But then Chloe took it out of my hands. Apparently she shared my most personal secret with some friend of hers, who decided to tell Rob last night. Rob came over here in a rage. I was blindsided by the whole thing.'

A friend of hers. Shelby thought of Barbara, and instantly realized that Rob had been deliberately vague with Lianna. He was keeping secret the fact that Chloe was in AA.

Just then the front door opened and a voice called out, 'Hey, I'm home.'

'We're in the sunroom,' Lianna called out.

Harris came into the sunroom, carrying his briefcase and loosening his tie. 'I have to go to the hospital later,' he said. 'This is just a breather. Hi Shelby,' he said, and then put his arm around Lianna's shoulders, kissed her forehead and patted her belly. 'How's junior?' he said.

Lianna looked up at Shelby with narrowed eyes. 'A little agitated if you want to know the truth. Shelby's here hurling all kinds of accusations. She knows about Rob's visit here last night. And about Molly's real father.'

Harris immediately looked guiltily at Shelby. 'We probably should have told you last night. But it was awkward. We didn't want to make things worse with Rob.'

'That's not all,' said Lianna. 'She thinks I might have hired someone to kill Chloe. To keep it quiet.'

Harris laughed. 'Oh come on, honey,' he said. 'She didn't mean that. You're being overly sensitive.'

'That's what she said,' Lianna cried.

Harris frowned. 'All right. All right. Let's climb in off the ledge, ladies. We're all stressed out these days.' He turned to Shelby. 'Tell me, how is Rob? Is he awake?'

'Not yet,' said Shelby, somewhat shaken by his matter-of-fact response to her earth-shattering news.

Harris sighed. 'I felt so badly for him last night. When he came over I think he was really hoping to hear that it wasn't true.'

'I'm sure,' said Shelby stiffly. 'He loves Molly.'

'And he's been a wonderful father to her. I'm sure he would have been a wonderful father even if he had known the truth,' Harris said, frowning at Lianna. 'You should have had a little faith in him.'

'OK. I know. I should have told him,' said Lianna irritably, raising her hands as if in surrender. 'I should have, but I didn't. I was having an affair with a married man before I started seeing Rob. A man who was incapable of being a father to Molly.

'Whereas Rob . . . well, he was so proud of her. I let him believe that Molly was his. I'm a bad person. I admit it. Believe me, I paid for it last night when Molly found out. She was furious with me,' said Lianna.

'Darling, with all due respect, you deserved it,' said Harris.

Lianna raised her chin defiantly. 'I did not deserve to be outed by Chloe. What she did was wrong. It's my own fault. The minute I saw that she worked there, I should have gone somewhere else. I should never have stayed with Dr Cliburn.'

'Well, I guess it's normal to be curious, under the circumstances,' said Harris.

'Tell me you wouldn't fire a nurse who did that to one of your patients,' Lianna shot back. 'I should have found another doctor. I knew it was a mistake.'

'He's the best,' said Harris gravely. 'We wanted the best.'

'Even so,' said Lianna.

Harris patted her on the shoulder. 'Luckily, Molly is wise beyond her years.' He turned to Shelby. 'Her first thought was for Rob. She said to him right away, "I don't care about that guy. You're my Dad and that's final." It was very touching.'

Looking at him now, Shelby could understand why Chloe had always admired Harris when she worked in his office. He was a voice of calm and compassion.

'So, yes,' said Lianna. 'Rob was here, he was angry and, no matter what Chloe did, I guess I am to blame. Right now my daughter thinks I'm a horrible person and I suppose I deserve that. My husband seems to be a little more forgiving.' She gazed ruefully up at Harris, who smiled back at her. 'I don't know what else I can tell you. I'm actually relieved that it's all out in the open now. I just want Rob to get well so that we can all start to mend some fences.'

Shelby suddenly felt ashamed of her own outburst. She had taken a morsel of information and jumped to an extreme conclusion. However embarrassed Lianna might have been by her secret, it was clearly not something that had to be hushed up at any cost. Shelby didn't know whether she was disappointed, or relieved.

Shelby stood up. 'I shouldn't have said what I did,' she said.

'No, you shouldn't have,' said Lianna balefully.

'My daughter's death . . . it tortures me,' said Shelby.

Lianna sighed and was silent for a moment. 'I know it. I can imagine. It's all right.'

'No. I'm sorry. I was really out of line.'

Lianna looked at Shelby with sorrowful eyes. She placed one hand protectively on her own belly. 'No harm done,' she said.

Shelby took a deep breath. 'I do think, if it's all right with you two, that I will call the police and tell them that Rob was here last night. Before his accident. The detective said it might be important to know where he was.'

Lianna shrugged.

'Sure. Of course,' said Harris.

'I'd better go get Jeremy,' said Shelby.

Lianna nodded. 'I suppose we'll see you at the hospital.'

'Why?' Shelby asked.

'Visiting Rob?'

'Oh yes,' said Shelby, ashamed to have forgotten. 'Of course.'

TWENTY

Shelby walked up to where Darcie stood, guarding her small charges as they clambered on the jungle gym and flew skyward on the swings. Jeremy was in the thick of it, whooping that he had a sword and he was ready to use it.

'He seems to be doing OK,' said Shelby hopefully.

Darcie nodded without looking at her. 'Everything considered,' she said. 'How is Rob doing?'

'I called earlier. His condition is stable.'

'The church managed to contact his parents last night. They're in some tiny village in Indonesia. It's going to take them a while to get to a flight. They'll be back in a couple of days.'

'I'm just glad they got a hold of them,' said Shelby. 'Rob needs them here right now.'

'I agree.'

'I've never met his parents,' said Shelby. 'Rob and Chloe had a very small wedding, and they couldn't get here for it. They came once to see Jeremy, but I was in Paris while they were here.'

'They're very nice people,' said Darcie. 'Always cheerful. I remember them from when I was a little girl. They're very tough. They've lived in all kinds of conditions.'

'You've known Rob's family that long?' Shelby asked.

'All my life.'

'Rob must be kind of like a big brother to you,' she said.

Darcie watched Jeremy playing. 'Jeremy wants to go and see his dad.'

Shelby shook her head. 'Not yet. Not while Rob's unconscious, certainly. That will only scare Jeremy. He's just lost his mother. If he sees his father so messed up, it will give him nightmares.'

Darcie turned and looked at Shelby with wide, blue eyes. 'So you're not going up there tonight?'

'I'll run up in the morning,' said Shelby.

Darcie turned and looked back at her charges. 'I'll go tonight,' she said.

Shelby heard a note in Darcie's voice that took her by surprise, but she did not mention it.

'Time to get Jeremy home,' Shelby said.

Shelby's phone rang as she was beginning to usher Jeremy off to the bathtub. It was Elliott Markson's secretary calling. Mr Markson wanted to see her in his office the next morning at ten o'clock. Shelby said that she would be there. She had an idea of what this summons was about. At best, Elliott Markson was probably going to confront her about all the work she was missing, and he would surely dress her down for enlisting the help of Perry Wilcox. At worst . . .

Now that she knew that Rob's parents were arriving and would certainly move in here with Jeremy for the length of their stay, she would be free to return to her job, if she still had one. Perhaps it was time to think about working again. All her efforts to make sense of Chloe's accident were running into nothing but dead ends. The question was, would she have a job to go to? She had a feeling that she would know the answer tomorrow.

The evening routine with Jeremy proved difficult. It took all her wiles to convince the child that his father was still too sleepy for visitors, and that he was really going to be fine and they would see him soon. His usual storybook turned into three, and he wailed each time she tried to leave him alone in his room. By the time she had gotten Jeremy in bed, Shelby was almost ready to crawl into bed herself.

The doorbell rang at eight thirty, and she rushed to answer it, not wanting its peal in the night to wake Jeremy from his restless slumber. Detective Camillo, whom she had met at the hospital, was standing on the doorstep with a uniformed officer.

'Detective,' said Shelby, frowning.

'May we come in?' he asked.

'Of course,' said Shelby.

She stood aside as the two men entered the house and stood in the living room. Shelby invited them to sit and offered them a drink. Both men declined the drink but sat down in the living room, perched on the edge of their seats. Detective Camillo leaned forward in the chair, and rested his elbows on his knees.

'I want to thank you for your phone call earlier today,

Mrs Sloan. Once we knew where your son-in-law had been last night, it made our job a lot easier.'

'I'm glad I could help,' Shelby said.

'So, since I spoke to you, there have been a few developments in your son-in-law's case that I thought you would want to know about,' he said.

Shelby nodded. 'OK.'

'I wanted to talk to you before you heard about this on the eleven o'clock news.'

Shelby was instantly alarmed. 'Heard what? Is Rob all right? I called the hospital before dinner. They said he's still stable.'

'Yeah. I spoke to the doc about an hour ago. Apparently, he'll be all right. But, we still want to charge these guys with attempted murder.'

Shelby's eyes widened. 'Guys? You found out who did this?'

The detective's weary eyes glinted with satisfaction. 'It looks that way. Actually,' he said, 'we caught a few breaks on this one. Which is not to minimize the excellent legwork by my squad.'

'So what happened?'

'Well, it was much as I originally suspected. Because Rob's car had nearly a full tank of gas, we proceeded on the assumption that he had filled up on his way home. When you told us that he had been out in Gladwyne, we were able to determine his route. After that, it was easy to narrow down the possibilities. We checked the surveillance videos for everywhere you could buy gas along the route. We found him on the third try. Your son-in-law stopped for gas and got into an altercation with some kids who were hanging around just looking for trouble.'

'An altercation? About what?' Shelby asked.

'We don't know. All we have is the video – no sound. Anyway, when he drove away, they followed him. They followed him on to the Schuylkill and forced his car off the road. They had a gun. He was lucky he wasn't killed.'

'Oh my God,' Shelby said. She exhaled and sat back in her seat. 'I can't believe it.'

Camillo shook his head. 'Even the most minor argument turns lethal these days. They're not happy just insulting you. They gotta kill you now.'

Shelby shook her head. 'Don't they even think about the consequences?'

'They don't think about anything. Believe me,' he said.

'I'm just really amazed that you found them so quickly.'

'Well, like I say, we were lucky. The surveillance camera at the pumps gave us their license plate. From that, it was easy to track them down.'

'I see.'

'I don't mean that there's anything lucky about this,' Camillo demurred.

'I understand,' said Shelby.

Camillo frowned. 'There's just one more thing. From what we saw on the video, your son-in-law really got up in their faces. Is he normally kind of a hot-tempered guy?'

Shelby shook her head sadly. 'No. Usually he's pretty mild-mannered.'

'Any particular reason why he would have been edgy last night?'

Shelby was silent. She felt extremely grateful to the police for finding the people who had forced Rob off the road, but she didn't really relish the idea of divulging the reason Rob had been in a belligerent mood. What if it ended up on the news? Molly would be humiliated at school and every-where else. She was a teenager, awkward and self-conscious like most teenagers, and she didn't deserve that. She was the innocent victim in this whole thing. Shelby suddenly under-stood exactly why Lianna had not offered this information up to the police.

'Did something happen last night?' asked Detective Camillo.

Shelby shook her head. 'No. Not really. There was a family argument. You know. Between exes. Normal stuff.'

'I'm not asking to be nosy ma'am. Your son-in-law's state of mind is going to make a difference if this thing gets to trial.'

Shelby frowned. 'Why?'

'Well, the defense might try to say that he provoked these guys. Challenged them maybe.'

'You don't believe that, do you?' she asked.

'What I believe is not important. It'll be what the jury believes.'

'That is horrible. A man is minding his own business and

he's dragged into this situation. He's pursued and run off the road by criminals. And now you're saying they might blame it on Rob?'

'I'm saying that it's important to know what kind of a person he is. Is he prone to violent outbursts?'

'No. I mean, not normally. Last night, he'd had a bit of a shock. He was probably not completely himself,' said Shelby carefully.

'No criminal convictions. No . . . domestic violence. Nothing like that.'

Instantly, Shelby thought about Chloe and the cruise. Wasn't this what she had secretly wondered and feared? How could you ever really know a person from the outside? To the world Rob was a churchgoer, a social worker, a kindly father, a good husband. But people like that had been known to snap. Isn't this exactly what she had suspected? That there was a hidden side of Rob that was capable of violence? Of murder?

The thought of it filled her with despair. She realized that she had just about gotten to the point of acceptance. For a while she had suspected Rob, and then, everything she learned had made her see him as nothing more than a grieving husband. He had been honest about Chloe's alcoholism, and passed a lie detector test. Even Perry Wilcox, an experienced detective, had judged that Rob was being truthful, and that Chloe's death was probably an accident.

Now, with his question, Detective Camillo had set her brain ricocheting in her skull again, like that of a shaken baby. Was there no respite from this doubt, she wondered? She didn't know how she could go on living with it. She had to resolve this in her mind. She had to learn how to accept it and move on. For her sanity.

'Mrs Sloan?' Detective Camillo asked worriedly.

'What?' she asked.

'Anything you want to tell us?' he asked.

Shelby stared straight at him. 'No,' she said. 'Nothing.'

TWENTY-ONE

S helby sat calmly in the waiting area outside of Elliott Markson's office. She had stopped by her apartment, and she was properly dressed for her own termination. A well-known designer had once told her that navy blue was the color of power, and she had taken that suggestion to heart. She had on one of her very favorite suits, a Ralph Lauren, with the faintest pinstripe, and some heels that were rather higher than she might normally wear. They would at least put her at Elliott Markson's eye level. She tapped one foot idly, and pretended not to notice the delay. Finally, the intercom on his secretary's desk buzzed.

The secretary turned to Shelby. 'You can go in now,' she said.

Shelby went to the office door, took a deep breath, turned the knob and strode in. She knew he would be seated, watching her, and she met his gaze without flinching as she crossed the large, paneled office and put a hand on the chair in front of his desk. The desktop was virtually empty, with no photos, awards, or even art objects to give any clues about the man behind the desk.

'May I?' she asked.

'Please,' he said.

Now that she sat and really looked at him up close, she realized that Elliott Markson was not as young as she had previously thought. He was probably about her age. He had gray at his temples, and she noticed reading glasses sitting on his desktop.

'You wanted to see me,' she said.

'Yes,' he said. He placed his elbows on the desktop, and steepled his hands in front of his face. Automatically, Shelby noticed the excellent quality of his suit and shirt. 'First of all,' he said, 'how are you doing?'

Shelby was briefly taken aback. For a moment she thought he wanted her to let her guard down. She wasn't about to. 'Fine,' she said.

'How about your grandson?' he asked.

This question surprised her. But she was not unnerved. 'He's doing well. Thank you for asking.'

Elliott Markson waved a hand as if to dispense with the platitudes. 'Now, Ms Sloan, I know that you've been under a lot of stress lately. But it came to my attention recently that you engaged our head of security to investigate your daughter's death. This was, essentially, a private matter.'

Shelby was not about to start making excuses, or protest that Perry had insisted on using company time for the job. She waited.

'And this is the sort of misappropriation of company time and funds which is no longer going to be tolerated here at Markson's. The culture at Markson's has to change in order for the business to survive. My uncle, before he died, had lost all perspective. He let his employees take their birthdays off and bought all their kids presents at Christmas. He would have approved of Mr Wilcox acting as your personal gumshoe. I am not that kind of employer. I am not Santa Claus.'

'I understand,' said Shelby. Part of her wanted to just stand up and announce that she was leaving, before he had a chance to fire her.

Elliott Markson held his hands open wide. 'No . . . protestations? Explanations?'

Shelby shook her head. 'It's terrible to me to think that Perry's job was jeopardized because he tried to help me. It was completely my fault.'

'So it seems. But Mr Wilcox has not lost his job.'

'I'm grateful for that,' said Shelby.

Markson nodded. 'Ms Sloan, you've missed a lot of work lately, and have given us no indication of when you plan to return.'

Here it comes, Shelby thought. She took a deep breath, and thought that there were a million things she could do with her experience and her qualifications. Sometimes it was best to make a change, and sometimes the only way to make a change was to be forced into it. Shelby raised her chin and waited for the blow.

'That being said, I realize that you have been thrown into some extraordinary circumstances lately.' Elliott Markson frowned slightly. 'Your grandson is suffering a terrible loss.

It's very difficult to lose your mother at such a young age,' he said. 'Very difficult.'

Shelby felt truly nonplussed. She had expected hostility. 'Yes, it is,' she said.

'I do realize how important it is for you to help him through this. There are times in life when one's career has to take a back seat,' he said.

Shelby stared at him.

Elliott Markson met her gaze. 'You seem surprised.'

'I . . . I was expecting . . .' she said.

'To be fired?' he asked.

Shelby hesitated. 'Frankly, yes. It crossed my mind.'

'Should you be fired?' he asked coolly.

Shelby remained calm. 'No. I'm good at my job. I will get back to it as soon as . . . as possible,' she said.

Elliott Markson did not look at her. 'My uncle had great respect for you, and he was a keen judge of character. I am trying to implement a lot of changes at Markson's to streamline operations, including in your department. But I think they can wait until you are ready to return.'

Shelby could hardly believe her ears. Part of her wanted to bow to him, murmuring thanks, and back out of the room. But some things had not changed and there was no use pretending that they had. 'This situation is still very complicated,' she said. 'In the coming months, years maybe, there are going to be times when my grandson will need me. He has no mother now. I'm always going to put him first.'

Elliott Markson's expression was impassive. 'As you must,' he said.

Shelby left Markson's office feeling lighter in spirit than she had in a long time. No matter how willing she was to walk away if need be, she had to admit that she did not want to lose her job. And now, it seemed, she was being allowed a respite. Her job was safe and she had even received a glimmer of understanding from an unlikely source. She felt almost happy.

She decided to stop at the hospital and look in on her son-in-law on her way back to Manayunk. She needed to evaluate for herself whether or not she could safely bring Jeremy to see his father. If Rob was still unconscious, or too frightening in appearance, she was going to have to continue making excuses.

She drove to Dillworth Memorial, and parked in the attached, multistory garage. She went up to the seventh floor and found Rob's room. When she walked in, she saw that the bed was empty.

For a moment her heart was seized with anxiety. She turned and rushed out to the nurse's station.

'Excuse me,' she said.

The nurse looked up.

'I'm looking for Rob Kendricks. He's not in his room.'

The nurse glanced at a chart hanging above the desk and then turned around and put her question to another nurse who was examining vials in a cart behind her.

'Oh, they took him down to x-ray. He'll be back up in about . . .' The nurse glanced at her watch. 'Half an hour.'

'Is he conscious?' Shelby asked.

'Yeah.'

'Really?' Shelby asked. 'That's great.'

'Yeah. He's doing much better,' said the nurse.

'Can I wait in his room?' Shelby asked.

The nurse grimaced. 'It could be longer than half an hour. We're backed up today. You can go down to the coffee shop and get some food. Try again after lunch.'

The moment she heard the words, Shelby realized how hungry she was. 'That's a great idea,' she said. 'I'll be back a little later.'

Shelby took the elevator back down to the first floor, and entered the cheerful, cafeteria-style coffee shop. The line was long, but moved quickly. Shelby got herself a sandwich and a cup of tea, and, after paying, exited the line into the dining area. Every table seemed to be at least half-occupied. For a moment she regretted not getting something to go. She looked around the room for a table with one occupant who might not object to sharing.

All of a sudden, to her surprise, she saw a familiar face. It was Talia's graduate assistant from the computer lab at Franklin. Shelby walked over to the table and spoke to the young woman with shaggy brown hair who was sipping at a cup of coffee and working on a computer notebook.

'Faith?' she said.

Talia's assistant looked up at her. Her face lit up slightly. 'Oh hi, Ms . . .'

'Shelby.'

'Right,' said Faith self-consciously.

Shelby gestured to the empty seat across from Faith. 'Would you mind if I sat down here,' she said. 'I don't mean to interrupt your work.'

'No, not at all,' said Faith, clearing her jacket off the chair. 'Please sit down.'

'It's just so crowded in here,' Shelby apologized.

'It is. I didn't see you come in,' said Faith. 'I'm trying to keep up with everything.'

Shelby nodded. 'What brings you to the hospital?' she asked, shaking out her paper napkin and putting it in her lap.

'I brought my mom for her physical therapy. She had a stroke years ago and she's still not completely well. My dad usually brings her but he's been under the weather lately, so I have to do it. Luckily, Dr Winter is really understanding about that. I know she takes care of your mother,' Faith said.

'Yes, she does,' said Shelby, forcing herself not to make excuses or explanations.

Faith shook her head. 'It's so hard to do everything. My husband and I bought a house. Well, more like a construction site than a house. There's so much to do,' she said, shaking her head. 'And we're doing it ourselves.'

'Whew,' said Shelby.

'Plus, it's kind of a hike to get here. So I'm just lucky to have a boss like Dr Winter. And, really, I don't mind. My parents need my help.'

Shelby thought about her sister's dour face, the accusation in her every word. She doubted very much if Talia was understanding. She never seemed to think about other people and their lives. When Faith mentioned her parents, it probably just gave Talia an opening to describe her own martyrdom, her brother's and sister's indifference.

'How about you?' Faith asked politely.

'What?' Shelby asked.

'What are you doing here?'

'My son-in-law is here,' said Shelby. 'He was in an accident,' she said.

'That's too bad,' Faith murmured.

Shelby thought about trying to explain but she could see Faith's gaze wandering back to her computer screen.

'You go ahead,' said Shelby. 'Don't let me interrupt you.'

'I'm always playing catch-up,' said Faith apologetically. She glanced at the clock. 'I need to finish before my mom gets done.'

Shelby nodded and picked up her sandwich as Faith returned to tapping at her keyboard.

In a few minutes, Shelby heard a voice from over her shoulder. 'OK, honey. I'm all done.'

Faith closed her computer and stood up. 'Hey Mom,' she said. 'How'd it go?'

'Oh they tortured me, as usual,' the woman said with a chuckle.

Shelby turned in her chair.

'Mom, this is Dr Winter's sister. Mrs Sloan. Mrs Sloan, this is my mother, Peggy Ridley.'

Shelby stared at the plump, older woman with a pink, unlined face, who was leaning on a cane. A few weeks earlier, in a police station in St Thomas, this same woman had told her about Chloe's last moments before her death.

The woman stared back at Shelby. 'Oh my word,' she said.

TWENTY-TWO

'You,' said Shelby.

Faith looked in confusion from her mother's amazed expression to Shelby's grim face. 'You two know each other?'

'Yes. Well, I'll be darned,' said Peggy. 'It's a small world, isn't it?'

Shelby was staring at the woman in disbelief. No, she thought. Not that small. How could it be? She did not understand it, and she could not organize the cacophony of thoughts in her head.

Peggy's surprise seemed perfectly genuine. But her genial amazement turned to wariness in the face of Shelby's silence and her frozen expression.

'How do you know each other?' Faith asked.

'We met when Dad and I were on the cruise,' said Peggy.

'You were on the same cruise?' Faith asked.

Shelby tore her gaze from Peggy's face and blinked at Faith as if she had just awakened. 'No. It wasn't me who was on the cruise. My daughter was. She died on that cruise,' she said.

'Mrs Sloan's daughter was the one who fell off the boat,' Peggy confided sadly.

Faith gasped. 'Oh my God,' she said. 'Oh, I'm so sorry, Mrs Sloan. I didn't know. My mother told me a woman fell off the boat. I just never realized . . .'

'Talia never said a word about it?' Shelby cried. 'That was her niece.'

'No.' Faith looked almost guilty. 'She doesn't really talk about personal things,' she said.

My God, Shelby thought with a mixture of disgust and disbelief. Even for Talia, that level of indifference was difficult to imagine. In Talia's mind, Chloe's death had not been worth mentioning to her own assistant.

'She did send me to the CVS to pick up a sympathy card for her,' said Faith. 'But that wasn't for you, I'm sure. No, of course not.'

Yes, Shelby thought. It was. The thought of it made her furious.

'What an amazing coincidence,' said Peg. 'I mean, to think that we were on that same trip where your daughter . . . Well, what are the odds?'

Shelby turned to Faith. 'Did Talia know that your parents were on that cruise?'

'I don't know. Wait. As a matter of fact, I think I did tell her. I mean, I thought it was an interesting story, about my parents spending time with the woman who fell off the boat. I'm sorry, I didn't know it was your daughter,' Faith said, grimacing apologetically. 'And she never said anything.'

'Maybe she didn't put two and two together,' Peg offered hopefully.

No, Shelby thought. That's impossible. Even for Talia. She was used to Talia treating the circumstances of her life as insignificant. But this was no ordinary circumstance. The parents of Talia's assistant were the last people to see Shelby's daughter alive. You would have to be stupid not to make the connection. And whatever else she might be, Talia was not stupid.

'Have you had any news?' Peggy asked kindly. 'Anything at all?'

Shelby's gaze returned to Peggy. 'No,' she said.

'We thought it was just awful the way the boat continued on after that,' Peggy said, shaking her head. 'We didn't feel right about that. Virgie and I couldn't get over it. People carrying on as if nothing had happened.'

Shelby was having difficulty forming the words for a response. All she could think about was their mutual connection to Talia. It was a coincidence that she could not reconcile. But, how could these people be involved? They seemed utterly guileless.

'We got a card from Virgie and Don the other day. Do you remember Virgie and Don Mathers? They were the other couple . . .'

'Yes,' said Shelby.

Peggy sighed and shook her head. 'Lovely people. Salt of the earth.'

Faith glanced at the clock on the wall. 'Well, Mom, we better be going. I've got to get back for class.'

'You're right,' said Peggy. She reached out a soft, dry hand and placed it over Shelby's. 'I'm glad to see you again,' she said. 'I never stopped praying for your Chloe.' There was something here that Shelby didn't know. Something that she needed to know. Perhaps, she thought, she was grasping at straws, still trying to make some sense of Chloe's death. But she couldn't just dismiss the fact that the Ridleys provided some kind of bizarre connection between Chloe's death and her life here at home. After all, she reminded herself, wasn't that why she had pored over the photos of people on board the ship? She was searching for a connection and now, here it was, even thought she had no idea what it meant. Shelby had to make a quick decision. 'Faith,' she said. 'I can take your mother home. Why don't you let me drive her and you can head back to the lab. Or . . . wherever . . .'

Peggy frowned. 'Oh no,' she said. 'We couldn't ask you to do that.'

'Please, I'd like to,' said Shelby. 'You were so kind to me in St Thomas. It's no trouble. Where do you live?'

'It's a bad neighborhood,' said Faith apologetically.

'You grew up there,' Peggy chided her.

'Still . . .' said Faith.

'Where is it?' Shelby demanded. She felt shaky and unsure of herself. She did not know what, if anything, she was hoping to find by taking this woman all the way across town. At the very least, she reassured herself, it was an opportunity to spend a little more time with the people who had last seen her daughter alive. Maybe in their last conversations Chloe had said something illuminating. Something that would help Shelby to understand.

'South Philly,' said Faith. 'It's called Hector. It's off of South Fourth Street.'

'Sure, I know it,' said Shelby. 'We used to live in South Philly when my Chloe was a little girl. I know just where it is.'

Faith looked relieved. She turned to her mother. 'I could use the extra time on this research.'

Peggy hesitated, and then nodded. 'OK, honey. You go ahead,' she said.

'I'll take good care of her,' Shelby promised.

Faith embraced her mother. 'Give Dad a hug for me. Tell him I'll see him soon,' said Faith.

Peggy held her daughter's arms and looked at her seriously. 'Don't forget. You know how he is. He needs bucking up.'

'I won't forget.'

'Shall we go?' said Shelby.

It was a laborious process to get Peggy to the parking garage. Once there, Shelby instructed Peggy to wait by the elevators while she brought the car around. Shelby drove up, got out, and relieved Peggy of her cane, gently getting her situated in the front seat while she placed the cane in the back. Then she went around to the driver's side and got in.

Peggy settled into the seat like a plump, feathery bird on her nest. She carefully put on her seat belt and folded her hands in her lap.

'This is really very nice of you,' said Peggy. 'My Faith works so hard. Too hard if you ask me. She and her husband bought a house that they're fixing up themselves. She's trying to finish that degree. Plus, she works for Dr Winter. And she has a part-time job cleaning houses on Saturdays.'

'That is a lot,' said Shelby.

Peggy sighed. 'That's for sure. And now she's trying to help me out as well. Bud, my husband, is not well. Do you remember Bud?'

'Of course,' said Shelby. 'What's wrong with him?'

Peggy sighed. 'He has a very serious condition. Lou Gehrig's disease.'

Shelby thought about the man she had met in the St Thomas police station. He had looked perfectly healthy. Rather robust even. And yet, Lou Gehrig's disease was about as grim a prognosis as one could receive. 'It just happened? Since you got back?' Shelby asked.

'Oh no. We've known about it for a couple of months,' said Peggy. 'He hardly has any symptoms yet. Most of the time he feels perfectly well. But, he has days . . . I keep thinking that if he remains in good health long enough, they may find a cure. He doesn't seem to have any optimism left though. I guess, maybe, when we had the cruise to look forward to, we were thinking about that. But now he's just very down. Hardly leaves the house.'

As Peggy talked, Shelby was driving south through the city, passing from the trendy neighborhood around the hospital through the bustling Italian Market area, now mostly Asian in flavor, and into the huge residential swathe of the city known as South Philly. Close to Washington Street, the two-story row homes were plain but well kept, with trees planted along the sidewalks. As she drove farther south, towards Snyder, the curbs became strewn with litter, and the run-down blocks were pockmarked with boarded-up buildings, covered with graffiti. One fact was inescapable. The Ridleys had just been on an expensive cruise. And yet, one had to be poor to live in this neighborhood. Nobody would ever live here by choice.

She found Hector Street. It was a narrow, one-way street. It was in better condition than some they had passed, but food wrappers and cigarette butts were wadded up on the sewer grates, thuggish teenagers clustered on the corner, and cars with duct-taped roofs and windows were parked along the curb.

Shelby parked a few doors down from the Ridleys' house. As she got out of the car and came around to the passenger

side to open the door for Peggy, she was trying to think of a
tactful way to frame the troubling question that was emerging
in her mind. Finally, she said, 'Well, it was lucky that you
had the means to take that cruise before your husband got any
sicker.'

'Oh heavens,' Peggy chuckled as she allowed Shelby to
help her out of the seat and accepted the cane which Shelby
retrieved from the back seat. 'We could never have afforded
that cruise. Not in a million years.'

'Oh?' said Shelby, although she was not truly surprised.

'No,' Peggy scoffed. 'My husband won that cruise in a
contest.'

'Really,' said Shelby.

'I know. Wasn't that lucky? Sometimes it seems like everything is going wrong. And then, something good happens.'

They had crossed the sidewalk and arrived at the foot of
the steps leading up to the Ridleys' house. 'I can't thank you
enough,' said Peggy. 'This was so nice of you.'

'Here,' said Shelby. 'Let me help you inside.'

'Oh, I can manage,' said Peggy.

'No, I promised Faith,' said Shelby.

Peggy beamed. 'Bless your heart. Can you stay for a cup
of coffee?'

Shelby tried to sound nonchalant. 'Sure. A quick half a cup.'

'Good,' said Peggy, as Shelby helped her, one by one, up
the steps. The front windows looked blank, covered, as they
were, with closed drapes discolored by years of sun, except
for a dusty arrangement of fake flowers in a greenish urn
which was propped on the inside window sill. Peggy unlocked
the front door, opened it, and called out 'Bud, I'm back.' There
was no answer.

Then she turned to Shelby. 'Come. Come on in.'

Inside the house was dimly lit and tidy. Peggy indicated a
well-worn chair at the scarred dining table. 'So, coffee?' Peggy
asked. 'It's instant.'

'Sure,' said Shelby, although she was not thirsty. Now that
she was seated in the Ridleys' home, she felt more confused
than ever. These were people of the most modest means who
had won their trip in a contest. It was purely a stroke of luck
in an unlucky life. How could it have anything to do with
Chloe's death? She did not even know what questions to ask.

Peggy limped back to the kitchen. Shelby looked around the tiny living room and dining area. It was a virtual shrine to Faith. Every wall and surface had photographs of her, from baby pictures to wedding photos of Faith, in a sensible knee-length dress and a short veil, holding a bouquet and tilting her head toward her gentle-looking husband. She had not been a young bride, but she was beaming with contentment in the photos. In a few moments Peggy returned with a steaming mug, and set it down in front of Shelby.

'Aren't you having any?' Shelby asked.

Peggy shook her head. 'Makes me need to pee. And the bathroom's upstairs.'

Shelby nodded, and blew on the steaming liquid. 'So, you won that cruise in a contest.'

'I didn't win it,' said Peggy. 'Bud did. Some sports radio station he listens to. You had to be the twentieth caller or something. At first I wanted to see if we could trade it in for the money, so we could help Faith and her husband out with the house. The place needs all new appliances and everything. And he's got two kids from his first marriage so the money is always tight.'

'Sure,' said Shelby. But she wasn't thinking about Faith's finances. She was thinking about the probability of someone winning such an expensive prize from a call-in radio contest. Shelby worked in the retail business. She knew a thing or two about advertising expenses. There was something wrong with this explanation.

'Bud wouldn't hear of it. He insisted that we go. We'd never been on a real vacation like that. When Faith was little we took some trips in the car, but then Bud lost his job. And I had my accident – it was always something.'

'I know how that is,' said Shelby absently.

'I'm glad we went,' said Peggy. 'We have good memories to look back on.'

'That's good,' said Shelby.

'I wonder where he is,' Peggy fretted. 'I did ask him to get me some coleslaw. Maybe he walked down to the corner deli. He hardly leaves the house anymore. He's very depressed. Well, who wouldn't be? Here he's been worrying about me all these years and then boom. But I tell him, look, you never know. It could take years for this thing to progress.

Meantime, you can't spend the rest of your life hiding in the house.'

Shelby sipped at the coffee. 'No, of course not,' she said.

'Usually I volunteer in the morning at the church. My friend, Judy, picks us up and we have lunch there. We know everybody there. Bud used to enjoy it himself. But now he doesn't want to go anymore.'

There was a sound of a key turning in a lock, and Peggy looked up at the front door. 'There he is,' she said, with real relief in her voice.

The front door opened, and Bud Ridley came in, a newspaper tucked under his arm, carrying a small, brown paper bag. He did not look like a sick man. He had the same hearty appearance that Shelby remembered from the police station in St Thomas, but the expression in his eyes was weary.

'Hey honey,' said Peggy. 'Guess what?'

'What?' Bud asked, tucking his keys into his pants pocket.

'You'll never believe who's here.'

'Who?' Bud demanded.

Shelby stood up and turned to face him.

Bud stared at her, and then recoiled, his eyes wide, as if he'd seen a ghost. He let out a strangled cry, dropping the bag and his newspaper.

'Bud,' Peggy exclaimed. 'What's the matter with you? That's spilling all over the rug.'

The carton of coleslaw in the brown bag had burst open and dumped out on the floor. The oily dressing was seeping into the well-worn carpet. Bud did not seem to notice. His face was a deathly white.

Shelby's heart began to race. His reaction was not simply surprise. It was something much greater. The sight of her had sent him into a complete panic. Why? 'Hello Bud.'

Bud's mouth opened and closed, like a fish. 'How did you find us?' he gasped.

'Find you?' Shelby asked.

'Faith,' said Peggy. 'Faith's boss is Shelby's sister. How is that for a strange coincidence?'

Bud averted his eyes, as if he was afraid to look at Shelby.

'Did you have one of those spells of weakness, honey?' Peggy fretted. 'You haven't had one in a while. It's all right. Don't worry. These things happen.'

Bud shook his head.

'I better clean this up,' Peggy sighed.

'I'll do it,' said Bud, avoiding Shelby's gaze.

Shelby was electrified by his discomfort. By his fear. Suspicion sharpened all her senses. There was a secret here. She could feel it. She was sure. She just didn't know how to confront him. How did you happen to be with my daughter, just before she died? she wanted to ask. How did you come to be on that boat? On that same cruise. And then, suddenly, she knew what to ask. 'Bud, Peggy was just telling me about how you won that cruise from a radio station,' said Shelby. 'I have to start listening to that station myself. What station was it?'

Bud did not answer. He scurried past her into the kitchen. Peggy was shaking her head at the mess on the floor. Shelby stood in the dreary living room, feeling like a tireless explorer at the hidden portal to an ancient tomb. The look on Bud's face at that first, unexpected sight of her, told her that she had stumbled on to the secret she was seeking. And no matter what it took, she was going to pry that secret loose.

TWENTY-THREE

'I don't know what happened to him,' said Peggy. 'Bud,' she called out toward the kitchen door. But there was no answer. 'It's not like him to be so rude.'

'It's all right. I need to be going anyway,' Shelby said. 'I have to pick up my grandson. Thank you for your hospitality.'

'Here, don't step in that,' Peggy said as she accompanied Shelby to the door, sidestepping the spilled coleslaw.

Shelby said good-bye and walked out on to the front step. Once outside, she was shaking so hard that she needed to hold on to the railing to descend. She managed to make it to her car. She climbed inside, turned on the engine, and locked the door. She needed to think. Bud Ridley had nearly collapsed when he saw her in his living room. And it wasn't because he was pleasantly surprised. No. He clearly had hoped never to set eyes on Shelby again.

Part of Shelby wanted to jump from the car, bang on the door to the house and demand that he tell her the truth. But she knew that would not accomplish what she wanted. She needed time to think. To plan her ambush. She needed to confront him when Peggy was not around. Peggy was oblivious. That much was clear. Shelby was going to have to take him by surprise, and alone.

Shelby picked up Jeremy and drove him to the park. On the way, he said, 'Are we going to see Daddy?'

In the chaos of the day, Shelby had forgotten her intention to visit Rob. But at least she knew now that Rob was conscious. So, even if he looked terrible, he would be able to reassure his son. 'Yes,' she said. 'We'll go and see Dad after supper.'

Jeremy let out a whoop of joy, and, when they arrived at the park, he burst from the car and clambered up the jungle gym in a frenzy of excitement. Shelby took a seat on a bench far from the other parents and the squeals of the children, and took out her cell phone. For a few minutes she thought about her strategy. Then she dialed information, took a deep breath, and placed her call.

'Sunset Cruises,' said the operator.

'Yes, my name is Erin Dodson. I'm in radio advertising. I'd like to speak to the head of your advertising sales department,' Shelby said.

'One minute, please.'

Shelby waited, and then heard a smooth, seductive male voice on the other end of the line. 'This is Craig Murphy. How can I help you?'

'Hi,' said Shelby. 'My name is Erin Dodson. I'm calling from radio station WLSP in Philadelphia. We're a twenty-four hour sports radio station, and I wanted to know if we could entice you to spend your advertising dollars at WLSP by running a promotional giveaway of a Caribbean cruise for two. We have an excellent demographic for your kind of customer and I'd be happy to meet with you—'

'Wait a minute. Whoa.' Craig Murphy chuckled. 'Are you new at this job?'

Shelby hesitated. 'I've been here for three weeks,' she said.

'Well, I appreciate your enthusiasm but we don't give away cruises on local radio stations. A giveaway like that is something we might do nationally with Coke or something. Local radio is definitely not a part of Sunset's advertising strategy.'

Shelby was silent. I knew it, she thought.

'In fact, we really don't do any radio advertising at all these days. We've found that, when it comes to cruises, there's no substitute for the visual image. We are strictly high-end magazines in print, and, of course, television. The occasional newspaper supplement entirely devoted to our product.'

'I can't talk you into a meeting to explore the possibilities?'

'Sorry,' said Craig Murphy. 'But you'd be wasting your time. It's just not going to happen.'

'Well, thanks anyway,' said Shelby.

Shelby tucked her phone back into her bag, and walked toward the jungle gym. Her gaze remained on Jeremy, but she wasn't really seeing him. Her thoughts, and her heart, were racing away.

It was a lie. She had suspected it the moment she heard it, but now she knew for sure. They had not won the cruise in a contest. That was something Bud had told his wife and daughter, and they had believed him. But it wasn't true. And if they hadn't won it, then how did they happen to be aboard that ship? More importantly, why did Bud lie? And why were they with Chloe on the night that she died?

A scream ripped through her distraction and she saw a cloud of dust and a crowd of children at the base of the jungle gym. She ran over and found Jeremy fighting and clawing at an older, larger boy. They were rolling around in the sand at the base of the apparatus.

'Jeremy, stop,' Shelby cried, as she tried to get between them. Jeremy was flailing away, although taking the worst of the fight. 'Both of you. Stop it right now,' Shelby insisted.

'He stepped on my fingers,' Jeremy cried tearfully.

'You pushed me,' the other boy accused.

'All right. All right, enough,' said Shelby. 'Let me see that hand.'

Jeremy displayed reddened fingers. 'It's his fault,' Jeremy yelled.

'I don't care whose fault it is. There's no need for a fist-fight. Come on, Jeremy. Come with me. We've got to get to the hospital.'

'The hospital! I'm not going to the hospital,' Jeremy protested, drawing back his fingers and hiding them behind his back. 'It doesn't hurt.'

'To see your dad,' Shelby reminded him.

'Oh,' the boy said glumly. And then he brightened. 'OK.' He brushed the sand and dust off his clothes and began to run toward the car.

Once Jeremy was out of earshot, Shelby turned to the other boy, who was snickering. 'And you,' she said, causing him to look up at her, wide-eyed. 'Next time, pick on somebody your own size. You hear me?'

Shelby tapped on the door of Rob's room, and then looked cautiously around the corner. Rob, bandaged up and attached to an IV, was sitting up in bed looking at some program on the television. He looked up at her.

'I brought someone to see you,' she said.

Jeremy barreled past her and headed for the bed. Rob's eyes lit up at the sight of his son. But Shelby practically had to tackle the boy in order to keep him from jumping on to his father's fractured body.

Father and son managed an awkward hug. Jeremy looked at his father in amazement. 'You look bad,' he said admiringly.

'I feel pretty bad,' Rob admitted. 'How are you? How's school?'

'Miss Darcie is nice. She said I did the best picture.'

'Did you bring it?' Rob asked.

Jeremy looked disappointed. 'I forgot.'

'It's OK. I'll see it soon.'

'I talked to your doctor in the hall,' said Shelby. 'Looks like they might spring you soon. Although you're going to need some help.'

Rob nodded. 'I'm sorry, Shelby, about what I said to you.'

'What did you say?' Jeremy asked.

'Nothing, honey,' said Shelby firmly. 'Your dad has had a lot on his mind. But I have some good news for him. Your grandparents are on their way here from Indonesia.'

Jeremy's eyes were wide. 'Are they Indians?'

Rob and Shelby both laughed.

'No, they're just working there,' said Rob. 'Really? Are they headed back?'

Shelby nodded. 'I think Darcie took care of it, through the church. They were able to locate them.'

'That's great,' said Rob, a catch in his voice. 'It'll be so good to see them.'

Shelby cast a glance at Jeremy. 'I figure they can handle things for a while.'

'I want to thank you for all you've done,' he said sheepishly.

'No thanks necessary,' said Shelby. 'It's my grandson.'

'I know,' said Rob.

'You might want to thank Darcie. I've really relied on her help.'

'She has been great, hasn't she?' said Rob. 'A lot of people say they'd do anything for you, but she really means it.'

'Well, she really cares.' said Shelby. She watched Rob's face to see if he understood what she was saying.

'I can't help it. I still think of her as a little kid,' said Rob.

'She's no little kid,' Shelby said. 'She's a very capable young woman.'

Rob looked at her in surprise. 'I'll be sure to thank her,' he said.

'Can I watch cartoons?' Jeremy asked, crawling up on to a chair beside Rob's bed. Rob handed him the remote, and Jeremy began to flip through channels with an authoritative ease, finally settling on a cartoon show that immediately engrossed him.

A nurse bustled into the room and took Rob's blood pressure. Then she handed him a paper cup with pills in it. 'Down the hatch,' she said cheerfully.

Rob swallowed the pills.

'Those are for the pain,' she said as she headed back toward the door. 'If you need more, push the call button.'

Rob thanked her and then looked back at Shelby. 'Look, Shelby. About this business with the detective you hired to look into . . .' He glanced at his son, curled up in the chair, staring at the television. 'What happened . . .'

'I went behind your back,' said Shelby. 'I can understand why you felt blindsided.'

Rob shook his head. 'No. I've been thinking about what you said. That I accepted the official version too readily. You may be right about that.'

'Why do you say that?' Shelby asked.

Rob's expression was rueful. 'Lately I found out that I can be too trusting. I believe what people tell me. I always think people are telling the truth.'

Shelby knew he was thinking of Lianna, and the truth about Molly's father. She decided not to mention it. 'I've found something out,' said Shelby quietly. 'Something you should know about.'

Rob frowned.

'Do you remember the people on the ship who were with Chloe during the bingo game? The Ridleys? She had a cane. They helped Chloe back to your state room?'

Rob nodded. 'Yeah. Vaguely.'

'They're here. In Philly. I ran into them.'

'Really? That is strange. Or, maybe not. I imagine there were a number of people from Philly on that cruise.'

'This guy said that he won the cruise in a radio contest. But that wasn't true,' said Shelby.

Rob's eyes were beginning to glaze over. 'Hmmm . . .' he said. 'How do you know that?'

Shelby did not tell him that their daughter worked for Talia. She wasn't prepared to say the words aloud. Not yet. 'It's a long story. I just know,' said Shelby.

Rob peered at her. 'Why would he say that?'

'I don't know. But, I plan to find out.'

'Hi Dad.'

Rob and Shelby looked at the door. Molly stood shyly in the doorway.

'Hey,' said Rob, holding his arms wide. 'There's my girl.'

Shelby edged away from the side of the bed to let Molly take her place. She glanced out into the hallway and saw Lianna waiting there. Lianna raised a hand in greeting and Shelby nodded.

Molly tousled Jeremy's hair, and then leaned carefully over the bed to give Rob a kiss. Shelby saw him blink away tears as he squeezed her hand. She was still his daughter, no matter what they both had learned about her actual conception. It was as if the revelation had never occurred. Their relationship appeared to be seamless in the face of that startling news.

Rob's medication was kicking in, and he was becoming

enveloped in the cushiony fog of pain relief. He held his children close, and the three of them seemed to form a complete
family. As if no one was missing from the picture.

Stop. That's so unfair, Shelby chided herself. They were
simply relieved not to have lost one another. As for Chloe's
death, they thought it was settled. Shelby was sure that it was
not.

TWENTY-FOUR

S helby stared at the late news without really seeing it. A
reporter with all the gravitas of a Barbie doll was
recounting how a man's body had been found floating
in the Schuylkill with two bullets in his head, and police were
trying to identify the decomposed remains. It was the kind of
news story which had become commonplace in the city. Every
night another horrible crime, and Shelby watched it without
caring. It only mattered, she thought, when it happened to
you.

Tonight she could not focus on anything but the thought of
Peggy and Bud Ridley. There was no escaping the fact that
Talia was a possible connection between Chloe and the Ridleys.
But Shelby's head began to ache when she tried to think of
a reason – any reason – that Talia could be involved in this.
Obviously she and Talia had their disagreements. If she was
honest, she knew that her sister was perpetually angry at her.
But angry enough to arrange the murder of Shelby's child?
She doubted it. Was it possible that it *was* a coincidence that
the Ridleys were on the same cruise as Chloe and Rob, whether
or not Bud was being honest about how he came to be on the
boat?

Glen had suggested that perhaps someone had drugged
Chloe's drink on the ship, so that it would be easy to throw
her overboard. And without Chloe's body, Shelby would never
be able to prove it, or learn who had done it. But the more
she pondered, the more she felt sure that Bud Ridley knew
the answer. She had to find out what Bud knew. There had
to be a way to trap him. She knew she should go to bed, and

try to sleep, but it was hopeless. There was no point in even trying.

Sometime around the break of dawn, Shelby passed out without realizing it, and luckily awoke in time to get Jeremy to preschool. It wasn't the sun that woke her – the day was gray and rainy. But some inner alarm clock caused her eyes to open in time. She automatically readied Jeremy for his day, and delivered him to the school. Then, she pulled a black baseball cap over her hair, turned up the collar on her jacket and drove back to South Philly. She parked, and waited near the corner of Hector Street. Some druggy-looking street people walked slowly by and stared into her car, but continued on their way. She remembered that Peggy had said that most days, her friend picked her up and took her to the church to volunteer, and that Bud no longer wanted to go. Shelby was lying in wait, hoping it was such a day.

She did not have to wait long. Peggy's friend, a bustling, gray-haired woman, arrived in her car and went inside. After a short while, she emerged, helping Peggy down the steps. Shelby sat tight until they drove away. Then, she got out of her car and approached the house. She rang the bell and turned her back on the front window.

There was no answer from inside.

Dammit, she thought. Could he have left the house today? Then, she thought she saw the front curtain move slightly. He was there. She had taken precautions for just this eventuality. Her baseball cap and turned-up collar obscured her face.

Shelby rapped again. 'Open up.'

Still no response.

'I'm here from the police. We want to talk to you about a Faith Latimer.'

There was a silence from inside the house. Then, after a few moments, the locks were turned, and the front door opened.

Bud looked out, worry written all over his face. Shelby did not give him a chance to close the door. She pushed the door open and wedged her shoulder against it. 'I thought that would get you,' she said.

Bud glared at her. 'Get out of here. You aren't the cops.'

'That's true,' said Shelby. 'But I'm not leaving.'

He met her gaze and tried to stare her down but it was no

use. He turned away from the door and Shelby followed him into the gloomy house, slamming the door behind her.

Bud sat down heavily in the Barcalounger in his living room, in front of the photographic shrine to his daughter, and licked his lips. He picked up the remote and switched on the television, staring at some frenetic game show. Shelby stared at him. He did not look up at her.

'I want to talk to you,' she said.

Bud had his palms planted on the arms of the chair as if he were trying to anchor himself in a gale. 'Got nothing to say to you,' he said.

The game show host's jolly patter and audience applause was deafening. 'Can you turn that off please?' Shelby asked.

Bud increased the volume in response.

Shelby walked over to the television, bent down and turned off the power button. She placed herself in front of the digital box. Bud pressed impotently on the remote. Shelby was blocking the signal with her body.

'Get out of the way,' he growled.

'Trying to win another cruise?' Shelby asked sarcastically.

Bud avoided her angry gaze.

'I saw your face when you walked in and saw me here yesterday. You looked like you'd seen a ghost. I want to know why,' Shelby said.

Bud did not respond, or look at her.

'You thought you'd never have to see me again, didn't you?'

'What do I care about seeing you?' he growled.

'I know that you didn't win that cruise in a contest. I called the cruise line. They don't do promotions like that. You lied to your wife when you told her that you won that cruise. You did no such thing.'

His defiant expression faded and he drew up his shoulders. 'What business is that of yours?'

'I want to know how you got on that cruise.'

'I bought tickets,' he said.

'Do you have a receipt?' she demanded. 'A credit card bill?'

Bud looked at her in outrage. 'Who do you think you are? I don't have to show you anything of my . . . business.'

'I think someone else paid for you to go on that cruise,' she said accusingly.

'You don't know anything,' he said.

'Well, I know you didn't pay for it. Let's not be stupid. One look around here makes that pretty clear.'

He pursed his lips, and his gaze was flinty. 'Must be nice to be rich and look down on everyone else,' he said.

Shelby was not about to respond to, or be distracted by, this guilt trip. 'Who paid for you to go on that cruise?' Shelby demanded.

Bud shook his head. 'It was a gift. Now, get out of my house. Mind your own business,' he said.

'From who? I can find out,' she said.

Bud shrugged, his eyes averted.

'Look at me, goddamit,' Shelby cried. 'What were you doing there? Why were you with my daughter? Did someone pay you?'

'You're crazy,' he said. 'I don't know what you're talking about. I never took a dime. From anybody. Now get out of my house or I'll call the cops.'

Shelby pulled her cell phone out and tried to hand it to him. 'Go ahead,' she said. 'Let's do that. Let's get the cops involved in this.'

Bud did not take the phone from her. 'Leave me alone,' he said in a weary tone. 'I'm a sick man. You barge in here, making threats . . . Just go away.'

Shelby hesitated, and then put her phone back in her pocket. She moved away from the TV, and sat down in a chair across from him. She took off her cap, turning it between her hands.

Bud rubbed his fingers over the remote, but did not turn on the television. For a few moments the room was silent. Then Shelby said, 'I have a bunch of photos in my apartment too. Of my daughter. A lot like the ones you have of Faith. Baby pictures and school pictures and even a wedding picture.'

Bud licked his lips.

'She was my only child,' said Shelby, her voice shaking. 'If you know what happened to her, you have to tell me. If it were Faith, you would want to know . . .'

Bud turned his head for the first time and looked at her directly. 'Don't try that on me,' he said.

'Try what?' Shelby asked.

'Try to make me feel sorry for you.' Bud shook his head. 'It's too bad you lost your daughter. But you should have raised her better.'

Shelby frowned at him. 'Raised her better? How dare you?'

He hesitated, and then seemed to make a decision. 'Your daughter got drunk on that boat and fell overboard.'

'No, Mr Ridley,' said Shelby slowly. 'I don't think that's what happened.'

Bud was shaking his head. 'Well, you weren't there. So you don't know.'

'What did you do to her?' Shelby breathed.

'I didn't do anything to her. Maybe she lived dangerously and paid the price.'

'Lived dangerously? You're out of your mind,' said Shelby through gritted teeth, 'Chloe lived in a row house in Manayunk. She was a mother of a toddler. Her hobby was quilting. She worked as a receptionist.'

'Oh really? You think that's how she afforded that fancy cruise?'

'For your information, that cruise actually was a present. I gave it to her.'

Shelby saw surprise and alarm flicker across Bud's face. And then, he seemed to clamp down on whatever the thought was that had scared him.

When he spoke again his tone was petulant. 'Your mistake,' he said. 'She was playing you.'

'No, Mr Ridley. You're the one who's playing. And I've had it up to here,' said Shelby, slicing the side of her hand across her own throat. 'Are you the one who pushed her? Did someone pay you to kill my daughter?'

Bud did not seem shooked by this terrible accusation. Instead, he shook his head, as if in disgust. 'Figures you'd say that,' he said in a withering tone. 'That's how you see life isn't it?' His tone was sarcastic. He seemed to be regaining his footing. 'Hooray for me, the hell with everybody else. Maybe that's where she learned it.'

'Learned what?' Shelby protested. 'What are you talking about?'

He glared at her through narrowed eyes. 'For your infor- mation, all people are not like that. Some people care about other people. They help people. They don't take advantage of other people. Like Chloe.'

Shelby gasped. When she heard Chloe's name, issuing contemptuously from his mouth, it was as if he were spitting on it. She could not stand it another moment. She leapt to her feet. 'That's enough. Shut your mouth. Just answer me. Did you kill my daughter? Did someone pay you to push her off that boat? Is my sister involved in this?' Shelby could feel herself growing hysterical as she brought her sister's name into the equation. She focused on calming herself down.

Bud turned away from her again with a stubborn finality. 'The chickens have come home to roost,' he said. 'How do you like it?'

Shelby growled at him. 'Tell me. Tell me what you did.'

Ridley shook his head. 'Leave me alone. I'm a sick man. I'm dying.'

Shelby stared at him. She knew it was true, although he looked hale and hearty, reclining in his chair. She suddenly realized that it didn't matter. He was no match for her wrath. Not in the long run. She took a deep breath, and pointed a shaking finger at him. 'All right. You listen to me now. You have a secret and it is not safe. It's all gonna come out. Everything. There's nothing you can do to stop me. I'm like a dog with a bone. Do you understand me, Mr Ridley? I know you did it. I don't know why, but I know you did. I will find the proof. You pushed my daughter off that boat. And you're going to pay for it.'

Bud raised his shoulders, as if to ward off her words. 'You're crazy,' he said.

Shelby had to ball up her fists and dig her nails into her palms in order to resist the temptation to strike him. She suddenly realized how she could hurt him more. 'What do you think Peggy will say? How will your wife like it when she learns what you did? What will Faith think about her father then?'

Bud stared at the photo gallery of Faith, his chin trembling. 'You're about to find out,' Shelby said.

TWENTY-FIVE

Shelby knocked at the front door of the house. She had a key to the front door, but she always knocked. It was one way of saying that she no longer saw this place, in any way, as her home. No one responded to her knock. Shelby frowned. Lately, her mother always had a caretaker during the day while Talia was at work. Maybe she couldn't hear the knocking from upstairs. Shelby didn't want to startle whichever caretaker was here. But she did want to establish her right to be in the house. Besides, Shelby thought, she didn't care about accommodating anybody else's feelings right now. She removed the key from a zipper compartment in her pocketbook and unlocked the front door.

'Mother,' she called out as she walked into the gloomy foyer. She knew her mother would not answer, but she figured that would give the caretaker fair warning that she was in the house.

No one answered. Shelby frowned. Was it possible that they had gone out? She had glanced in on Estelle the last time she was here. Estelle was in no shape to go out.

Shelby hung up her wet jacket and cap on a rack of hooks in the hallway, and glanced into the living room to the right of the foyer. Everything was as it had always been. The aged, fraying furniture, the drapes closed, the coffee table piled high with yellowing newspapers, the smell of mold. Shelby sighed, thinking how she had always hated this house.

Maybe not always, she thought. Maybe not when her father was alive. Her memories of him were like glimpses of a past that did not really belong to her. She had a vague memory of him returning home after school, the smell of his aftershave when he lifted her up in his arms. An image of his smile, which she could not fix in her mind, hovered at the edge of her memory. It would appear to her, from time to time, like a ray of sun through cloud cover, and then vanish again. She did not try to recall him very often. The thought of him, forever missing, was painful. But she could scarcely remember those days. Sometimes, it seemed as if her father had been dead forever.

There was no one in the living room. Shelby walked through to the pea green dining room with its massive mahogany set of table, chairs, and sideboards. It made a strange sort of office for Talia, a woman who was a computer whiz. The dining room table was covered with a humming computer, as well as piles of books, papers, and accordion folders.

Shelby glanced into the kitchen. A woman's denim handbag with a vinyl strap hung over the back of one of the kitchen chairs and there were dirty dishes in the scuffed enamel sink. The caretaker must be here, Shelby thought. Maybe she hadn't heard Shelby calling out.

Shelby went back through to the staircase and climbed the carpet-covered treads to the top. She walked down the hall to her mother's room and looked in. The caretaker, a skinny young woman with pale skin and dyed maroon-colored hair pulled back in a messy ponytail, was sitting beside the bed, leafing through a woman's magazine. She had an iPod on the arm of the chair and earbud headphones in her ears.

Estelle Winter was sprawled on the bed under her covers, her hair uncombed, her eyes half-open and glassy. She was in some sort of twilight state, snoring and yet blinking as if she were actually awake. Shelby's heart hardened at the sight. This was how she remembered her childhood home – the blinds down, the household chores undone, the rooms reeking of alcohol. Those memories were constant. The unstable center of it all was her mother, whining or snoring when she was tired, laughing hysterically when she was high, and then lashing out as the euphoria faded. It was an unending cycle.

And then, Shelby had a horrible, fleeting thought. Is this how Chloe would have ended up? No, she thought. No. Chloe would have conquered it. Jeremy was the center of her world, and she was a good mother. For his sake, she would have conquered it.

'Jesus!' The caretaker jumped from her seat, tearing off her headset, the iPod falling to the floor.

Shelby let out a cry.

'Who are you?' the woman demanded, in Eastern-European accented English.

'I'm,' Shelby pointed to Estelle, snoring on the bed, 'her daughter.'

The young woman frowned suspiciously. 'You frightened me.'

'I'm sorry,' said Shelby. 'I called out when I came in.'

'Well . . . I didn't hear you,' the woman complained.

'I'm really sorry. We haven't met. I'm Shelby.' She extended her hand.

The young woman took it unwillingly. 'Nadia,' she muttered.

'I'm really sorry, Nadia.'

'Hmmph,' Nadia muttered.

'Look, if you want to go out for a break, I can stay with her for a while.'

'Miss Talia doesn't want me taking breaks,' said Nadia.

'Well, Talia's not here. You go ahead if you want.'

Nadia looked at the big round-faced watch on her wrist. 'I could use a few things at the market.'

'Go ahead,' said Shelby. 'We'll be fine.'

'I just run down there for half hour or so.'

'Perfect,' said Shelby.

Nadia nodded agreement. 'OK. Estelle,' she announced in a loud voice. 'You be good. Don't get in trouble.'

Shelby looked warily at the woman on the bed. 'Do you think she understands you?'

Nadia shrugged. 'Sometimes she does. Other times . . .' She made a spinning gesture by her ear with her index finger.

'Yeah, I know,' said Shelby. She sat down in the chair that Nadia had just vacated. Estelle grunted, and turned over.

Shelby listened as Nadia went down the stairs, back to the kitchen for her bag, and finally, out the front door. Shelby heard the front door close behind her. Estelle suddenly startled her by reaching out a hand and groping instinctively, unconsciously, along the bedside table for the half-empty bottle of vodka which rested there. Her clumsy hand caught the side of the bottle and knocked it over. It toppled on to the matted carpet. Estelle moaned softly and closed her eyes again.

Shelby bent down, clucking in disgust, and picked up the bottle. At the least the cap was screwed on tight, and the vodka hadn't spilled. She was tempted to remove it from the bedroom, but what for? It was far too late for that. Estelle had chosen booze over life. At least she was consistent, Shelby thought.

Shelby replaced it on the table and, as she did, her gaze fell on a dusty framed photo of Estelle with her children that was pushed toward the back of the table, behind the alarm clock. In the photo, Shelby, Talia, Glen, and their mother were all sitting on a picnic blanket next to an old car. There was a picnic basket open beside them, and there was food spread out on the blanket. Shelby had seen the photo a million times, but it seemed to her that this was the first time she had ever really looked at it.

She and Glen were young in this picture, probably about four and one years old, respectively. Talia, the eldest by eight years, had an arm draped possessively around Estelle's neck. Not quite a teenager yet, she already had the solemn, knowing look of one who was no longer a child. Even at twelve years old, Talia seemed to treat her mother protectively. Estelle looked pretty, but distracted. Shelby did not ever remember her mother as pretty. Estelle was smiling at the photographer, who must have been their father. He would live only one more year after this photo was taken.

Shelby thought of her own bedside table in her condo. She kept a framed photo there of herself and Chloe. To her, it was like a talisman, reminding her, each time she looked at it, of what she lived for.

Were you a good mother once, Shelby wondered, looking at Estelle? Before your husband died, and life became too much for you to handle? Was that where Talia developed this unreasoning loyalty to you? A chill coursed through Shelby at the thought. Was it possible that they had been happy for a while, and Shelby simply could not remember it?

Estelle let out a noisy snore. Even in the dim light of the bedroom, Shelby could see that her skin was yellowish in color, as her liver disease moved into its final stages. Shelby tentatively reached out a hand. It hovered over her mother's shoulder. I wish I remembered you that way, she thought. She rested her fingers for a moment on Estelle's shoulder, and thought she heard her mother sigh.

Shelby pulled her hand back, got up from the chair and crept out of the room. She had come for a purpose, and she needed to get to it. She looked back at her mother before she pulled the bedroom door shut. Then, she went back downstairs, and straight to the dining room. She took a seat in one of the dining room chairs and looked at the top of the table. She often walked past this table, and noticed the glut of papers and folders on top of it. A computer, a Mac, sat in the middle, but it was surrounded by paperwork. Obviously Talia was capable of doing all of her business transactions online. But a perusal of the contents of the desktop clearly showed that Talia kept a hard copy of everything. It was as if she didn't trust her own area of specialization, or maybe it was just the prudent thing to do. It being tax time, Talia had all her physical receipts spread out across the table.

Shelby knew exactly what she was looking for, although, even as she searched, she could hardly believe that she was suspecting her own sister of such an evil deed. Part of her hoped that she would find nothing that could possibly implicate Talia in such a terrible plot. Talia was self-absorbed, but not cruel. Shelby could not think of one reason why Talia would want harm to come to Chloe. But someone had paid for the Ridleys to go on the cruise where Chloe died, and Talia was the link. Shelby was past caring how monstrous her theory might seem. She simply had to know. Two tickets on a cruise were not something you paid for in cash. If Talia bought them, she had to have charged it, Shelby thought. And she had to have purchased them after last December, because Shelby hadn't mentioned the cruise until some time after Christmas.

Shelby tried to think when she had told Talia about the present, and the fact that she would be minding Jeremy while Chloe and Rob were away. It was difficult to remember because Talia never registered any interest in anything you told her. But perhaps the information had registered with her.

With a little hunting, Shelby was able to locate the accordion folder with this year's credit card receipts and began to sort through them. They were not organized by month, so first she had to put them in order, and then examine each charge. And, she thought, she had to keep an eye on the clock. She didn't want Nadia coming in here and finding her rifling through the bills instead of attending to her mother.

Slowly, she worked her way through the charges, marveling at Talia's abstemious life. Amazingly, she did have charges for clothing, although, given the way she dressed, it never seemed that she wore anything new. She charged books and music, and sometimes groceries, but there were almost no restaurant charges. And no liquor bills. Talia could protest that she forgave her mother for her habit, but there was no doubt that she had avoided following a similar path.

There were many charges to charitable and political organizations that made Shelby stop and look again. Bud Ridley's words came back to her. Hadn't he been maundering on about good people who tried to help everyone? Was that how the rest of the world saw her sister, Shelby wondered?

She forced herself not to speculate any further about her sister's expenses, and simply search for the charges to Sunset Cruises. She had gotten halfway through the month of March with no luck when she heard the front door open.

Nadia was back. Would she would head right back upstairs, or come through toward the kitchen to leave her pocketbook there? Shelby hesitated, trying to ready some excuse, and then wondering if she really had to justify her actions in her mother's home to this young girl. She hesitated a moment too long.

Talia walked into the living room and stared at Shelby. Her eyes widened.

'What do you think you're doing?' she said.

TWENTY-SIX

Shelby stared back. 'I didn't know . . .'

'You're going through my papers?' Talia exclaimed.

Shelby licked her lips. 'I didn't expect you home,' she said.

Talia put her hands on her hips. 'Obviously,' she said. 'I decided to come home for lunch and check on Mother.'

'Look, Talia—'

'Don't "look Talia" me. That is my private business. I can't believe my eyes. Why are you going through my papers?'

Shelby was embarrassed to be caught. But she reminded herself that she was looking for proof of a crime. She had hoped to arm herself with black and white proof. But, now, looking at Talia, she felt a reckless sense of entitlement. She could not imagine why, or how it could be possible. But if it were, no amount of snooping she could do would ever compare to that sort of treachery. If Talia had done this, arranged for the murder of Shelby's child, there was nothing left to care about between them. 'I'm looking through your receipts,' Shelby said boldly.

'Looking for what? You've got a lot of nerve.'

'Faith's parents went on a cruise. I need to know who paid for it.'

Talia looked completely baffled. 'Faith? My graduate assistant?'

Shelby nodded. 'Her father claims that he won the cruise in a contest, but he didn't.'

'So?' said Talia.

'He's lying about it. Somebody paid for it.'

'What's that got to do with you snooping through my papers?'

Shelby hesitated. 'I wondered if you paid for it,' said Shelby flatly.

Talia shook her head. 'Have you lost your mind? Why in the world would I send Faith's parents on a cruise?'

'It was the cruise that Chloe was on,' said Shelby.

Talia looked at her blankly. 'So?'

'You tell me,' said Shelby stubbornly.

'I'll tell you this. I haven't got that kind of money, and if I did, I certainly wouldn't spend it on people I don't even know.'

'You have plenty of money,' said Shelby.

'And how do you know that?' Talia demanded. 'Oh, that's right. You've been going through my bank records.'

'Did you do it?' Shelby asked.

'Do what? I don't know what you're talking about.'

There was the sound of a key in the front door lock, and then the door opened, and Nadia came in, carrying a shopping bag and her umbrella. Talia turned and looked at her aghast. 'Where were you?' she demanded. 'Who is with mother?'

Nadia looked furtively at Shelby. 'Your sister. She said she would stay with mother.'

'I pay you to stay with her,' Talia cried. 'How dare you just go off shopping and leave my mother alone?'

'Your sister said—'

'You don't do what my sister says,' Talia cried. 'You do as I tell you.'

'I told her to leave,' Shelby interrupted. 'I said I would be here until she got back.'

Talia turned on Shelby with fury in her eyes. 'And this is how you stay with her? You leave her all alone and come down here to snoop through my accounts?'

Nadia stood in the foyer, uncertain about what to do next. All of a sudden there was the sound of a loud thud from the second floor, and then a weak, plaintive moan.

'Mother,' Talia cried. She turned away from Shelby and left the room, running up the stairs. Nadia followed dutifully behind her. As Shelby watched them go, she had a sudden revelation, both disheartening and, at the same time, comforting. Talia was not worried about what Shelby might find in her accounts. She had rushed off to her mother's side without a backward glance. She was not worried, Shelby realized, because there was nothing to find. Shelby heard Talia descending the staircase. She came back into the living room, glaring at Shelby.

'How is she?' Shelby asked. 'Is she all right?'

'How do you live with yourself?' said Talia through gritted teeth. 'You don't give a damn what happens to her.'

'This is more important,' said Shelby.

'She's your mother.'

'I know that,' said Shelby. 'I do my share.'

'The occasional check,' Talia said bitterly. 'I suppose you think you shouldn't have to help pay for her care. Your own mother.'

'My mother used to chase me with a hammer, crawling under tables and chairs to try to whack me. She humiliated me for sport. She was cruel. I lived in terror of what she was going to say or do next.'

'It wasn't that bad,' Talia scoffed. 'You always exaggerate.'

'Don't tell me what I remember. Don't tell me what I should feel about her,' Shelby insisted.

Talia sighed. 'You never cared about her feelings. You walked away and never gave us a thought. Mother always said that about you. Shelby does exactly as she pleases and the hell with everybody else. But I never thought you would stoop to this. Is that what you're really doing here? Trying to figure out how your pitiful contribution to her care has been spent?'

Shelby stared at her sister's face which was devoid of any recognizable emotion. 'This has nothing to do with Mother,' she said. 'I'm here because somebody paid for Bud Ridley to go on that cruise. I think somebody sent him there to throw my daughter overboard,' she blurted out.

Talia looked stunned, and for a moment she did not speak. And then she shook her head. 'And you think I did it?'

'I was just . . . I didn't know,' said Shelby, but even as she spoke, she was wishing she had never started this conversation. For a moment she felt frightened of her sister. Frightened to see that same fury blooming in her sister's eyes that she had so often seen in her mother's.

'So, wait a minute. That's why you're looking through my papers. To see if I paid for someone to take that cruise and kill your daughter?'

Shelby nodded. 'Yes.' Even as she uttered the word, Shelby realized that it was the worst accusation she could ever make. To level it at her sister was tantamount to breaking every tie between them that ever existed. There was no taking it back, no matter what. The word hung in the air between them.

'Oh, for heaven's sakes,' said Talia.

Shelby stared at her.

'Why would I do that?' Talia demanded.

'To get back at me,' said Shelby. 'For leaving you with all the responsibility for Mother. For not helping you.'

Talia sighed, and her shoulders heaved. 'Look, Shelby, if you feel guilty, that's your problem. Personally, I will never have to ask myself if I did enough for Mother, if I made her happy. It's you two who will have to suffer. You and Glen. Just don't come crying to me someday, saying that you're sorry. If you're sorry then, it will be too late.'

Shelby stared at her sister. It was as if her heinous accusation had not even penetrated. Talia was not offended. She did not understand that Shelby had suffered the most grievous loss in the world. She did not even grasp that Chloe was the most important thing in Shelby's life. Shelby thought about that impersonal sympathy card which Talia had sent Faith to buy for her. Chloe's death had not really registered with Talia. To Talia, only one person mattered. She was devoting her life to the person she loved most, and, if she felt chagrin, it was because her brother and sister didn't see it her way. They were missing their chance.

'I'm sorry,' said Shelby, suddenly ashamed of the enormity of her mistake. 'I shouldn't have said that.'

'Said what?' Talia asked.

'Well, I shouldn't have come here and rifled through your papers. I shouldn't have implied that you might have made a deal with Faith's father.'

'I don't know Faith's father,' Talia complained. 'Why in the world would I make a deal with him?'

'You're right,' said Shelby. 'It makes no sense.' Once again, she felt as if the answer to her questions had slipped from her hands and evaporated into the air.

'So if you're not going to help, why don't you just go?'

'I guess I will,' said Shelby. 'I need to get Jeremy.'

Talia looked puzzled, as if she didn't know whom Shelby was talking about. And then her gaze cleared and she looked bored. 'Well, go ahead then,' she said. 'You're no help to me here. As usual.'

TWENTY-SEVEN

The next morning, before dawn, someone pounding on the front door of Chloe's house awakened Shelby. She rushed down the stairs, tying the knot on her robe, and opened the door.

A couple stood on the doorstep surrounded by suitcases. They were both tall and thin, with glasses and short gray hair. His was in a crew cut, and hers was in a little silver cap. They both wore baggy pants, soft shirts, and sneakers. 'Shelby?' said the woman.

'You must be Vivian,' said Shelby. 'And Hugh. Come on in.'

The Kendricks, though missionaries by vocation, did not dress in clerical garb or brandish Bibles. They both had a relaxed, genial appearance. Vivian did not leave the heavy lifting for her husband. Together she and Hugh picked up their assorted bags and wedged themselves through the front door. Vivian set hers down in the hall with a sigh. 'There we go.'

She looked at Shelby with concern. 'This is a terrible way to finally meet, isn't it?'

'It's a very tough time,' Shelby admitted. 'But I'm glad you're here.'

'How are you holding up, dear?' Vivian asked kindly. 'I'm so sorry about Chloe. Such a lovely girl.'

'It's been tough,' said Shelby. 'I'm lucky to have Jeremy. He keeps me so busy I . . . I don't have much time to think about it.'

'Still,' said Vivian. 'The Lord doesn't give us a more difficult trial than that – the death of a child. I can't tell you how my heart aches for you.'

Shelby thanked her.

'I know this is an uncivilized time to be showing up at the door,' said Hugh. 'But we've been in transit for the better part of twenty-four hours.'

'You must be exhausted,' said Shelby.

They looked at one another and nodded. 'We're pretty tired,' Hugh said.

'You should lie down,' Vivian said to her husband. She turned back to Shelby. 'He's had some problems with a heart arrhythmia. He needs rest.'

'Well, you can go upstairs to Rob and Chloe's room and stretch out on the bed.'

'I think I'll do that for a few minutes,' said Hugh.

Vivian rubbed her husband's shoulder tenderly. 'That's a good idea. Go and rest for a while.'

Once Hugh had climbed the stairs, Vivian settled herself on the living room sofa and sipped some tea that Shelby had brought her.

'I'd love to hear about your life in Southeast Asia,' said Shelby, trying to stifle an early morning yawn.

'Oh, there'll be time for that,' said Vivian. 'You and I need to get to know one another. After all, we have a grandchild in common. I'll just be so glad to see Jeremy and Molly again. The last time I saw Jeremy he was an infant.'

'They'll be glad to see you, too,' said Shelby.

'Do you know when Rob can come home?' Vivian asked.

'The doctor said maybe today,' said Shelby. 'But he's pretty beat up. He may not even be able to climb the stairs. I figure he can sleep in that recliner if it's necessary.'

'Do they know how it happened?' Vivian asked, frowning.

'Actually, they do,' said Shelby. 'Apparently he got into an argument with some kids when he was buying gas. They followed him and ran him off the road. Luckily, the police have them in custody.'

Vivian shook her head. 'Oh my God, that's awful. Poor Rob. All he's been through. Losing Chloe, when he'd finally found happiness. And now this.'

Shelby felt the color rise to her cheeks. 'They did seem happy together.'

'Oh definitely,' said Vivian. 'Lianna was never the right woman for him. Just between you and me and the lamppost, the only reason he married her was because she got pregnant and he wasn't about to walk out on his responsibilities. Not that he regretted it, mind you. He adored Molly from day one. But the marriage . . . let's just say, it wasn't the best of times for him. He didn't complain, but I could tell. He would have stuck it out, of course, if she hadn't left him. He's honorable that way.'

Shelby certainly wasn't going to be the one to break the news about Molly's parentage. Rob could tell his parents about that. More than anything, she was stunned to hear Rob's mother's perspective on his marriage to Lianna. An unhappy alliance, that only occurred because Lianna told him she was carrying his baby? Chloe, Shelby thought sadly, had worried for nothing.

'But when he got together with Chloe – well, the whole tone of his emails changed. Chloe was just so much more right for Rob than Lianna ever was. That time we came to visit, after Jeremy was born, was the happiest I'd ever seen my son. And now she's gone. He's lost her.' Vivian's eyes welled with tears. 'He's had to endure so much.'

'Chloe adored him,' Shelby said honestly. 'He's a fine man.'

Vivian sighed. 'Well, we'll have a bit of a rest and then we'll go and get him at the hospital. Do what we can to ease the burden for him.'

Shelby nodded. 'I think once I get Jeremy up and dressed I'll go back to my apartment.'

'I'm sure you could use a break,' said Vivian.

'No that so much as I want to give you folks a little extra space. And time to get to know Jeremy. He's a wonderful kid.'

'He goes to preschool, doesn't he?' Vivian asked.

'Yes. His teacher is an old friend of your family's – Darcie Fallon?'

'My goodness. Little Darcie is teaching school? She was an adorable child. Always following Rob around like he was her big brother.'

'Well, she's very devoted . . . to both of them. Rob and Jeremy. If you need anything, I know you can rely on her,' Shelby said.

'That's good to know. We'll all have to pitch in to help Rob now. Jeremy will need all the love and support he can get. Especially from his grandparents,' said Vivian pointedly.

'I'm always here for him,' said Shelby, her voice shaking a little.

Vivian reached out and grabbed Shelby's hand with her own. 'I know you are,' she said.

Shelby was only able to return to her apartment by promising Jeremy that she would see him the very next day. He was uncertain about these strange new grandparents until Vivian assured him that they were going to pick up his dad at the hospital and bring him home. He immediately forgot Shelby's departure in the excitement over his father's return home. Shelby felt incredibly grateful to Vivian and Hugh for the kind, low-key way that they handled their grandson. She knew she was leaving him in loving hands, even if it was only for a little while.

Shelby was running a load of laundry in her kitchen and putting together a simple supper for herself when the phone rang. To her complete amazement, it was her sister, Talia, sounding almost cheerful.

'I'm surprised to hear from you,' Shelby said. 'I thought maybe you weren't speaking to me.'

'Why wouldn't I be speaking to you?' said Talia.

'Never mind,' said Shelby.

'I'm calling because I thought you might want to know, since you were accusing him yesterday.'

'Who are you talking about?' Shelby asked. Her sister had never called her to discuss someone other than their mother or Glen.

'Faith's father,' said Talia, and Shelby could hear the

satisfaction in her voice. Far from being angry at Shelby, she was proud to have this information to offer her sister. 'He killed himself last night.'

Shelby's knees went weak. 'What?'

'Yeah. Faith called to say she wasn't coming in. Apparently, he hanged himself.'

'Oh my God,' said Shelby, recoiling from the mental image.

'Faith said he had a terminal illness,' said Talia offhandedly. 'Probably wanted to avoid the slow decline.'

Shelby's mind whirred. She thought about her confrontation with Bud Ridley and felt a nagging sense of culpability. Had her threats sent him over the edge? No, she thought. If she had been wrong about his part in Chloe's death, it wouldn't have affected him at all. It was because she was right that he had taken this drastic step. His actions actually confirmed her suspicions. She was certain now that someone had hired him – it just wasn't Talia.

'Did you hear me?' said Talia.

'I heard you,' said Shelby.

'I couldn't tell. You didn't say anything.'

'I'm thinking,' said Shelby. Bud's suicide seemed to say, louder than words, that she had confronted him with at least part of the truth. But Shelby had to know if Bud had admitted to anything before he died. Left a note. Something to implicate the person who had engaged him.

'What is there to think about?' asked Talia.

'I'm just wondering . . .' Shelby realized that she needed to see Faith or Peggy. To question them. But their hour of shock and grief was no time to start making accusations against their dead father and husband.

'Wondering what?'

'Are there services? Or a wake?'

'I don't know,' said Talia impatiently.

'If there's a wake, you should really go and pay your respects,' said Shelby slowly.

'Why?' said Talia. 'I said I was sorry. That's enough.'

Sometimes Shelby wondered how her sister managed to function in the world. The conventions of life had no meaning for her. 'Talia. Come on. You work with her every day. It's the least you can do. You'd expect Faith to show up if the tables were turned. If it were mother.'

'Mother would never kill herself,' Talia said indignantly.

'I meant, if she were to die. That's how people show that they care about you – by showing up.'

'I don't care about Faith that way,' she insisted.

That's probably true, Shelby thought. She heard no sympathy or compassion in Talia's voice. Even Shelby, who sincerely believed that Bud had pushed Chloe overboard, was able to imagine Peggy's shock and sympathize with Faith's grief.

There was a component of empathy missing in Talia, but that was hardly news to Shelby. And she was not about to let her sister off the hook. She intended to go to the visitation with Talia, so that her presence there would seem natural. 'Do you want to hurt her feelings?' Shelby asked. 'Because if you don't show up, her feelings will be hurt. And that's not a good way for an assistant to feel.'

Talia was silent for a moment. 'She is a good assistant,' Talia admitted.

'Exactly. I'll go with you.'

'Why?' Talia asked.

Shelby wasn't about to explain that perhaps the link to Chloe's killer could be found at Bud Ridley's wake. 'It'll make it easier,' Shelby said. She was already searching for Bud's death notice on her computer as they spoke. She located it. 'The first viewing is tonight. We'll go and get it over with.'

'I can't leave mother,' said Talia.

'Get Nadia to stay with her,' said Shelby. 'Tell her I'll pay her double.'

TWENTY-EIGHT

Shelby and Talia hurried past a half a dozen smokers who were huddled, collars up, under the eaves and entered the vestibule of the funeral home, shaking the rain off of their umbrellas. Shelby consulted the board with names of the dead who rested inside. She had heard of wedding factories, but this facility seemed to be a funeral factory with a dozen or more of the departed ensconced in the variously themed rooms inside. 'The Columbus Room,' she said to Talia. 'Come on.'

Talia followed her sister into the wide, dimly lit hallway with its thick carpet and imitation-Venetian chandeliers. There were letter boards beside the double doors, indicating which of the deceased rested in that room. Between the double doorways were thickly padded faux-leather benches where people could sit for a while and escape the grief of the other mourners, the cloying smell of the funeral flowers, or the sight of the departed.

Shelby went down the hall until she located the Columbus room. She gestured for Talia, who was hanging back near the doors to the vestibule, to join her. Reluctantly, Talia shuffled over to her sister.

'I'm not staying here for long,' Talia said in a normal speaking voice that was startling in the hush of the funeral home.

'We don't have to stay long,' said Shelby. 'Just speak to the family and sit for a few minutes.'

'I don't want to.' Talia squirmed like a child. 'You made me do this.'

'Just take it easy,' said Shelby. 'It's rude to be in too big of a hurry.'

Shelby led the way. The room had folding chairs which were set up to accommodate a crowd of a hundred or more. There was no need for that many chairs tonight at the viewing of Bud Ridley. There were about a dozen people scattered in the front few rows, in pairs or groups of three or four.

The open casket was at the front of the room, flanked by gladioli in urns. In the front row, facing the casket, Peggy, Faith, and Faith's husband, whom Shelby recognized from the wedding picture in Peggy's house, were seated, wearing black. Shelby gestured to Talia to follow her, and they went down the side aisle and walked up to the casket. Shelby looked in at Bud. It was hard to believe that she had seen him alive just the day before. The undertaker had liberally pancaked his face and neck so that his complexion was an orangey-pink, and the bruises around his neck were minimized. The embalmed body looked like a life-size, homely doll, lying stiffly on a bed of satin.

You killed my daughter, Shelby thought, looking at him.

Your suicide is the proof. She closed her eyes for a moment, as if she were praying, and took a deep breath.

Talia glanced at the body and then turned away. She walked over to Faith and stiffly muttered 'Sorry, Faith.'

Shelby turned around.

'Oh, Dr Winter, how nice of you to come. This is my husband, Brian. And this is my mom.'

Talia grimaced as she shook hands with each of them. Peggy was slump-shouldered, her face puffy from weeping. She greeted Talia politely, wiping her eyes with a balled-up Kleenex.

Talia hastily excused herself, and took a seat halfway to the back of the room. She indicated to Shelby that she should hurry up about it. Shelby ignored her sister. She greeted Faith, who seemed surprised and almost flustered to see her again. She murmured her condolences to Faith and her husband, and then moved on to Peggy.

Peggy grasped both of Shelby's hands in her own. 'Shelby,' she said wearily. 'It's so good of you to come.'

'Well, it seems that we've both suffered a terrible loss lately.'

Peggy shook her head. 'I don't how you get through the day,' she said.

Shelby hesitated, and then sat down in the chair beside Peggy's. She knew very well that Bud had not told his wife about her visit – she would have bet anything on that. Still, she thought Peggy might find her presence odd; after all, she was virtually a stranger. But it was not as if there were a line of mourners behind her, and Peggy seemed to welcome the opportunity to stop counting the people who had, and had not, showed up this first evening.

'What a shock this has been for you,' Shelby murmured sympathetically.

Peggy dabbed at her eyes. 'Oh, that's for sure.'

'He didn't give you any indication?' Shelby asked. She was relying on the fact that Peggy was a garrulous woman, and she knew that most people welcomed an opportunity to exorcise their misery by recounting it, over and over.

Peggy sighed. 'Well, as I told you, he was depressed. I mean, anyone would be with that diagnosis, but he wasn't even showing many signs of the illness yet. Hardly at all.'

She glanced over at her husband's body in his coffin and shook her head. 'To look at him, you'd think he was the picture of health.'

Shelby murmured agreement. She knew that she had to try and walk the line between sounding concerned, and overly curious. She had to pose each question carefully. 'Did he say or do anything that would make you think he might . . .'

'No. No, of course not,' said Peggy. 'If he had . . .' Peggy shook her head and started weeping again.

Shelby felt a little bit cruel to be pressing this distraught woman. But she reminded herself that Bud Ridley had been her enemy. He had killed Chloe. And, in truth, Peggy seemed content to be speaking about her late husband. All too soon, people would avoid mentioning his name to her. Shelby persisted.

'Did he leave a note, anything like that?'

'That's the horrible part,' Peggy confided. 'He did. He said . . .' Peggy had to collect herself. Then she continued. 'He said he couldn't live with himself. As if he was somehow to blame for this. I mean, it's an illness. It wasn't his fault. I know he worried about me having to try to care for him as it got worse. I know that. But I never would have blamed him.' Once again, Peggy was weeping.

'Of course not,' Shelby murmured. He couldn't live with himself. That wasn't about the illness, Shelby thought grimly. He couldn't live with himself because he threw an innocent girl off of a cruise ship for gain.

Shelby felt almost guilty about continuing. But not guilty enough to retreat. 'I hope the insurance pays up. I've heard that they can be miserable about paying when a person commits suicide. And at a time like this, you don't want to be worried about money.'

Peggy was not a woman given to secrets and circumspection. 'Oh no, we've had this policy for years. Of course it doesn't amount to much. Once we pay for the funeral . . . Well, there won't be anything left.'

'Really?' Shelby asked. Her face flamed as she posed the question. It was none of her business and she knew it, but she was asking anyway. If Bud had enjoyed a big payday for throwing her Chloe overboard, surely he would have let his wife know where to find the money. After all, it was not as if he had been hit by a car. He had done this deliberately. He had the time and the foresight to leave his wife access to all that money before he took his life.

'Nothing,' said Peggy. 'In fact, I'm gonna have to sell the house and move in with Faith and Brian. If I can find a buyer. I tell you, Shelby, it's a nightmare. I don't know what I'm gonna do. Really, I don't.'

This isn't getting me anywhere, Shelby thought. The suicide's implicit admission of guilt made it seem as if the mystery of Chloe's death was almost solved. But now his wife maintains there is no money? A contract killing costs more than the price of two cruise tickets. And it was only weeks ago. Bud couldn't have spent it all before he died. Or could he? Did he have a secret mistress, or a love child? And then she thought of that shrine to Faith in their living room. No. It was much simpler than that. Peggy and Faith were this man's whole life. If he had money to leave anyone, he would leave it to them. So where was the money? Shelby's head was beginning to ache.

'Excuse me,' said Talia impatiently, leaning down to speak to Peggy. 'My sister and I are going to have to leave. My mother needs me.'

Talia's words made Shelby jump. What are you doing, she thought? But Talia was oblivious to Shelby's purposes. She was simply not going to put up with this discomfort any longer.

'Oh, of course,' said Peggy. She attempted to pat Talia's hand, but Talia whisked it away. Startled, Peggy was nonetheless gracious. 'It was very nice of you to come. I know Faith appreciates it, and so do I.'

'Yes, really,' Faith whispered. 'Thank you, Dr Winter.'

'Get back to work as soon as you can,' said Talia.

It was possible that Talia was trying to be kind and encouraging, but it sounded like an angry command the way she said it. Faith blanched and looked away. 'It might take me a little time,' she said.

Talia frowned. 'There's a lot of work to do,' she said.

'And you,' said Peggy, turning to Shelby, who had risen reluctantly to her feet. Peggy took Shelby's hands in her own. 'It was brave of you to even come here. After just losing your Chloe like that. It's such a hard time.'

'It isn't easy,' Shelby admitted.

'When it's sudden like this, there are so many things you wished you'd have said. Or done. So many regrets.'

In spite of herself, Shelby felt the tears rising to her own eyes. Tears of sorrow, but also of frustration. She was no farther along than she had been when she first arrived. Just more confused. She nodded. 'That's so true,' she said. 'But you can't go back. And second-guessing yourself . . . well, there's no use in it.'

Peggy's gaze was far away. 'His doctor told me that this diagnosis was very difficult to accept. I mean, they're trying to find a cure and all, but until they do, it was really hopeless. And Bud knew it. His doctor wanted to give him anti-depressants, but Bud wouldn't hear of it. Said he didn't want to become dependant on pills. I should have insisted. If only I had insisted. Or recognized the signs.'

Faith put an arm around her mother. 'Come on, Mom. You can't blame yourself. Dr Janssen saw him every week. If Dr Janssen didn't recognize the signs, how could you be expected to know?'

Shelby stared at Faith. 'Dr Janssen?'

'Dr Harris Janssen,' said Peggy proudly. 'One of the finest neurologists in the country. He treated me when I had my stroke years ago. Saw me every year for a follow-up. So, when Bud started having weakness in his side, and dropping things every now and then, I said to him, let's go see Dr Janssen. Let's not wait another minute. Isn't that right, Faith?' Peggy asked. Then she looked around the Columbus Room. 'I wonder if he knows about this. I'm sure he'll come by to pay his respects if he hears about it. Did you call him, Faith?'

Faith shook her head. 'I still have a lot of people left to call.'

Peggy shook her head. 'When I think of how good he was to us.'

'Come on,' Talia whispered, nudging Shelby in the side. Shelby ignored her.

'It's rare to find a doctor like that.' Shelby managed to sound impressed.

Peggy nodded solemnly. 'When I had my stroke, we had no insurance. Dr Janssen . . .' Peggy pressed her Kleenex to her eyes and sniffed. Then she drew herself up and continued.

'Never charged us a single dime. Same with Bud. He can't go on Medicare for two more years. Dr Janssen told Bud he would see him through this illness, until he got on the Medicare. That's the kind of person he is.'

'Wow,' said Shelby, feigning admiration.

'Of course, I shouldn't be telling you this.' Peggy said.

Shelby wondered if her secret thoughts were showing on her face. 'I'm . . . uh . . . I don't know why not . . .'

'Well, he always said to us, "Don't go telling people that Harris Janssen will treat you for free. I'll be broke in no time." Still, it's unbelievable, isn't it? In this day and age. For a doctor to be so kind?'

'Truly,' said Shelby.

'I'm sure Dr Janssen will show up,' said Faith, patting her mother's knee.

'There's a lot of good people in this world,' said Peggy, her lips trembling. 'You always have to remember that.'

TWENTY-NINE

Shelby and Talia got back in the car, and Talia turned on the engine and the lights. 'Phew,' she said. 'I thought we'd never get out of there. I didn't realize Faith's mother would be such a gabber.'

Shelby did not reply. She stared through the rain-spattered windshield as the wiper blades cleared it, over and over again.

After a few minutes of silence in the car, Talia glanced over at her sister as she drove. 'How come you're so quiet?' she said disapprovingly.

'I'm wondering something,' Shelby said.

Talia did not bother to ask what it was.

'Could you . . . hack into a person's bank records?'

'Of course,' said Talia, now in her comfort zone. 'The banks are constantly changing their systems to try to prevent it, but no sooner do they get them changed than some hacker gets through their firewalls. I've often thought that the answer to that would be . . .'

Shelby swiveled in the seat and looked at her sister. 'No,'

she interrupted. 'I mean can you, personally, hack into someone's bank records for me?'

'What?'

'I need to look at someone's credit card receipts.'

'No,' Talia bristled. 'I cannot do that. That's illegal.'

'Please Talia,' said Shelby. 'You're the only person I know who would be able to do it. Who would know how to do it. I'm sure you do know how.'

'Whose records are you trying to pillage now? I take it you're finished poking into mine?' Talia asked.

'I'm sorry about that, Talia. I should never have . . . I was wrong to think that of you. But I don't think I was wrong entirely. Faith's father got on that cruise because someone bought him a ticket, and after I accused him, he killed himself and left a note saying he couldn't live with the guilt.'

'So?'

'So, when Faith's mother mentioned that doctor, Harris Janssen, I suddenly realized . . .'

'Realized what?' Talia demanded.

'There's a connection. He's married to the ex-wife of Chloe's husband. Chloe used to work for him, some years ago.'

'That doesn't mean anything,' said Talia impatiently.

'It does. I know it does. I don't know why yet, but there's something. Talia, you're the only one I can ask to help me,' Shelby said.

'Oh no you don't,' said Talia. 'Don't try that on me. If I ever got caught I'd lose my tenure at Franklin. No way.'

'I wouldn't ask you if it weren't important, Talia.'

Talia shook her head. 'I don't care how important it is. I'm not doing it.'

'Talia, I think he must be the one who paid for the Ridleys' cruise.'

'Oh, now he's the one. Yesterday you thought I was the one who paid for their cruise,' she sniffed.

'I was wrong about that. But after what Faith's mother said about Dr Janssen, I realized that it must have been him who arranged . . .'

'La, La, La, La, La . . .' Talia was chanting in a loud, singsong voice.

'Stop that,' said Shelby.

'You stop it,' said Talia. 'I'm not doing it no matter what

you say, and I don't want to hear about what you think. You think everybody and his brother are buying cruise tickets for people so they could kill your daughter. You're starting to sound like a crackpot.'

Shelby gazed at her sister's pale face, rigid with defiance. Talia was not kidding and she was not about to change her mind. Shelby turned in her seat and resumed staring through the rainy windshield. Maybe I am a crackpot, she thought.

I just don't care.

Talia dropped her off and they parted without so much as a word of good night. Shelby was not angry at her sister for refusing to help her. It was, in fact, perfectly in keeping with Talia's character, and with their relationship. But it reminded Shelby of how strained was the bond between them. Nothing had changed about that. Each one was relieved to be rid of the other. As Talia pulled away, Shelby entered her building and rode the elevator up to her floor. It felt as if she were riding in slow motion, it took so long to arrive. She could not wait to get inside and just think, with no distractions.

Jen Brandon was waiting when the elevator doors opened. 'Shelby,' she said with genuine pleasure. 'Hey, I'm going out to meet a couple of friends for a drink. Do you want to join us?'

'Not tonight, Jen. Thanks.' She hurried past her friend, fumbling for her apartment keys.

'Are you back for good?' Jen called after her.

'I don't know,' said Shelby. 'Maybe.'

Jen shrugged and hopped on the elevator. Shelby let herself in to the apartment and collapsed on to her living room sofa with a sigh.

Dr Harris Janssen. Lianna's husband and the Ridleys' doctor. Up until tonight, the images Shelby had of Harris in her head were all admirable. Well, mostly. He had stolen Rob's first wife, but Shelby realized that she had always more or less blamed Lianna for that. And Chloe had thought the world of Harris when he was her boss. She always said how generous he was. It was this very generosity that Peggy Ridley was extolling tonight at the funeral home.

Shelby did not doubt for a minute that Harris had treated Peggy for free when she had her stroke, years ago. Chloe had often reported that Dr Janssen was known to be charitable, and to donate his services to people who were struggling or in need. He had taken care of Peggy, and he was taking care of Bud, without looking for compensation. Certainly, that was an act of charity. The US health insurance quagmire being what it was, there were millions of people with none or minimal coverage, particularly worthless when one needed a specialist like Harris Janssen. But something had changed in Harris Janssen's life during those years. For some reason, Chloe had come to present a threat or obstacle to him. When he searched through his options, had he realized, at some point, that the Ridleys had incurred a debt that they could never repay? When he needed an enormous favor – a monstrous favor – had he turned to Bud Ridley?

Slow down, Shelby chided herself. You don't know any such thing. And why in world would Harris Janssen want to hurt Chloe, of all people? He had been kindness itself when it came to Chloe. It was true that Chloe had dipped into Lianna's medical files and uncovered the secret of Molly's real father. But no one in the Janssen household seemed all that put out by her discovery. So why? Why would Harris Janssen enlist Bud Ridley to end Chloe's life? For once, she had to agree with Talia. It made no sense.

It didn't matter how much she reminded herself of that. Chloe was dead, and the last people to see her alive were the Ridleys, who owed their very lives to Harris Janssen. It was a chain – the link that she was seeking. But she had to find proof before she went any farther.

If only Talia had agreed to help her. There was no use thinking about it. She had refused, and that was the end of it. And Shelby didn't know the first thing about hacking into a computer. Or anyone else who did either.

Even as she tried to imagine how she was going to obtain the truth she sought, an anguished word kept running through her mind: why? Stop, Shelby thought. Right now, it doesn't matter why. The important thing is that you've found a connection. The 'why' is bound to reveal itself sooner or later. Right now you need to think about getting your proof – proof that Harris paid for the Ridleys to go on the Sunset Cruise. Once that is done, you can enlist the police to find out why.

Shelby closed her eyes and tried to think. If Harris had paid for the cruise, who else might know about it? Lianna, if she paid the bills. A charge for two cruise tickets would be rather a glaring expense on a monthly bill. For that very reason he probably charged it through the medical practice. So, his nurses or receptionists? She couldn't very well ask them. They would never jeopardize their own jobs to give her that information without asking Harris. She thought about trying to break into his office and gain access to their computers. But it was a doctor's office with a supply of drugs – it was probably wired with alarms that went off directly at the police station. It seemed impossible.

And then, suddenly, she realized that she was looking at this problem from the wrong angle. There were lots of places where Harris's financial transactions were no secret. The bank knew about them. So did the credit card companies. And Sunset Cruise lines knew about it, in the sense that they all had records. All she had to do was to become one or the other, and soon, she would know too.

THIRTY

'OK, now explain this to me again,' said Rosellen. Shelby pulled her chair up beside that of her assistant. All the day before she had contemplated her plan. It had to happen on a Sunday, when the medical office was closed. Now, it was seven o'clock on a Sunday morning and they were sitting in Rosellen's office at Markson's. It felt as if they were alone in the enormous building, although the custodial staff were finishing up their work and a couple of diligent sales and display people were drifting in to get ready for the day. The store opened for business at eight, to get a jump on the competition. To the sales staff of Markson's, Sunday was just another work day. When Shelby had called Rosellen at home last night and asked her to come in early, Rosellen had agreed without even asking why.

'All right,' said Shelby. 'This is the toll-free line, right?'

'Right,' said Rosellen.

'OK, so I need you to call my cell phone on that line,' said Shelby.

'Why?' said Rosellen

'I want to be sure that nothing but the toll-free number registers on the caller ID when you use this line.'

Rosellen dutifully punched in the number from Shelby's iPhone and the phone in Shelby's hand began to ring. Shelby looked at the caller ID window.

'Good,' she said.

'OK, now what?' said Rosellen. 'What should I do?'

'Well, that depends. Are you working today? I didn't even ask when I called you last night.'

Rosellen shook her head. 'I'm catching a train to Baltimore. My aunt's having a family party this afternoon.'

'I'm sorry I got you up so early,' said Shelby.

'I told you,' said Rosellen. 'Anything you need, just ask.'

'I won't forget this,' said Shelby. 'So, what you should do is get out of here, and pretend you never even saw me.'

'What are you doing, Shelby?' Rosellen asked. 'You're making me nervous.'

'Believe me, I'm the one who's nervous. Hopefully I will be able to explain it to you very soon. Right now, I just need access to a toll-free number.'

Rosellen stood up. 'OK. I trust you. I hope everything goes the way you want it to.'

'Fingers crossed,' said Shelby.

Rosellen looked up and down the hall, and then waved as she slipped out.

Shelby assumed Rosellen's vacant chair, and picked up the receiver on the phone. She dialed Lianna and Harris's home number and waited as it rang. Her heart was pounding. She had received this kind of a call herself one time, and it came early on a weekend morning, when she was barely awake. She remembered feeling confused by it, and that was the effect she was hoping to have on Harris Janssen. Last night she had practiced repeatedly, using a fake British accent as she recited the scenario. People were always intimidated by a British accent. Besides, she couldn't take the chance that they might recognize her voice.

She listened to the ringing, hoping that Harris was still asleep, or only just waking up. She held her breath, and reminded herself that she was not the one who had committed a crime.

'Hello,' said Lianna. Her voice sounded slurry with sleep.

'Hello, may I speak to Dr Harris Janssen.' Shelby was pleased with her British accent. It sounded natural. All those British television series that she liked to watch, she thought.

'For you,' Lianna murmured.

There was the sound of fumbling on the phone, and Shelby heard Harris saying, 'Who is it?'

'Dunno,' Lianna said.

In a minute his voice came through the receiver loud and clear.

'Dr Janssen here.'

'Hello, Dr Janssen. My name is Kim Teller and I'm calling about your credit card account.'

'For God's sakes, it's Sunday morning. Don't you people know what time it is? Spare me the special rates. Whatever it is, I'm not interested.'

This was precisely the reaction Shelby had anticipated. 'Please don't hang up, sir,' said Shelby calmly. 'This is not a solicitation. This is account security. I'm sorry about the hour but I needed to be sure to reach you. If there's a problem, we need to address it immediately. I am calling about some suspicious activity on your account.'

Harris hesitated. Everyone knew about identity theft these days. Everyone had heard of someone whose account number was purloined by thieves. Shelby could visualize him recalibrating his attitude. 'What activity?' Harris asked in a meeker, more worried tone.

'Well, as you may know, we monitor the charges on all our customers' accounts so that we can alert the customer to any charges that seem uncharacteristic. It's a precaution we use to attempt to avert identity theft, which, as I'm sure you know, has become epidemic.'

'Yes, of course,' said Harris.

'Now, Dr Janssen, you recently used your card to make several routine purchases for goods and services in the Philadelphia area, which is normal activity on your account. However, an account manager noticed that a cruise on Sunset Cruise lines for two was charged for that same time period and, since one can't be in two places at once, it set off an alert process, which is why I'm calling you.'

Harris was silent. For a moment.

Shelby's hand was damp where it held the receiver. 'Now let me hasten to assure you, Dr Janssen,' she said in a soothing tone, 'we're simply trying to protect your interests. Identity theft is an enormous problem in our industry. All we want to do is to check that these transactions are all known to you and that you have no wish to query them.'

Harris hesitated. 'There's no problem with my account,' he said firmly.

'You're quite certain that all these charges are legitimate.'

'It's fine.' His tone was terse and edgy, as if he couldn't wait to hang up the phone.

'All right. Thank you very much for your time Dr Janssen. I'll take the warning off this account. And I am so sorry to have disturbed you.'

'No problem,' said Harris gruffly.

Shelby hung up the phone. She was trembling all over. You bastard, she thought. It *was* you.

For a long time, Shelby sat hunched over in Rosellen's chair, shaking from head to toe, trying to absorb this new reality. Harris Janssen had arranged her daughter's death. Somehow she had thought that when she found out this information, she would spring into action, ready to avenge herself and her child. But now that the moment had arrived, she felt completely empty and sick at heart.

Last night, all she could think about was her desire to expose the plot that had led to Chloe's death. She had vaguely imagined herself bringing her information to the police and enlisting them to arrest this man. Now that the moment was here, she realized that she could not walk into the nearest police precinct and expect someone to listen to her tale. Her theory was based on the flimsiest of evidence. She had a dead man who had lied about winning a trip, and a respected doctor whom she had conned by pretending to work for a credit card company. It was all speculation. And it related to a crime that had been committed thousands of miles away, in the middle of the sea. The police of Philadelphia had their hands full. Bodies riddled with bullets were routinely found floating in the river or buried under trash in the vacant lots of the city's worst neighborhoods. Hadn't she just heard about one on the news? If she tried to explain about Chloe, they would probably laugh at her.

It was as if she had made the whole journey for no reason at all. She had hunted for Chloe's killer, and now that she knew his identity, she felt utterly bereft. There was no one who shared her conviction, or even shared her life enough to care. What now, she thought? No answer rose in her mind. The inside of her head felt fogged over. All she could feel was an immense depression descending on her.

She was too late. It was all too late. If only she had insisted that the police pursue all the possibilities when the crime occurred . . . But there was no way she could have known. She thought back to the perfunctory investigation in St Thomas, the bland reassurances of Chief Giroux and Agent DeWitt. And then, a possibility occurred to her and, with it, a flicker of hope. Agent DeWitt, who had aided Chief Giroux, was from the FBI. The FBI probably had a computer database of all their investigations, as well as an office right here in Philadelphia. They had offices in every big city in the U.S. Maybe if she went there, she could find a sympathetic ear – someone who would be interested in the idea of a planned murder. Of course the first question they would ask her was 'Why?' And she had no answer. Still, the prospect of visiting the FBI gave her a mission. After all, they were already involved. Perhaps she could reengage them.

'You're an early bird.'

Lost in her thoughts, Shelby had not heard Elliott Markson enter the office. She looked up at him guiltily. She had worn her workout clothes in, not expecting to see anyone but Rosellen and some maintenance people at that early hour. 'Mr Markson,' she said. 'I didn't expect to see you here on a Sunday morning.'

'I don't sleep well. And I have a lot of time on my hands,' he admitted. 'At least if I come in to the store, I feel like I've made something useful of my day.'

'I know what you mean,' Shelby said.

Markson, dressed in one of his expensive suits, looked at her steel gray tank top and warm-up jacket with raised eyebrows. 'This is an odd time to return to work,' he said.

Shelby was ready to start making excuses, and suddenly it all seemed too much for her. She wanted to speak the truth out loud, even though she knew where it would lead. Her boss would think she was losing her mind with this tale of a contract murder in exchange for health care. And, he would be angry that she was using the company's facilities to pursue some fantasy of vengeance.

'No,' she said, 'I'm not here for work.'

Elliott Markson folded his arms over his chest. 'Then what are you doing here?' he asked.

Shelby sighed. She was fresh out of lies, and decided to be frank. If he fired her for it, so be it. 'Well, you know that my daughter disappeared on a cruise. Since it happened, I've come to believe that she was murdered. I'm attempting to find a way to prove it. I devised a plan to try and trap the man I suspect in a lie. I needed to use a toll-free number so I used the one here,' she said bluntly.

She waited for an angry, or at least a sarcastic response, but it didn't come. She looked up at him.

He was gazing at her without rancor. 'Did it work?' he asked. 'The phone call?'

'You think I'm crazy, don't you?' she said.

'I barely know you,' he said. 'But, you don't seem crazy.'

Shelby looked away from him, and placed a hand on the phone receiver, remembering the shock of that conversation with Harris. The affirmation of every horrible thing she suspected. 'Well, yes. In a sense, it did work. I'm more convinced than ever that I am right.'

'What are you going to do about it?' he asked.

His matter-of-fact response surprised her. She thought about it for a moment, and then made up her mind. 'I think I will go to the FBI,' she said, with a decisive nod. 'They were involved in the initial investigation.'

Elliott frowned and then he looked closely at her. 'Perhaps I can help,' he said. 'I have a personal connection actually, at the FBI, here in Philly.'

Shelby frowned. 'Really?'

'If you like, I can give him a call.'

Shelby looked at him in surprise. 'I thought that was against the new company policy.'

Elliott looked pained, and Shelby immediately regretted her flippancy. 'I'm sorry,' she said. 'I appreciate that. I really do. I am all alone in this.'

'If you think it would help,' he said stiffly.

'That would be great,' she said. 'Really. Having someone, a name, to contact there would be a huge help.'

'I'll call him at the office tomorrow,' Elliott said. 'I'll have him get in touch with you.'

Tomorrow, Shelby thought. This can't wait until tomorrow. But she knew better than to say it. It would have to wait. 'I can't tell you how grateful I am,' she said sincerely.

'Happy to help.' He turned to leave the office and then he turned back. 'We need to get you back to work,' he said.

THIRTY-ONE

Shelby drove into the parking garage in the basement of her apartment building, inserted her card which raised the barrier bar and slowly cruised down the rows of parked cars toward her space. She didn't know how she was going to stand the wait for twenty-four hours to speak to Markson's contact at the FBI. But she knew she had to wait. This was her best hope for some real help with muscle behind it.

Shelby knew she had to resist the overwhelming urge to drive directly to the Janssens' house and confront Harris, throwing it all in his face. As tempting as it was to imagine herself shouting at him, exposing him, she knew it was a bad idea. A man who was ruthless enough to arrange a murder was way too dangerous to be confronted on his home territory. Besides, he would only deny it, and there would be no satisfaction in that. She would lay it out in front of the proper authorities. She wanted justice for Chloe. She couldn't let her anger rule her actions.

Shelby glanced at the dashboard. It was still only eight thirty. She suddenly realized that she was starving as she pulled into her space beneath the building. She had been up for hours already, and had hardly slept the night before. The other tenants of her high rise were obviously getting a slow start on this gray, chilly April Sunday. Why not sleep in, Shelby thought? She wished she had someone to sleep in with. She was not one to bemoan her lack of a lover, but since

Chloe's death she had realized how lonely her life had become. Chloe was not only her daughter, but her closest confidante. You need to get out and see people, she told herself. You need to get back to work.

She decided that once she had placed everything she knew in the hands of the FBI, she should consider getting back to work at Markson's. She found herself thinking about Elliott Markson, wondering why he too was free to come to work early on a Sunday morning. He was proving to be more complex than the overbearing boss she had heard about through the grapevine. True, he was not a genial *paterfamilias* like his uncle. But there was something honorable and genuine about him. She had thought this morning, when she hung up on Harris, that there was no one she could explain all this to. But during that brief interlude, when Elliott Markson stood in the office door, she had the sudden sense that she could explain herself to him.

Shelby's stomach growled, and she hoped she had something edible in the cupboards or the refrigerator in her apartment. She'd been away so much that she hadn't had time to stock the place. She and Jen had made tentative plans for a Sunday lunch, but she was too hungry to wait for lunch. She'd find something to throw together, she thought. She got out of her car and locked the door. Just as she was about to turn in the direction of the elevators, she felt something press her in the back.

'Do not scream,' said Harris Janssen.

Shelby jumped, and dropped her keys on the concrete floor. 'What are you . . . ?'

'It is a gun,' he said. 'Don't make me use it. Just come with me.'

Shelby shook her head. She had to feign ignorance. 'What in the world are you doing?' she asked.

'Don't,' Harris whispered. 'Don't pretend.' As he spoke he was nudging her toward the entrance to the garage. Shelby looked all around her, longing to see another resident who might come to her aid. But the garage was as quiet as a cemetery.

'Harris, there must be some misunderstanding,' she said.

'No. No misunderstanding,' he said. 'I admit you did catch me off guard this morning. The mention of those cruise tickets really threw me. I was so anxious to get off the phone I wasn't thinking straight. And then, when I collected myself, I decided to check the number. All toll-free numbers can be traced, you know. I traced yours back to Markson's. Now come with me,' he said, 'and don't say another word.'

Shelby's heart sank; to think she had been so easily found out. Her cleverness was not cleverness at all. She thought about screaming, but the garage remained deserted. The building had no attendant at the booth, just an automated arm. Holding the gun against her, Harris pulled Shelby around the lowered arm and over to his car which was parked in a visitor's space.

She expected him to open the passenger door, but she had misjudged his intent. He pushed a button on his keys and the trunk lid popped up.

Shelby reared back and cried out. 'Oh no,' she said, struggling to get away from him. He pushed her down roughly and she cracked her head on the lid. Shelby reached up automatically to press on the throbbing spot where she had struck her head. Something warm and sticky seeped over her hands. She felt him grab the waistband of her sweatpants and tug.

Dazed, she had the sickening, confusing thought that he was going to rape her. 'Stop it,' she cried. She held on to the waistband of her pants and with her bloody hands.

Harris reached inside his jacket and pulled something out. Suddenly, in the fold of still-exposed skin above her hip, Shelby felt a pinprick, and then everything went black.

Vivian Kendricks carefully raised the footrest on her son's chair and Rob lowered his slippered feet gingerly on to it, wincing as they touched down.

'How's that?' Vivian said.

'Good. Much better,' said Rob.

Jeremy started to clamber up on to his father's chair.

'No, Jeremy, don't do that,' said Vivian. 'Your Dad's hurting too much.'

Jeremy's expression was crestfallen.

'Oh, it's OK,' said Rob. 'Come on, slugger. You can sit with me. Just not the lap. Not yet.'

Jeremy cautiously wriggled into the seat beside Rob. Rob did his best not to let the pain in his ribs show on his face.

He draped his arm around his son's shoulders. 'There we go,' she said. 'Now we're comfortable.'

Vivian smiled in spite of herself. 'All right you two. But no jumping around.'

'We're just gonna watch a movie,' said Rob. 'Right?' Jeremy's eyes were wide. 'Right. How about *Pirates of the Caribbean*?'

'How did I know you were going to pick that one?' Rob said.

'I'll get it,' the child crowed. He crawled down from the chair and began to sort through the DVDs in a rack beside the set.

'So, I understand that Jeremy's teacher in preschool is Darcie Fallon,' said Vivian.

Rob nodded, watching fondly as his son expertly navigated his video collection. 'She's a great teacher. She really loves the kids.'

'She always had a crush on you,' said Vivian.

'Mother,' Rob cautioned her, nodding at Jeremy who was too busy with his DVDs to be listening to their conversation.

'I'm just saying,' said Vivian. 'You were the only one who didn't know it.'

'That's not true,' said Rob. 'Is it?'

Vivian rolled her eyes and smiled. 'All right. I'm going to set the table for lunch in the kitchen. When Dad gets back from church, we'll eat.' She started for the kitchen, and called back, as she reached the door, 'I made egg salad.'

Jeremy grimaced in distaste, but Rob said, 'Your grand-mother makes the best egg salad in the world. Wait till you try it. You're gonna love it.'

Jeremy shrugged, noncommittal. He was forcing open a DVD case and pulling out the disc. He inserted it into the DVD player, and pressed the play button on the remote, as Rob put his head back and let the relief of being home with his son and his parents wash over him. For a moment he pondered what his mother had said about Darcie. Was she right? To him, Darcie was always that little kid, hanging around the edges of what the bigger kids were doing. He had just never thought of her any other way. Although she had turned into a pretty young woman.

Rob felt his eyes drifting shut. As often happened, when

he closed his eyes, he relived his accident. The fear he felt, as
that jalopy-load of delinquents chased him on the expressway,
ramming the side of his truck with their car while he tried to
maintain control of the wheel, coursed through him again.
Other drivers had whizzed by, not knowing or not caring what
was happening to Rob as his truck began hydroplaning and
heading for a tumble down the embankment along the highway.

Rob took a deep breath and forced himself to think about
something else. He found himself picturing Darcie again, in
a new light, and the thought of her gentle face was strangely
soothing. Jeremy was getting ready to climb back up on to
Rob's chair. Suddenly, the doorbell rang.

'Hey buddy, can you answer that?' Rob asked. 'I can't get
up that fast.'

'Sure,' said Jeremy eagerly. He turned and raced toward the
front door. Vivian, hearing the bell, came out of the kitchen
wiping her hands as Jeremy led a pair of men into the living
room.

'Cops,' Jeremy whispered to his father.

The two officers tried not to grin. 'I'm Detective Ortega,'
said the dark-haired man. This is my partner, Detective
McMillen.'

Rob nodded to them both. 'Is this about my accident?' he
asked.

The two men frowned at one another.

'OK,' said Rob. 'So this is not about my accident.'

'What happened to you?' said Detective Ortega.

'I got into an argument with a couple of kids who were
drugged up,' said Rob. 'They followed me and ran me off the
road. Your guys collared them. I thought that's why you were
here.'

'No. We didn't know anything about that. We're here in
regards to a man who was found murdered a few days ago.'

'Murdered!' Vivian exclaimed.

'You gentlemen probably should sit down,' said Rob.
'Jeremy, why don't you run up to your room and play for a
little bit. We'll watch the movie when the policemen leave.'

'I want to hear this,' said Jeremy, wide-eyed.

'Go on, young man,' said Vivian, ushering him up the stairs.
'Scoot.'

Detective Ortega waited until Jeremy had disappeared up

the stairs and then he continued. 'Actually, I believe we've met before. We stopped by here one night when you were getting back from a trip. We were looking for information about a guy who had gotten a ticket on your street. An escaped convict named Norman Cook.'

'Oh, right,' said Rob. 'I do remember that.'

'A few days ago, we found his body, floating in the Schuylkill. Somebody had put two bullets in his head and dumped him.'

Rob shook his head. 'Why are you telling me this?'

'Well, it turns out this Norman Cook was parked on your block because he was looking for your wife.'

'My wife?' Rob exclaimed.

'Yes. Is she home? We'd like to speak to her.'

'No. Actually. She . . . died.'

'She did? When?' asked Ortega.

'On that trip you mentioned. We were on a cruise. She fell overboard.'

'Oh yeah,' said McMillen. 'I heard something about that.'

Detective Ortega looked in his notebook, frowning. 'And she never mentioned to you that this Norman Cook was here? I mean, I'm guessing, just from the fact that he got a parking ticket on your block, that he found her.'

Rob shook his head. 'She never mentioned it to me. Why would an ex-con be looking for my wife?'

'We were hoping you could tell us that.'

Rob shook his head. 'I don't know anything about it. What makes you think he was looking for her?'

'Well, it seems he went to the main branch of the library and asked the librarian to help him with the computer. He hadn't had any internet access in prison. He asked her to Google somebody for him. The librarian remembered him because it was unusual – a man his age not knowing how to use a search engine. After they found his body in the river, she saw his mug shot on the news and contacted us. Your name is Kendricks, right?'

'Yes, but . . . I just . . . I can't understand why Chloe wouldn't have said something to me. I mean, if she met with this man . . . If he came to the house . . .'

'Who's Chloe?' said Detective Ortega.

'My wife,' said Rob.

Ortega frowned at what was written in his notebook. 'Your wife isn't Lianna Kendricks?'

'That's my ex-wife,' said Rob.

'This guy was looking for Lianna Kendricks. It says she lived at this address.'

'Well, she did, when we were married. She's remarried now. She lives in Gladwyne.'

Detective Ortega shook his head. 'I guess our boy came calling and found the wrong lady,' he said.

'I can't imagine why she wouldn't have mentioned it to me,' said Rob.

Detective Ortega looked at Rob. 'I don't know. But judging from this parking ticket, I'd say they had themselves a visit.'

THIRTY-TWO

'How long this time?' Talia asked. She had just returned from the market and was putting groceries away in the kitchen.

Glen broke off a piece of the coffee cake which Olga, one of Estelle's caretakers, had left on the counter. He stuffed it in his mouth and rolled his eyes.

'That is fantastic,' he said, pointing at the maimed cake.

'Glen, I asked you a question,' said Talia.

'What?' Glen asked impatiently.

'How long are you staying this time?'

'A little longer this time,' said Glen. 'I had to get out of the place I was living and it might take me a while to find something.'

'You're going to have to do your own shopping,' said Talia. 'I just got back from the store and I don't have enough for you.'

'Oh, we'll make do,' said Glen, breaking off another piece of the cake.

'I mean it, Glen. This time I mean it.'

Glen came around the counter and tickled his older sister, who squirmed away from him. 'Quit it,' she said, irritably.

'I'll even cook for you,' he said. 'I'll make my specialties. We'll call Shelby.'

'She won't come. She's mad at me.'

'Why?' Glen asked.

'I wouldn't do something she wanted.'

'What?'

'Oh, it's not worth talking about,' said Talia wearily.

'No, really, I'm interested.'

'She keeps trying to find somebody to blame for her daughter falling off that boat. First it was me. Now, she's on to someone else.'

'What has all that got to do with you?' Glen asked.

'Nothing,' said Talia exclaimed. 'I don't want anything to do with it. But she's got it into her head that it's some guy . . .'

'What guy? That's kind of vague.'

'I don't know. But she wanted me to hack into his bank records. As if I would do that. I could lose my position.'

'Really?' said Glen, frowning. 'This sounds serious. Who was it?'

Talia sighed. 'I don't know. Somebody Faith knows.'

'Faith, your assistant?'

'Yes. Some doctor. Now leave me alone.'

'I think I'll call Shelby and invite her over,' said Glen. 'I want to hear about this.'

'Glen, I told you, there's not even enough food for you.'

'Maybe I'll pay her a visit.'

'Why don't you go stay at her place? She's got room,' Talia said.

'Oh, come on now,' said Glen, mischievously. 'You'd miss me.'

'No, I wouldn't,' said Talia.

'You don't remember who it was? Who Shelby was tracking?'

'No. I wasn't paying attention. I have to go check on Mother. And stop eating that cake.'

Talia left the kitchen. Glen sat at the counter, thinking. He walked over to the wall phone and picked up the receiver. Thumbtacked to the wall beside it was a list of numbers. Shelby's home number and her cell were listed. Glen tried them both. There was no answer. Both went directly to voice mail.

'Shelby,' he said. 'It's Glen. I'm at Estelle's house. Give me a call. I'm . . . Just give me a call.'

He hung up and sat back down at the counter. He broke off another piece of the cake and chewed it meditatively. Then he went back to the phone and ran his finger down the list of numbers. Talia's assistant's number was listed there. He thought about calling her, but then decided it would be too hard to explain who he was, and what he wanted to know.

Better to wait for Shelby to call back. He couldn't help feeling a little proud of himself. He was the one who suggested that maybe there was some kind of conspiracy around Chloe's death. Even though she had dismissed him at the time, Shelby had obviously paid attention to what he said. Come around to his way of thinking, so to speak. Not that he was going to rub it in that he'd been right. But what was that old saying – sometimes even paranoid people do have enemies? She was seeing it his way now.

Shelby awoke lying on her back, with a bright light in her face, and no idea where she was. Everything was a blank. She tried to move her arms, and realized that she was immobilized on some sort of table. And then she remembered. Harris Janssen. He had given her a shot that knocked her out. She had no idea how long she had been out. Or where he had taken her. She tried to let out a cry, but there was a handkerchief across her mouth, which was tied behind her head. She blinked rapidly, trying to clear her blurry vision, and turned her head to the side. She was looking at a beige wall, on which hung a framed painting of a seashore scene in pastel colors.

Shelby struggled, but could not move. She turned her head to the other side and saw a counter and cabinets. On the countertop were syringes, test tube racks, and a blood-pressure cuff hooked on a metal stand.

'Oh, you're awake,' he said. He came and stood beside the table, looming over her. He was not wearing a lab coat, but simply weekend casual clothes. He met her gaze apologetically.

'Please believe me, Shelby,' Harris said. 'I never meant for any of this to happen.'

Shelby tried to speak behind her gag, but it was no use. All that came out were noises and grunts.

'Turn your head,' Harris said.

Frowning, Shelby did as she was told. Harris untied the gag and gently pulled it loose from Shelby's mouth.

Shelby began to scream. Or at least, she tried to scream. What came out was a hoarse, strangled cry.

'Don't. Don't bother with that,' said Harris. 'We're all alone here. Nobody's going to hear you.'

Shelby tried to lick her lips with her tongue, although her tongue felt swollen, and too dry to moisten her cracked lips. Harris frowned. Then he disappeared from her field of vision, and she heard water running. In a moment, he returned, and dabbed her lips with a swab that looked like a large Q-tip.

She started to thank him, and then realized how ridiculous that was. It was his doing that she was a prisoner here. 'Is this your office?' she asked. She remembered that Harris's office was only a few blocks from the neuroscience center at Jefferson Hospital. On weekdays it was a bustling area. On Sundays you could park a Winnebago on the street with no problem.

Harris nodded. 'This is my examining room. The office is closed on Sunday. There's no one here. There's no one in the whole building.'

Shelby closed her eyes. 'How did you get me in here? Someone must have seen you.'

'There's a service elevator at the back of the building,' he said. 'It really wasn't difficult. Look, I'll be honest with you. I don't know what I'm going to do with you. After your call, I just knew I had to act quickly. I need some time to think. I didn't know where else to take you.'

Shelby felt sick at heart, realizing she inadvertently let him know that she suspected him. Now, it seemed, all her effort was for nothing.

Harris fiddled with some apparatus on the examining table, and Shelby was startled to feel the table starting to rise at her waist. In a few moments, she was in a sitting-up position, though still securely strapped to the table, her hands pinned with cloth wraps.

'There,' he said, sitting down in a swivel chair opposite her. 'It makes it easier to talk. I don't want to hurt you. I didn't want to hurt Chloe. You have to believe me. Things have spun completely out of control.'

Shelby gazed at him balefully. 'My daughter thought the world of you,' she said. 'She admired you so much.'

Harris lowered his gaze.

'How could you do this?' Shelby asked. 'You had her murdered.'

Harris's face bunched up, almost as if he was experiencing pain. 'How did you know? How did you find out? I mean, that 800 call was no shot in the dark. You already suspected me.'

Shelby felt a small, worthless feeling of satisfaction, to think that she had stumbled across the clues that led her to his terrible secret and he didn't know how. She was not about to satisfy his curiosity. At least, not until he satisfied hers. 'Why did you have my daughter killed?' she asked.

'Look, Shelby, you probably won't believe me,' said Harris. 'But if it had just been about me, I wouldn't have . . . I would never have hurt Chloe. She was a lovely girl. I was fond of her. But she was always a little bit jealous of Lianna. And a little vindictive, to tell the truth.'

Shelby stared at him. 'You killed her because she was jealous of Lianna?'

'No, no, of course not,' said Harris. 'And by the way, just to set the record straight, you were all too quick to assume that your daughter had gone through Lianna's medical records to find out about Molly's father. Chloe would never have done that. She was far too professional to do something like that. It would never have occurred to her. You should have realized that.'

'Don't you dare,' said Shelby. 'You're defending my daughter to me. You bastard.'

'I don't blame you for being angry,' he said.

'Why?' she pleaded. 'Why did you have to . . .' She couldn't continue. Tears slid down her cheeks and fell on her shirt.

He sat on the swivel chair, frowning. His feet, in sturdy shoes, were planted on the floor, his arms folded across his chest. He looked, for all the world, like a doctor trying gently to reveal a difficult diagnosis to a patient.

He sighed. 'A few weeks ago, a man named Norman Cook showed up at their house – Chloe and Rob's house. He was Molly's real father. He had come looking for Lianna, but he found Chloe, who was only too happy to listen. Imagine her surprise – Molly was not Rob's child! She finally had some-thing major on Lianna. Chloe gave Norman Cook our address. Told him how Lianna had left Rob and married me. After he left, she started thinking it over, and I guess she got a little worried. She showed up at my office determined to tell me all about it.'

Shelby shook her head helplessly. 'I don't get it. None of you seemed to care that much about Molly's real father. Why did Chloe have to die, just because she knew?'

Harris sighed. 'Because by the time Chloe came to see me, Norman Cook was already dead. I had killed him.'

Shelby gasped. 'You . . . Oh my God.'

'What Chloe didn't know – what Norman Cook didn't tell her – was that he had escaped from prison a week earlier. He was doing life for killing a clerk and a customer at a conveni-ence store. One of the people he killed was a medical student – some Indian kid with a wife and young baby – tragic. The police knew he had an accomplice, but he never gave up the name of his accomplice. The police thought it was another boy. Actually, it was a young woman. It was Lianna. Cook knew Lianna was pregnant with his child, so he took the fall, and kept quiet. At least, that's how he saw it. He thought he was her knight in shining armor.

'I'm sure she didn't have anything to do with the killings. She's much too gentle a creature. But, she was there. She did run.

'Anyway, after Cook was arrested, Lianna married Rob. She told Norman it was just to have someone help her support the baby. He wasn't happy about it, but he endured it. Then she stopped writing to him and he started getting angry. That's no way to treat a knight in shining armor.

'When he arrived in Philly, and Chloe told him that Lianna had married again, was pregnant again, he became incensed. He came to our house. I was the only one home at the time. I was completely stunned. He was raving. He told me that he was going to expose Lianna as his accomplice in that conveni-ence store killing. He said it would almost make it worth it to go back to prison. Just to know that she would have to go to prison too. That she would have to suffer.

'I tried to reason with him. I offered him anything he wanted. I offered to fix him up with a car and money and time to get

away, but he wasn't interested. He knew the cops were hot
on his tail, and would catch up with him before long. The
only thing he wanted in this world – the only desire he had
left – was for revenge. He wanted Lianna to pay.

'I knew he meant it. I couldn't let that happen,' Harris said.

'You killed him?' Shelby said.

'He had a gun. I used it. I dumped the body in the Schuylkill,'
Harris said. Then he sighed. 'Chloe was the only one who knew
he had come to our house. Because she sent him. Of course
she was itching to tell Rob about Molly's real father, but she
wanted to wait until the cruise was over. I'm listening to her
tell me this, and thinking that I had to do something quickly.'

Shelby closed her eyes. 'Oh God.'

Harris shook his head sadly. 'I decided to arrange for Chloe's
accident to happen during the cruise. I was thinking of trying
to hire someone, but I didn't have the first idea of how to do
that. And then, I was treating Bud Ridley and he was saying
how he could never repay me. That's when I thought of it. I
told him that Chloe was blackmailing me. I asked him to
accept the cruise tickets and take care of it for me. He knew
he had no choice.'

'He could have gone to the police,' Shelby said bitterly.

The room was silent for a moment.

Then Harris said, 'I knew he wouldn't. He wouldn't betray
me. He was too honorable.'

'Oh very honorable,' Shelby groaned. 'He killed an innocent girl whom he didn't even know.'

'I told him to meet her. To find an opportunity. Peggy
helped with that – without meaning to, of course. She's just
one of those people who makes friends easily. Anyway, that
night, after the Ridleys and that other couple helped Chloe
back to the state room, he wedged something in the door so
that it wouldn't lock behind him. I just want you to know
that I gave him a drug to sedate her. When he went back to
the state room, she was out. Completely unconscious from
the drug he put in her drink during bingo. Chloe wasn't aware
of anything that was going on. He threw her over the balcony.
She never knew what happened. Never even cried out,
according to Bud.'

Tears ran down Shelby's cheeks. 'Do you know what Bud's
suicide note said?' she demanded.

Harris raised his eyebrows. 'Do you?'

'It said that he couldn't live with himself,' Shelby spat at him. 'Because of what he'd done for you. How can you live with yourself?'

'Honestly,' he said grimly, 'that remains to be seen. I know you don't believe me, but I am so sorry about Chloe. And about Bud's death. I used to be . . . good. A good man. I was an idealist.'

'Chloe admired you,' Shelby said.

'Once you start down this road . . .' he said, shaking his head. He peered at Shelby. 'It's almost a relief to be able to tell someone. How did you find out about me?'

'I uncovered your connection to Bud Ridley,' she said.

'How?'

'We know someone in common,' she said. 'I kept pushing it. And it was partly luck. If you can call it luck,' she said.

'I admire you for that, Shelby. For being so determined.'

Shelby was somewhat amazed at the quiet tone he was taking, but the air in the room was electric with danger. He had told her his secrets. Keeping her alive meant jeopardizing his own life. She knew she had to try to save herself. Despite her deep desire to make him suffer, she also tried to maintain the most reasonable of tones.

'You know, there's no reason,' Shelby said, 'to make this worse than it already is.'

Harris, who was sitting with his arms crossed over his chest, his head lowered, looked up at her skeptically.

'Look,' said Shelby. 'Anybody could understand what happened with Norman Cook. That was probably self-defense.'

'I never thought for a minute that I would kill him,' Harris admitted. 'It was his own gun. I didn't even have a gun.' He glanced over at the gun which was lying on a metal cart beside his stethoscope. 'Now I have his gun, of course.'

'But you understand what I'm saying,' Shelby persisted, trying not to look at the deadly firearm on the rolling tray beside him. 'You might not even have to go to prison for that. Anyone in your position might have done the same thing.'

'And Chloe?' he said.

Shelby was silent for a few moments, and then she replied in a voice that shook despite her best efforts. 'I'll admit I was desperate to know what happened to her. But nothing we say or do will ever bring her back.'

'Sadly, no,' said Harris.

'As for Bud. He killed himself. Believe me, his family does not want to know the reason why,' said Shelby.

'You're right about that,' said Harris. 'But it doesn't change the facts.'

'You can't get away with this,' Shelby cried. 'People already know that I suspected you. That I was trying to trap you. At Markson's. They know. My sister knows. I was supposed to meet a friend this afternoon. Pretty soon she is going to sound the alarm and they are going to come looking for me. If you let me go now I will not make it worse for you.' Shelby was bluffing. Her lunch arrangement with Jen had been vague, and she had not told anyone but Talia whom she suspected. Talia never paid a bit of attention to what she said. But Harris didn't know that.

Harris seemed to ponder her suggestion. Then he shook his head. 'If you aren't alive to tell them what happened to you, I might be able to finesse this. People respect me. I'm a doctor. That will count for something. If I go to prison I'll lose everything. My life with Lianna. The baby . . .

'You know, everyone thinks Lianna married me because I was a doctor, and because I was well off, but that's not actually true. It was a love story, pure and simple. I never thought something like that would happen to me. But it did.

'And now, we have a baby on the way. A son. That changes a person,' he said. 'I don't even recognize myself. I've done things I never could have imagined. As you can tell, I would do anything to keep this life I have with them. Have you ever loved someone that much? Loved someone so much that you'll kill in order to protect them?'

Shelby hesitated. 'Only my daughter,' she said.

'That's what I thought,' he said. 'That's why I felt I had to tell you. You were pretty dogged about this whole thing. It seems only right that you should know the truth about what happened. But there's no way you would just let it drop. No way you would let them go easy on me. After all, I am responsible for Chloe's death.'

'You have to believe me,' she said, trying to keep her voice from shaking.

'I'm afraid not. But I promise you,' he said picking up a hypodermic needle from the metal tray table beside him, and holding that needle aloft, flicking the tip with one finger. 'This will just be like going to sleep.'

THIRTY-THREE

Alex Ortega looked down at the awkward-looking teenager who had answered the door. 'Molly?' he asked. 'Yes,' said Molly frowning.

'Is your mother at home?'

'Yes. She's at home,' said Molly.

'Can you get her for me?'

Molly nodded and disappeared. A minute later she was back. 'She'll be here in a minute.'

'Molly, you might want to go out to the squad car out there. There's somebody in that car who wants to see you.'

'Who?' asked Molly suspiciously.

'Your dad. He's kind of banged up, but he came along for the ride.'

'Really?' Molly took off down the walk through the gardens of the bewitching front lawn. When she was almost to the car, she stopped, and looked back suspiciously at the detective.

The rear window of the car rolled down, and Rob looked out. 'Molly,' he called out anxiously.

'Dad!' Molly rushed over to the car, just as Lianna arrived at the front door. She saw her daughter leaning into a strange car.

'Hey,' she demanded. 'What the hell . . . Molly!'

Molly straightened up and waved at her mother. 'It's Dad,' she said.

Rob gazed at her, unsmiling, out the car window, and lifted a hand in greeting.

'What's my ex doing here?' Lianna asked nervously.

'May I come in?' asked Detective Ortega. 'I have a few questions I'd like to ask you.'

Lianna frowned, but stepped out of the way. Detective Ortega came inside, and waited for her. Lianna led the way down the hall to the sunroom. She flopped into a wicker chair and pointed to another one. 'What's this all about?' she asked.

Detective Ortega took a moment to absorb the sight of her. She was curvaceous and lissome at the same time. Her face had a symmetrical perfection that was rare to see, although she seemed unconscious of her beauty, and did almost nothing to enhance it. Her clothes were faded, and she had no visible make-up, although one didn't ordinarily see such a flawless complexion, even with make-up.

'Mrs Janssen,' he said. 'Are you acquainted with a man named Norman Cook?'

Lianna blanched. 'Why are you asking me about Norman Cook?'

'Mrs Janssen?' said Ortega politely but firmly.

Lianna sighed. 'Yes. I mean, I was, years ago. I knew him. A lifetime ago.'

'When's the last time you saw him?'

'Not for years,' she said. 'What is going on?'

'Do you know where he is?'

Lianna glowered. 'Why?'

'Just answer the question,' said Ortega.

'He's in prison,' Lianna said. 'Serving a life sentence. Why are you asking me about Norman?'

'Have you heard from him lately?'

'No,' said Lianna. 'Why would I?'

Detective Ortega stared at her. 'What was your relationship with Norman Cook?'

Lianna sighed. 'All right, look. I was involved with him. It was a lifetime ago. He was a guy with a wild streak, and I was young and very naive, when we met. I did whatever he told me to do. I shouldn't have, but I did. It was a terrible mistake to ever get mixed up with him in the first place. I'm not the same person now. I have moved on.'

'Are you aware of the fact that he escaped from a prison work detail a few weeks ago and stole a car?'

'Norman escaped?' she cried.

'Yes.'

Lianna shuddered.

'You seem uncomfortable with that idea.'

'I am uncomfortable,' she said. 'I don't want Norman Cook to be trying to find me. Or anyone else.'

'Do you think it's likely that he would try to find you?'

'I don't know. It's possible. I stopped answering his letters years ago.'

'Mrs Janssen, we have reason to believe that Norman Cook did just that. He came here looking for you a few weeks ago.'

'Came here?' Lianna yelped. 'No.'

'Apparently, he went first to the home of your ex-husband in Manayunk. Then he was directed here, to your present address.'

'Directed by whom?' Lianna asked suspiciously.

'By Chloe Kendricks,' he said.

Lianna's eyes widened. 'Oh my God. Wait a minute. She talked to Norman? Oh my God. Was he the one who told her? Of course, he did. Jesus . . .'

'Excuse me?' said Detective Ortega.

Lianna sighed. She got up and walked over to the door of the sunroom and glanced into the house. Then she closed the sunroom door firmly. 'Look, I was just a teenager myself when I got involved with Norman Cook. OK? I was young and I got pregnant. Before long I found out that he was still married to somebody else. But, by then, I was afraid of him. He was a very violent man. He killed two men. Two perfectly innocent men who just happened to be in his path. That's what he was like. I mean, I was relieved when he went to jail. He begged me to wait for him. Of course I said I would but . . . well, I didn't mean it, as you can imagine. I got away as soon as I could.'

'What happened to your child?'

'You met her,' said Lianna flatly. 'At the door.'

'The young girl with the glasses?'

Lianna exhaled a noisy sigh. 'Yes. My daughter, Molly. But she doesn't know about the terrible things her father did, and I don't want her to know.'

'Did you see Mr Cook when he came looking for you?'

'No,' said Lianna. 'God, no. I had no idea he had escaped from prison, let alone was in the area. And, of course, Chloe did not see fit to tell me.'

'So, you're telling me that you did not see Norman Cook, or speak to him.'

'No. Why are you asking me this? What difference does it make if I saw Norman Cook or not?'

'Mr Cook was shot to death. His body was found floating in the Schuylkill.'

'WHAT?' Lianna jumped to her feet. She put a protective hand over her belly as if to hide her pregnancy from view.

If her surprise was not genuine, Alex thought, she ought to be in movies.

'Do you know anything about his death?'

'Do I . . .' Lianna was gasping for breath, shaking her head. 'No. No, I don't know anything. I never even . . . Who shot him?'

'Well,' said Detective Ortega. 'I was wondering if you did.'

All the color drained from Lianna's face, and her eyes became unfocused. Then, her irises rolled back and her knees gave way. Ortega jumped to his feet and reached out to try to catch her but he was too late. Lianna fell, with a thud, to the floor.

THIRTY-FOUR

Faith Latimer sat cross-legged on a canvas tarp, putty knife in hand, staring glumly at a bucket of sheetrock mud. Her husband, Brian, humming to himself, came into the room wearing paint-stained clothing and a painter's hat. He looked down at his wife's slumped shoulders sympathetically.

'Hey babe,' he said, leaning down and placing a hand on her shoulder. 'Don't try to do that today. Go on up and lay down. You're exhausted. When this is all over with your dad, there'll be time to get this done.'

'When this is all over my mother is gonna have to move in with us. Where will we put her? We haven't got one room done in this house.'

'Yes, we do,' he said. 'I just finished painting that little room off the kitchen, so your mom can have that. She can't really make the stairs.'

'My parents' bedroom was upstairs,' said Faith sadly.

'I know but this will be easier for her,' said Brian.

'I'm sorry about all this, honey,' Faith said.

'Hey, it's your mom,' said Brian kindly. 'And as moms go, she's not bad.'

Faith managed a crooked smile and her eyes glistened. 'You're the best. I'm so lucky.'

'I'm the lucky one,' he said.

The doorbell sounded. Brian frowned at his wife. 'You expecting anyone?'

'No, and I don't want to talk to anyone either,' she said.

'I'll get rid of them,' said Brian. He started to pick his way past the mud buckets to the front door.

Faith sighed, and stood up. At least there was no viewing tonight. Her mother was staying with her friend, Judy, and Faith and Brian would be there early tomorrow. The service began at ten. She still could not believe that her father was gone. And a suicide. She hadn't been the one to find him. That dreadful sight had greeted her mother when she walked in the door from one of her meetings. Her partner in life, dangling from the light fixture in the kitchen. The chair tipped over beside him. Faith squeezed her eyes shut, trying to block out the thought of it. She couldn't bear to imagine it. Tears began to splash on her mud-covered hands.

Brian leaned into the room. 'It's ... um ... your boss's brother?'

'Dr Winter's brother?'

'Yeah,' said Brian.'

'Why is he here?'

'I don't know. Do you want me to send him away?'

'Yes,' said Faith. And then she shook her head. 'No, wait. I probably should see what he wants.'

'I'm going to tell him that you're tired, and not to stay too long.'

Faith nodded. Brian was right – she didn't have the heart to do anything today but grieve for her father. She cleaned off the putty knife, and pressed the lid back on the bucket of joint compound. All of this could wait.

'Faith?'

Faith looked up and saw a shabbily dressed man in his thirties, with thick, graying hair and strong features. She could see the resemblance to Dr Winter, although the facial features looked better on a man than they did on her boss. Faith nodded. 'Yeah.'

'I'm Glen Winter. My sister is your ... I understand you are my sister's assistant.'

'That's right.'

'Sorry about your father,' he said.

'Thanks.'

'Listen um, I don't want to bother you at this time. But I'm trying to find some doctor that took care of your parents.'

'Why?' said Faith.

'For my sister,' said Glen evasively.

'Dr Winter?'

'No. No. Actually for my other sister. It's kind of complicated.'

'Why didn't Dr Winter just call me?' Faith asked.

Glen shrugged. 'She told me to do it. Kid brothers. We do all the errands.'

Faith was looking skeptical. 'You know, if you need a doctor and you don't have insurance, those urgent care clinics don't require it. You could try them,' Faith said.

Glen looked perplexed. 'What?'

'Well, pardon me for being suspicious, but Dr Winter and her sister came to my father's viewing and I heard my mother telling them about this particular doctor. It's true that he is a very wonderful doctor who never charged them. He's been treating my mother on and off for years, since she had a stroke. And more recently, my dad had to go to him also. He's just a rare person who wants to help others. I mean there are not many doctors like that. He really did it out of the kindness of his heart. But if that's what you're looking for – a doctor who won't charge you – you should really look elsewhere.'

'Hey, I didn't even know about that,' said Glen. 'But, now that you mention it, that's pretty radical. A doctor who treats patients for free!'

Faith frowned. 'Obviously he can't do that for everyone. I think he just felt sorry for my parents. My dad was hard working, but he could never afford the insurance once he lost his job. Anyway I really wouldn't want this doctor to think that you heard about this from us. That would be no way to pay him back for his kindness.'

'Of course not,' said Glen solemnly. 'But I assure you, this is not for me. I know I look a little bit . . . down at the heel. But my sister, Shelby, has money and insurance and all that good stuff. I think she just wanted to see this particular doctor – maybe it's because of his specialty or something like that.'

'What's wrong with her?' Faith asked worriedly.

Glen spread his hands wide with a smile. 'Hey. They never tell me anything. They send me to do the dirty work. It's always been that way. So, I'm just here to get the name.'

'But what are your sister's symptoms?' Faith asked.

Glen shook his head sadly. 'I don't even know,' he said.

'I'm sorry,' said Faith. 'Please. You'll have to go now. There are lots of doctors in the city. Find someone else.'

THIRTY-FIVE

Shelby opened her eyes. She lay on her side, curled up in a fetal position. All around her was blackness, and, for one moment, when she realized that it was not the grave, but a dark enclosure, and that she was still alive, she felt a giddy exhilaration. And then it quickly passed. Her head felt like it was being pounded with a hammer. There was tape covering her mouth. Her hands were tied behind her and her ankles tied together. When she tried, groggily, to straighten out her legs, she realized that she was being restrained in a cramped, tiny space. And beneath her, in the darkness, she heard something humming.

An engine.

Shelby's eyes widened. Part of her brain was still sedated, but her natural adrenalin was kicking in, overwhelming whatever tranquilizer he had given her. She remembered now. He was coming toward her with a needle and she was struggling, trying to free herself from the bonds that held her to the examining table. And then, everything else was a blank. Somehow he had moved her out of his office – probably under cover of darkness – and now she was back in the trunk of his car, and he was driving her somewhere. She did not know where, but she knew that he meant it to be her last stop.

Was it worth it, she asked herself? Now, she knew everything, but she would not live to tell about it. Or to see justice done for Chloe. Jeremy would not have his Shep, and her promise to Chloe, to always be there for her son, would be void and broken. Would anyone seek justice for her, as she had for Chloe? Shelby could not imagine it. She had never felt such a failure.

She thought about her captor. Harris Janssen was still trying to regard himself as a victim and a decent man, but there was no decency left in him. Killing Norman Cook had been one thing. If he had only stopped then, he might have found absolution. But he had gone ahead and methodically arranged for Chloe's death. He had given Bud Ridley an assignment too grievous to bear – and Bud had carried it out. Bud was unable to live with his conscience. At least he *had* a conscience, Shelby thought. Harris Janssen had lost his somewhere along the way.

When did it happen? He had been an admirable man when Chloe worked for him. When did character begin to crumble in the face of desire? Was it at the moment when his patient, Lianna, looked helplessly, admiringly into his eyes and he decided that he had to woo her away from her husband? Was that when he started down the slippery slope to the gutter without principles where he now existed? Or was it when he learned that she was bearing him a son? What did it matter anyway? He was ruthless now, and Shelby was his prisoner.

No, she thought. Don't give up like this. It's not over yet. You have to keep fighting. Frantically, Shelby began to try to pry her hands apart. As she strained to pull the bonds loose, her heart began to hammer wildly, and she could not get enough breath through her nose to fill her lungs. The panic was about to overwhelm her. Stop, she thought. Calm down. She lay still for a moment, trying to let the panic subside and let her breathing return to a semblance of normal. If she suffocated from her own fear, he would win. She wasn't going to make it any easier for him.

Once she managed to get her heart to stop pounding, she began to try again with her hands and her feet. Pretend it's an exercise, she thought. Pull them as far apart as you can, and hold them there. She was able to do that, as long as she didn't try to think. Once she let her thoughts take over, they began to race away, and that was too dangerous. She concentrated, very deliberately, only on the small space she was making between her hands and her feet. Even as she held her hands apart, she felt around with her fingers for some loose scrap of fabric or rope that she could pull. Mostly they grasped at the air.

Where is he taking me, she thought? No one will even be

looking for me. I will disappear and no one will even know. Her heart began to race again, and she forced herself not to think about it. The car stopped and then started again, rolling along silently. It was a good car. A new car. It would make a lovely hearse. NO. No, she thought. Don't go there. Pull your hands apart.

The car continued to move.

THIRTY-SIX

'She's probably taking a walk,' said Talia.

Glen shook his head. 'I don't think so.'

He bent down and inserted the key into the lock of the front door to Shelby's condo. The key turned.

Glen reached for the doorknob and turned it. The door opened inward. 'Shelby,' he called out. There was no answer.

Talia frowned. 'I'm going to get a ticket. That place I parked was a loading zone.'

'It's Sunday,' said Glen, looking around as he entered the apartment. 'There's nobody loading anything on Sunday.'

Talia followed him down the hall to the large, comfortable living room with its panoramic view. Glen went directly into the kitchen and began looking for some note or indication of where Shelby might have gone.

'Maybe she just went somewhere. She's a grown woman. She doesn't have to tell you where she's going,' said Talia. Talia's gaze was drawn to the bank of windows, but she frowned at the gray river, the bridge, the buildings, and the treetops, as if she found the sight of them offensive.

Glen was rummaging through note pads and takeout menus which were piled on the counter. 'Look, she doesn't answer her phone, or her cell. She doesn't answer the door. And her car is in the garage.' Glen had insisted that Talia drive him over to Shelby's when he returned from his fruitless visit to Faith. 'And what about these?' Glen held up a key chain and jingled the keys. He had found them on the floor of the garage, under the driver's side door of Shelby's Honda. He tried them on her car, and unlocked the door instantly. 'These are her car keys and her house keys. You think she just left them there and walked away?'

'She dropped them. Or they fell out of her purse,' said Talia irritably.

Glen shook his head. 'No. There's something going on.'

'I don't know why you think that,' said Talia.

Glen had given up on the kitchen and moved to Shelby's glass top desk in the living room. He sat down on the steel and leather desk chair and began to search through her papers. He stopped long enough to look up at Talia.

'Are you serious?' he said, shaking his head. 'Is it possible that you really don't know?'

Talia returned his exasperated stare dispassionately.

'You know, Talia, if you had interceded, and insisted, Faith would have had to tell me the name of that doctor. We could have settled this all by now.'

'It's none of your business, Glen. People's doctors are a private matter. I wasn't going to force my assistant to tell me that.'

'Can't you try to remember?' Glen asked.

'I did try,' Talia complained.

'Try harder.'

'This is a wild goose chase. I have to get back to Mother,' Talia insisted.

'No, you don't,' Glen snapped. 'Estelle is fine. She doesn't know if you're there or not. She doesn't need your help. Your sister needs your help. Now sit down. If you can't do anything constructive, then just sit there quietly.'

With a sigh, Talia sank down on to the nearest chair, turning her own car keys impatiently in her hands. 'What are you looking for?' Talia demanded of her brother.

'I don't know. Something to tell me where she went.'

Glen sat in front of Shelby's computer, his fingers poised over the keys. He typed in a few combinations. 'I wonder what she would use for a password,' he mused aloud.

'People use their birthdays,' Talia said, sounding bored.

'I tried that,' said Glen.

'You know her birthday?' Talia asked.

'I know yours, too,' said Glen. 'Now be quiet. Let me think.'

Suddenly, they heard a knock at the front door of the apartment. 'Shelby?' a voice called out.

Glen and Talia exchanged a surprised glance. Glen got up from the desk, went to the door and opened it.

A pretty woman with shoulder-length chestnut-colored hair and gray eyes was standing there. She frowned at the sight of Glen's wild hair and layers of shirts. 'Who are you?' she said to Glen. 'Where's Shelby?'

'I'm Shelby's brother. Who are you?' Glen demanded.

'I'm Jen. I live down the hall. I heard voices in here. I've been waiting for her to come home. We were talking about having lunch after she got back from Markson's. When I heard the voices, I thought it was her.'

'What was she doing at Markson's?' Glen asked.

'She works there,' said Talia.

Glen turned away from the door and looked at Talia. 'She hasn't been to work in weeks,' said Glen impatiently. 'Don't you pay any attention at all?'

Talia sniffed.

Glen looked back at Jen. 'Did she tell you why she was headed to Markson's?'

Jen shook her head. 'I don't know. She didn't say. She was planning some scheme. I think it had something to do with what happened to Chloe. She said she'd tell me all about it if it worked.'

Glen turned back to Talia who was listening to their exchange. 'I told you,' he said. 'There's something wrong.'

Jen frowned. 'What do you mean?'

'Come in, come in,' said Glen, heading back down the hall. Jen followed him cautiously. 'This is my other sister, Talia. I made her bring me over here when we couldn't reach Shelby. I found Shelby's car in the parking garage, and these were on the ground not far from the car.' He jingled the keys.

Jen reared back. 'Her car is here? And her keys were on the ground? That's not right.'

'Thank you. My point, exactly,' said Glen, giving Talia a meaningful look.

'So what do you think happened to her?' Jen asked anxiously.

Glen peered at Shelby's neighbor. 'Shelby told Talia that she had her suspicions about some doctor. Did she mention a doctor to you? Someone who might have had some involvement with Chloe?'

Along with the thousand fabrics, tiles, and paint colors that she kept in her head, Jen was the sort of friend who kept the details of all her friends' lives in her head as well. 'Chloe worked for a doctor. An ob-gyn named Cliburn.'

Glen turned to Talia. 'Does that ring a bell? Dr Cliburn?'

'No. Besides, she just said he was an ob-gyn,' said Talia scornfully. 'Why would an ob-gyn be treating Faith's parents? They're old people.'

'True,' said Glen. 'What was wrong with those people anyway? Faith said that her mother had a stroke. Now, the father . . .'

Suddenly, Talia's eyes seemed to light up. 'Lou Gehrig's disease. ALS. Amyotrophic lateral sclerosis. Ultimately, the neuromuscular system in the body completely fails . . .'

'Good work, Talia. So the doctor for that would be a . . .' Glen fumbled for an answer. He avoided things medical. He planned to live forever, like Peter Pan.

'A neurologist,' said Jen firmly. 'My uncle had a stroke. He saw a neurologist.'

'All right,' said Glen. 'Now we're getting somewhere. We can get a list of all the local neurologists. There can't be that many. It's a specialty.'

'Don't bother,' said Talia.

'Why not?' Jen asked.

'Janssen,' said Talia bluntly. 'I remember now. His name was Janssen.'

THIRTY-SEVEN

She did not know how long it took, but she knew that it took every ounce of her patience and determination. Finally, nearly crushing the bones of her hand in the effort, Shelby was able to pull one hand free. One hand was all she needed. The first thing she did was to rip the tape off her mouth. The next was to untie her ankles. She rolled over on her back, and for a moment she allowed herself to feel the physical bliss of not having her arms and legs bound and twisted unnaturally behind her.

But she only allowed herself a moment. She was still a prisoner. She had to get free of this trunk. She thought about pounding on the underside of the lid to try to attract attention. But for all she knew, they were out in the country somewhere, and there would be no one to hear her but Harris. If he heard her making a commotion he would know she had gotten loose from her bonds. He might pull over, get out, open the trunk and kill her then and there. Her mind was still cloudy and she did not know if she had the strength to resist him. Certainly, not without a weapon, especially if he was still carrying Norman Cook's gun.

She was aware that she was lying on a piece of carpet trimmed with rubber to fit the floor of the trunk. She rolled up, and began to tug at it. Sooner or later, he was going to pop the lid of that trunk. There might be a jack underneath the carpet that she could use for a weapon when that happened.

There was no light to aid her, so she felt around and found the edge of the carpet. She lifted it up and felt around beneath it for the tire well, where a person would naturally keep a jack or a lug wrench. She ran her hand over the cold metal floor beneath the trunk until she found it. She had to feel around for the mechanism to open it, but when she did, and the lid over the well opened, she felt her heart sing with hope.

She felt around, first with one hand, and then with both. It did not take long to realize that he was one step ahead of her. The jack and the lug wrench had both been removed. Only the tire remained.

Shelby wanted to cry. She rested her face on the floor of the trunk with a groan. There was nothing. He had made sure of that. Not even a screwdriver or a flashlight. Nothing.

She realized now that she should never have pursued this alone, without someone to help her. I had to, she thought. Chloe, darling, no one else cared. I had to find out what happened to you. Weary, she started to ruminate on all she had learned about Chloe's last days and moments. The thought of it was so upsetting that she had to put it out of her mind.

Are you going to just give up, she asked herself? Are you going to let the man who killed her get away with it? By killing you? She used all her mettle to summon some will. She pulled back the carpet once again, and studied the floor of the trunk. There were coated wires running along the sides beneath the carpet. Her eyes were adjusting to the dark, and she could see that they were leading from the back of the back seat to the exterior sides of the car.

To the lights, she thought. To the signal lights. To the brake lights.

The answer came to her. The smart thing was not to bang on the lid to attract attention. The smart thing was to attract attention without making a sound.

She just had to hope that someone out there would be paying attention. Shelby wound her hands under and around the wires, braced herself as best she could, and jerked on them with all her might.

'Jesus Christ, look at all these cops,' said Glen uneasily.

Talia pulled up in front of the Gladwyne house and parked.

Glen chewed on a cuticle. 'I wonder what they're all doing here.'

'I'm sure I don't know,' said Talia, but she sounded far less defiant than she had at Shelby's apartment.

'You think I should go up there?' said Glen.

'If you want. But I'm staying here,' said Talia. 'I'm not talking to them.'

Glen chewed the inside of his mouth. 'I'll do the talking,' he said. 'Just wait for me.'

Glen jumped out of the car and loped up the lawn to the house. There were two officers standing on the front steps. 'What's going on here?' Glen said.

The two officers looked askance at him. 'Move along,' they said. 'Nothing to see here, mister.'

Cops. They always looked at him with contempt. As usual, it irritated him. 'Hey I'm not some rubbernecking bystander,' said Glen, his voice rising. 'I'm involved in this. I came here to see Dr Janssen.'

'What do you want with Dr Janssen?' said one of the officers.

'That's my business. I want to speak to somebody in charge,' said Glen, trying to sound entitled.

The two men looked at one another, and then one of them picked up his two-way radio and spoke into it. The other one motioned for Glen to get down off of the steps. Glen considered refusing. Reluctantly, he stepped down.

After a few minutes the front door opened and Detective Ortega appeared. He looked out. 'What is it?' he said.

'This guy says he's looking for Dr Janssen.'

'Actually, I'm looking for my sister, Shelby Sloan,' said Glen.

Ortega hesitated, peering at the man on the step. 'Why do you think your sister would be here?' Ortega asked.

'She was trying to find Dr Janssen and now she's missing,' said Glen.

'Why was she looking for Dr Janssen?'

'It's a long story,' said Glen. 'It's to do with the death of her daughter, Chloe—'

'Chloe Kendricks?' said Ortega.

Glen frowned at him as if he just fooled him with a three-card monte. 'Yeah. How do you know that? What are you guys doing here anyway?'

'We're conducting a search,' said Alex Ortega.

Glen held up Shelby's car keys and shook them in front of the detective. 'Well, I don't know what you're searching for, but you better start searching for my sister. I found these on the floor of the garage beside her car. But she is not in her apartment and I'm worried that something has happened to her.'

Detective Ortega took the keys from Glen and frowned. 'You found these beside her car.'

'Yes. And look, her apartment keys are on them. She didn't get inside her building. Something bad is going down here. She would never just leave her keys on the ground and walk away.'

Ortega held the keys in the palm of his hand as if he might be estimating their weight. Then he nodded at Glen. 'Come inside,' he said. 'I'm afraid you might be right.'

Shelby heard the siren, and her heart leapt. Don't pass me by, she thought. Don't pass me by.

Her silent prayers were answered. She felt the car slowing down and pulling over. It bumped to a halt. The sirens stopped as well. For what seemed like a long time, there was nothing. Nothing at all. And then, she heard it. The sound of voices. Muffled. But definitely voices.

One of them had to be the cop. She strained to listen.

'Your lights,' she heard a man's voice say.

Yes, she thought. Yes. He had seen the lights which she had pulled out, and given chase. She was saved.

And then, she realized. Not exactly. She was still locked in this trunk, and no one knew it. Now, it was time to pound. She had no weapon, but she had strength. Strength she never knew she possessed. For all she was worth, she began to smash her fists against the lid of the trunk and scream.

'I'm just going to give you a warning this time. But you need to get those lights fixed,' shouted Officer Terry Vanneman handing Harris back his license and registration. Traffic was whizzing by on the expressway, trucks thundering like stampeding elephants. A Flyers game had just let out, and fans were screaming out their windows as they flashed by.

'I will,' Harris promised. 'I certainly will. All I can say is, they don't make cars like they used to.'

'What?' the officer shouted.

Harris waved his registration. 'Sorry. I will,' he shouted.

'You really shouldn't be driving this car around in that condition.'

'Of course not. My car must have been vandalized. That's the city for you.'

'Does happen,' said the officer. He was looking warily around himself. Even though they were pulled all the way over, the expressway traffic was so fast and relentless that a person felt completely exposed to danger, even on the shoulder of the road. Only the week before a good Samaritan who was trying to help with a tire change got killed by a speeding truck.

'Well, as I say,' Harris proclaimed loudly. 'I'm on my way to the hospital. After that, I will head home directly.'

Officer Vanneman slapped his palm against the roof of the car. 'OK, Doc, steady as you go.'

'Thank you, officer,' said Harris. He fired up the engine with a roar.

Inside the trunk, Shelby felt the car start to move again. No, she cried out.

But no one heard.

THIRTY-EIGHT

The next time the car turned, and began to slow, Shelby had heard no sirens. All she could hear was the fearful thudding of her own heart. Ever since the car had pulled away from its police stop, her hope had faded to nothing. She did not know how it was possible that no one had heard her cries and frantic beating on the inside of the trunk lid. The thought that she had been so close to rescue, and not been saved, seemed like a sign that she was doomed. Shelby didn't know what was coming, but she feared it. Harris was desperate, with everything to lose.

The car was moving slowly down a bumpy road or path, and Shelby knew, with a sickening certainty in the pit of her stomach, that they had entered some sort of desolate area. She was completely disoriented as to where she was, and where she was being taken, but she could tell by the car's jerky motion that they were no longer on the highway, or even the paved streets of the city.

The car slowed, and came to a full stop. The engine was turned off. Oh Lord, she thought, where has he taken me? She waited in the darkness of the trunk, trying to prepare herself for the fight of her life, until, at last, she heard the click of the trunk's lock. The lid opened a crack. Shelby felt almost crippled by having been cramped so long in the trunk, but she turned her legs so that she could try to rear up when the lid lifted.

Suddenly the trunk lid flew up and Shelby blinked, and tried to peer out. Harris was standing over her and in his hand he held the gun. Wherever they were, it was completely dark, and quiet except for the sound of crickets, the wind, and rushing water. 'Get out,' he said.

Shelby clambered to the edge of the trunk and tried, with shaking arms, to hoist herself up and over the top. Her first try failed.

'Hurry up,' he said, looking all around in the darkness.

Shelby was finally able to realign her weight and throw

one leg over the raised edge, and then push herself up and over. She tumbled out and fell on to a bed of gravel which made her cry out as the rocks embedded themselves in the heels of her hands and her knees.

'Quiet,' he demanded. 'Get up.'

Shelby crawled to her feet, balancing herself against the back of the car, and looked around. Now that she was out of the trunk she saw that it wasn't completely dark. There were some widely spaced gaslights along a wooded path. She could hear the sound of water burbling nearby, but couldn't see it.

'Where are we?' she asked.

'Never mind,' he said. 'Walk that way. And don't cry out or I will crack this thing over your head, so help me.'

Shelby thought about defying him, but who would hear her? Wherever it was that he had taken her, it was the most desolate and heavily wooded of spots. The air smelled of honeysuckle and evergreens, but there was no one but themselves to inhale the heady scent.

Shelby began to walk on her cramped, shaky legs. The black night was growing cold. Harris prodded her in the back, but she did not need much prodding. Being out of the trunk at last was such a relief that she did not care, for one moment, where he might be pushing her. She was just glad to be walking, to be breathing, to be free of that miserable enclosure.

'That way,' he said. 'Up that path.'

'Harris, please,' she pleaded.

'No,' he barked. 'No more talking. Go.'

She walked in the direction he was pointing up a gravel path and, as she passed under one of the lights, she saw a printed wooden sign where the paths ahead diverged.

Forbidden Drive, said one of the signs. The Monastery. Lover's Leap. The Devil's Pool.

She recognized the names. The Wissahickon, she thought. It was a huge swath of wooded park that flanked the Wissahickon creek. The Monastery Stables were horse barns, open to the public for riding lessons, and located in a lovely clearing near the edge of the park. Automobiles were not allowed in the park. It was crisscrossed with paths for walking or running or just enjoying the sun-dappled beauty of it on a lovely day. It was not meant for night. Shelby could hear the water more clearly now. They were close to the creek.

'That way,' he said.

Shelby read the sign aloud. 'The Devil's Pool,' she said.

'You're going for a dip,' he said.

Shelby closed her eyes. She saw little reason to hope, and she was weary of the fight. She suddenly remembered being in her apartment and looking out at the river in the dark. She remembered thinking how each body of water emptied into the next body of water, on and on, all the way out to sea. She didn't know if it was true or not, but it seemed true. All water is connected, she thought. And in that one, insane moment, she felt comforted. She almost felt ready. Ready to give in. Ready to join her lovely, lost daughter down on the floor of the sea.

Officer Terry Vanneman did not have long to wait for the next offender. A Toyota doing eighty-five mph. He fired up the blinking lights and siren, and gave chase, signaling for the driver to pull over. Almost immediately, the driver obeyed, and when he slowed and pulled on to the shoulder, Officer Vanneman nosed up behind him and parked by the edge of the road.

It's like trying to pull somebody over on the track of the Indy 500, he thought.

It was a duty he particularly disliked. Too damn dangerous. He sat in the car for a while, making the guy sweat. He knew what people thought. They thought that cops just sat there listening to the radio and eating a doughnut while the driver stewed in his own juices. That was somewhat, but not precisely, true.

It was true that Officer Vanneman took longer than was absolutely necessary to get out and approach the offending driver, but before he did, he always checked the license plate to be sure it was not a stolen car. He wanted his drivers contrite, not desperate. He did not fancy walking up to the car and being met with the muzzle of a gun.

As he punched the numbers into his cruiser's computer, his response was preempted by an urgent message, flashing for the attention of all officers.

They were to be on the lookout for a late-model Lexus, with doctor's plates. The number of the plates flashed on the computer screen. The driver was Dr Harris Janssen. He might have a hostage with him, and he was considered to be armed and dangerous.

Terry Vanneman felt a prickling over his scalp as he read the words. Shit, he thought. How long ago had he stopped that car? It could be anywhere by now. Terry felt sweat pooling around his belt and under his arms. What a collar that would have been! What a fucking coup! How could he have missed it? All he had noticed was that the rear lights were out. Otherwise the guy seemed like the model citizen. He wasn't even speeding.

Terry immediately radioed in and reported his position. He told the dispatcher that the car they were searching for was last seen heading west on the Schuylkill. He told them that the car's taillights were not functioning. The dispatcher thanked him before going to the next call.

Terry looked up at the car stopped in front of him, and hesitated. The next exit was for Lincoln Drive and the Wissahickon. The guy had been stopped once. He probably wouldn't chance being stopped again. He would probably get off the road as quickly as possible. Like, at the next exit.

Terry gave it a moment's thought. He was the last man to have seen the car, and there could be a hostage involved. He had not yet even approached that driver in the Toyota. One thing was certain. Hostage trumped speeding ticket.

Officer Vanneman made his choice. He turned his flashing lights and siren back on, waited for an opening and shot back out into the traffic lane, roaring by the startled, grateful driver in the Toyota at the side of the road.

'What are you up to?' Harris asked.

Shelby sat on a rock beside the black-shining pond, and began to remove her shoes.

'I didn't tell you to take your shoes off,' he said.

'I know. I don't know why I'm doing it,' she said dully.

'Maybe that's what a person would do,' Harris mused. 'I need it to look like you took your own life. So go ahead. Take them off.'

'They're going to wonder how I got here,' she said idly. 'Without a vehicle.'

'Let them wonder,' Harris growled.

She stopped, holding one shoe in her hand, and looked up

at him quizzically. By the light of the moon, she could just make out his face. 'Why did the cop let you go?' she asked. 'I was making so much noise.'

'We were on the Schuylkill. Between the trucks and the Flyers fans, you couldn't hear yourself think,' he said.

'Oh,' said Shelby with mild interest, as if they weren't talking about the turning point of her very survival.

'That was a neat trick,' Harris admitted. 'Pulling those wires out.'

Shelby shrugged. 'For all the good it did me,' said Shelby. They were like any two people under the moon by the side of a lake, making desultory conversation. Looking at him in the dark, with his round face and balding head, she was reminded of certain boys she knew in high school. The kind of shy, studious, unathletic boys who could make you laugh in homeroom or math class, but never met your eye in the hall or the cafeteria. And never got asked to parties.

Shelby continued removing her shoes. She put her socks in them and placed them neatly beside a rock. Then she stood up. She unzipped her jacket calmly, and removed that too, folding it and laying it atop the same rock.

'Don't you care?' he said. 'I mean, don't misunderstand me. I'd prefer it if you didn't. I have no desire whatsoever to see you suffer. I've made you suffer already and I'm sorry for it.'

Shelby stared at the glimmering surface of the Devil's Pool. 'I'm just very tired of fighting,' she said. 'I admit I would like to see you rot in jail. I would throw away the key myself. But I can't do this alone. I guess this is what it feels like to give up. Just . . . empty inside. At least I know what happened to my daughter now. No one else seemed to care as much about that as I did.'

'Not Rob,' Harris said scornfully. 'I never thought he was good enough for Chloe.'

Shelby let out a strangled laugh. 'That's almost funny, coming from you.'

'I know. Look, when they find you, it will seem like it was a peaceful death. Believe it or not, Shelby, that's what I want for you. You deserve that. I mean, of course I don't want any evidence that I killed you, but the truth is, I want you to die peacefully.'

'Fuck you,' she said. 'You ruined any peace I ever had.'

'All right,' he said. 'Never mind. I have no right to even say it. Go. Go in.'

'Maybe I should make you shoot me,' said Shelby absently.

'I will, if you insist,' said Harris. 'Believe me, I've gone this far . . .'

Shelby shook her head. More than anything else, she wanted to get away from him. She wanted to block out the sight of him, and the sound of his voice. She climbed up on the rock and looked into the depths. She couldn't actually see anything but the mesmerizing movement of the surface. She thought of Chloe, hitting the dark water, falling down, never knowing. Did she come to for an instant and flail against her fate? It was torture even to think of it.

'Go,' he said. 'Hurry up. I have to get back.'

'To Lianna,' she said. And anger at him flared anew in her weary heart. She turned to face him. Don't give in, she thought. He doesn't deserve that. Leap on him. Force him to shoot you to be free of you, she thought. Don't give him any other option. Make it hard for him. Resist. For Chloe's sake. For her memory.

'What are you waiting for?' he said.

'You're going to have to kill me,' she said. 'I won't help you.'

And then, in the distance, red and blue lights flashing through the trees, caught her eye. There was more than one car. Shelby's heart leapt. 'Look,' she cried out.

Harris saw the look on her face and turned in the direction where she was gazing. In a moment, he saw them too. They were closing in. Quickly. The sirens started to wail, one after another. They must have spotted his car, parked illegally near the entrance to Forbidden Drive. Voices were shouting and car doors were slamming shut. When he turned back to Shelby, Harris looked stunned, as if those lights flickering in the woods were fire. As if, as he watched, he saw all that he lived for going up in flames.

THIRTY-NINE

Hugh Kendricks, standing in Shelby's kitchen, handed his granddaughter, Molly, two drinks he had just poured. 'Take this one to your grandmother,' he said. 'And the other one to Dr Winter.'

Molly frowned. 'Who's Dr Winter?'

Hugh pointed to the dove-gray sofa in Shelby's living room. 'The woman sitting next to Grandma.'

Molly obediently took the glasses from Hugh. 'When do you think Mom will come back?' she asked worriedly.

Hugh patted his shaken granddaughter on the shoulder. 'I'm sure it won't be too long,' he said. 'They had to ask her a lot of questions about your stepfather.'

'Is Mom in trouble?' Molly asked.

'I don't think so. I don't think she had anything to do with . . . all this. Anyway, don't you worry. Your dad is with her,' said Hugh. 'He'll make sure they treat her fairly. He knows your mom would never have wanted to hurt Chloe.'

Molly sighed and nodded. Then she got on with her task of serving the drinks to the people assembled in Shelby's apartment. Tonight, Molly needed to be kept busy. In fact, everyone gathered there seemed in need of the distraction of company and a little camaraderie. Glen had offered to make his famous hobo's stew for dinner, but Shelby had talked him into ordering take-out and they were waiting for it to arrive. Jen was drinking wine and questioning Glen about his life and his prospects. Glen was at his most evasive, and charming, best. Shelby smiled to herself. After all their conversations together, Shelby knew, when it came to men, that Jen had a weakness for a lost cause.

'What's funny, Shep?' Jeremy asked.

She was resting on the sofa, with Jeremy perched on the arm beside her. 'Nothing. I'm just glad to be with you,' she said, squeezing his little arm.

Someday, when he was grown up, Shelby thought, she might explain to Jeremy how very close she had come to never seeing his angelic face again. Thanks to the timely arrival of the Philadelphia police, she was not dead at the bottom of the Devil's Pool, but comfortably ensconced in her own apartment, surrounded by the murmur of people who cared about her.

In the end, Harris had given up without a struggle when the police surrounded them in the Wissahickon. He had been dragged off in handcuffs, hanging his head, without a backwards glance at her, while EMTs hustled Shelby into an ambulance and rushed her to Dillworth Memorial Hospital. Talia and Glen had been waiting for her when she was released, after an examination proved that she was physically unharmed. Glen had embraced her tightly, and Talia, in a gesture which was expansive for her, had briefly patted Shelby's shoulder. At that, to Talia's alarm, Shelby had burst into tears.

That was just an hour ago. Rob was still at the police station with Lianna, who was being questioned. Rob's parents had brought Jeremy and Molly over to Shelby's apartment. Somehow, Vivian seemed to be making easy conversation with Talia. Shelby felt peaceful in the midst of the hubbub. She could not remember the last time there had been so many people in her home.

'Somebody's at the door,' said Molly offering Shelby a glass of sparkling water.

'Maybe it's dinner,' said Shelby. 'Hand me my pocketbook, will you? It's on the kitchen counter.'

As Molly approached the counter where Jen was sitting, Jen looked up from her conversation with Glen. 'Oh, no you don't,' she said. 'This dinner is on me. I'll get the door. Molly, why don't you help me carry the food?'

Molly seemed happy to have another job to do. She followed Jen to the door and then rushed back into the room, wide-eyed. 'It's an FBI man.'

'FBI?' said Shelby.

'That's what he said,' Molly reported.

Jen came back into the living room followed by a tall, clean-cut, gray-haired man in an open-necked shirt and a sports jacket. Shelby struggled to get up from the sofa.

'Ms Sloan?' he asked. 'Don't get up. Pardon my casual appearance but I'm here unofficially. My name is Chuck Salomon. I'm from the FBI. I'm in charge of the Philadelphia office. I didn't mean to interrupt the party.'

'It's not a party,' said Shelby. 'We're all just taking shelter, you might say.'

'Could I speak to you for a moment?'

'Sure.' Shelby turned to Molly. 'Molly, can you take Jeremy in the den? You two can watch a movie. I've got a collection of his favorites.'

'I know where it is,' Jeremy said importantly. 'It's my room when I come to Shep's. Follow me.' Molly obediently trailed her brother down the hallway.

Shelby offered the FBI agent a seat. 'Is there something wrong?' she asked.

'Well, I got a call from Elliott Markson. He's very concerned about you and asked me to personally reopen the investigation into your daughter's death.'

'He did?' said Shelby.

'Yes. He called me at home. His late wife was my niece, so we have a family connection. Anyway, I said I would stop by and see you.'

His late wife, Shelby thought. She was sure she had detected sadness beneath Elliott's detached exterior. 'Well, as it happens,' said Shelby. 'There won't be any need for that. I now know what happened to my daughter. Chloe's killer has just been arrested.'

'Really? Down in St Thomas?'

Shelby shook her head, her lips pressed together. 'No, actually. Right here, in Philadelphia.'

Salomon raised his eyebrows in surprise. 'Someone she knew then?' he said.

'The man who threw her overboard was a man named Bud Ridley. He was a stranger on the cruise who pretended to be trying to help my daughter. In fact, he was planning all the while to kill her.'

Salomon frowned. 'So he's been arrested?'

'No. Bud Ridley hanged himself. Apparently, the guilt was too much for him to bear.'

'So, I don't understand. Who was arrested?' Salomon asked.

'A man named Harris Janssen. He paid Bud Ridley to kill my daughter. Well, to be accurate, Ridley owed him an enormous debt, which he was trying to repay.'

'And your daughter knew this fellow Janssen.'

'Yes. We all did.'

'How terrible,' Salomon said, looking genuinely distressed by this news.

She thought about telling him that Harris Janssen had kidnapped her, and that he was a confessed murderer, but she felt too weary to answer the questions that might follow. 'It is. Many lives have been torn apart by this,' said Shelby.

'Ms Sloan, I'd like the agency to get involved in following this up,' Salomon said. 'I don't know what kind of evidence has already been amassed, but murder for hire is a federal crime and we have all the technological tools in our arsenal that one could ever need to make sure that this Janssen fellow pays a heavy price for his crime.'

Shelby sighed. 'Well, I don't want to step on anybody's toes – especially not the Philadelphia police department. It was one of their officers who stopped this man, when he was getting ready to shoot me and toss my body in the Wissahickon.'

'Good God. You have had a day,' he exclaimed.

Shelby smiled weakly. 'Yes, I have.' Before he could question her further she said, 'As for Chloe's death, I don't know under whose jurisdiction that crime might fall. Or any of that . . .'

'I understand,' said Salomon. 'I assure you, we have a history of cooperation with the Philadelphia department. We can work in tandem. In any case, it's not for you to worry about. Chloe's murder was our case to begin with, but it was clearly not investigated as thoroughly as it should have been.'

'No. It was not,' she said firmly.

'Let me see what I can do to make amends for that,' said Salomon kindly. 'I'll have a discussion with the Philadelphia authorities and we'll sort this out.'

'That would be wonderful,' said Shelby.

'It must be a relief to know the truth now – about what happened to your daughter.'

'Yes. I guess it is. I mean, if I had a choice I'd rather have my daughter back, but, obviously . . .' Shelby sighed.

'Justice is the next best thing,' he said.

'I suppose. Can I offer you a drink or something?' Shelby asked.

'No. I'll just head back home if you're sure you're all right.'

Shelby looked around at the people in the room. 'Yes, I'm all right.'

'I'll let Mr Markson know that the agency is going to be getting involved.'

'All right,' Shelby said. 'No. Wait. I'll speak to him myself. I want to thank him. That was so kind of him.'

'Well, he's a good man. Our family knows that for a certainty.'

Agent Salomon extended his hand, and Shelby shook it. 'I'll see you to the door,' she said.

Shelby walked Agent Salomon to the door, and wished him a good night. As the elevator doors opened for him, the delivery man appeared with dinner. Shelby invited him in. She was going to limp back down to the kitchen to get her purse, and then she decided against it. All these people were here, wanting to take care of her. Let them, she thought, and it was as if Chloe's voice were whispering in her ear, urging her to accept the love she was offered.

'Jen,' she called out. 'The dinner is here.'

Jen appeared in a minute, followed by Glen, who was fumbling in his pants pocket and bringing up dollar bills. 'I've got this,' Jen said firmly. 'You can help carry.'

'Happy to,' said Glen. He gathered up the bags and headed back to the living room calling out, 'Soup's on. Come and get it,' while Jen settled up with the delivery man. Jen closed the door behind him and turned to Shelby.

'Let me help you back down the hall,' she said.

'I'm OK,' Shelby assured her. 'You go ahead. I'll be down in a minute.'

'Don't take too long. You need to eat,' said Jen sternly.

Shelby gave her a quick hug, and Jen followed Glen down the hallway.

Shelby went into her bedroom, and pulled out the phone book from a drawer in the bedside table. Before she did anything else, she needed to thank Elliott Markson. It was a comfort to her to know that the FBI would be involved, and there was no chance of Harris Janssen squirming out of this. The police had promised her, at the scene, that he would never get out of jail, but there could be loopholes when expensive attorneys were involved. It was a good thing that the FBI had something to prove in this case. It should guarantee justice for Chloe. Shelby would remain involved in the legal process for as long as it took. That she knew for certain.

She sat down on the bed and leafed through the phone book, pondering what Chuck Salomon had said – that his family knew all about Markson's goodness. A long illness perhaps, that led to his wife's death? Some sort of ordeal that tested a person? She knew something about that, she thought with a sigh. Shelby ran down the list of Marksons, and located his name. He lived in a new high rise on Rittenhouse Square. She recognized the address. She punched his number into her cell. The phone rang and then went to voice mail. Shelby was almost relieved.

'Mr Markson – Elliott,' she said. 'This is Shelby Sloan. Chuck Salomon from the FBI was just here. He said you had asked him to help me. I just wanted to thank you for that. That was really . . . extremely kind of you.' For a moment she was silent, thinking about how important that genuine show of concern had been to her. She felt foolish, trying to express her appreciation in a voice mail. 'OK, um, I will . . . speak to you soon. Thanks again, Elliott. Really. It means a lot.'

She ended the call, glad that he had not answered, and that she didn't have to explain the whole story tonight. Sometime, perhaps, if he wanted to know it, she would find the will to tell it. Perhaps she would ask him about his own ordeal. They say we ease one another's burdens by sharing them, she thought.

Shelby could hear the movie playing in the den, the kids laughing, and people talking in her living room. She felt safe. Surrounded. It was still hard for her to believe that Glen, and even Talia, had searched for her. That Jen had helped them. That Rob had sounded the initial alarm. She was not completely alone, after all.

As she replaced the phone on the bedside table, she picked up the framed photo that always sat there, beside her reading lamp. It was taken when Chloe was eight, and they had had Chinese banquet day at her elementary school. Shelby had arranged for a long lunch hour and had arrived at school in time to eat with the other mothers and their children. Someone had taken a photo of her and Chloe, wielding chopsticks and beaming into one another's eyes. It had always been one of her favorite pictures. They both looked so perfectly happy.

Shelby kissed the photo and held it to her aching heart, tears rising again to her eyes. She wondered if the pain would ever fade. She closed her eyes and, in her heart, she spoke to the girl in the picture. I'm sorry, my darling. For all the ways I failed you. I'll miss you forever, she thought. I'll never get used to living without you. But at least I fought for you. As hard as I could. At least I did that. She gazed at the photo and kissed it again. Then, she set it back down on the table in its permanent place beside her pillow.